IBSN: Paperback 979-8-9932830-0-5 | Ebook 979-8-9932830-1-2

Edited by Leslie Colley

Book Cover by Sydney Langley

Illustrations by Sydney Langley

First edition 2025

DEVOURANCE

"I want you to believe... to believe in things that you cannot." Bram Stoker (1897)

Jacquelyn Marquez

Jacquelyn Marquez Books

DEVOURANCE

Jacquelyn Marquez

For Juan and Sirenita. Everything I do is for you. I couldn't have done this without you.

And for my mom and sister. Thanks for believing in me.

Thanks Daddio for letting me borrow your Dean Koontz books and always supporting my work.

And for my Twinzie, Booktok brought us together and thank you for taking such care with my story.

INTRODUCTION

Trigger Warning: This novel contains scenes of violence, assault, explicit sexual content, strong language, references to depression, grief and post partem depression, bloodplay and bloodshed.

Reader discretion is advised.

CONTENTS

Prologue — 1

1. Lost — 6

2. Intruder — 14

3. Muerte (Dead) — 28

4. Sickly — 40

5. Sombra (Shadow) — 47

6. Stranger — 54

7. Poderoso (Strength) — 62

8. Famished — 82

9. Sire — 89

10. Visions — 100

11. Condenado (Cursed) — 114

12. Bruja (Witch) — 126

13. Yield   148

14. Clarity   153

15. Ache   166

16. Espanto (Ghost)   174

17. Savage   178

18. Confessions   182

19. Marcadas (Marked)   194

20. Bloodline   202

21. Chupasangre (Bloodsucker)   210

22. Sol (Sun)   216

23. Alma (Soul)   224

24. Mate   232

25. Caged   242

26. Intrusive   254

27. Estrellas (Stars)   260

28. Breach   272

29. Esposo (Husband)   282

30. Hija (Daughter)   286

31. Broken   292

32. Fortune   305

33. Terca (Stubborn)   319

34. Imbuement   329

35. Lechusas (Owl) — 340

36. Chupacabra (Mexican Goat-sucker) — 344

37. Oblivion — 355

38. Volver (Come back) — 367

Epilogue — 374

ANGELOUS — 379

Glossary — 380

Glossary (SPELLS) — 383

Acknowledgements — 386

About the Author — 388

Prologue

The whispers became a ravenous buzzing inside his head, like flies around an animal carcass. It made it impossible to think, let alone drive. He gripped his steering wheel so hard that his knuckles were white.

The car lights in his windshield were blurring and he blinked hard to regain clarity.

His skin began to itch as the voices echoing around him grew to a cacophony of sound.

He had to pull over.

Barely managing to hit his blinker, he edged his old Dodge Avenger to the side of the road. Traffic was not as bad as usual, which was surprising given the time, peak commuter traffic. Everyone else was leaving work, while he was going in.

Trying to anyway.

A light mist began outside, and the water raked the

air as they passed through the beams of his headlights. He pressed his emergency lights, and both arrows began to blink on his dashboard.

He let out a shaky, steadying breath as the mist turned from red to white and back to red. And yet, the whispers only grew impossibly louder, drowning out all the traffic noise.

Could anyone else hear it too? Was it all in his head? Was he having a stroke?

Cold wind hit the back of his neck like a caress, and gooseflesh pebbled down his spine. All the windows were up and his air conditioner was perpetually broken, so where did that wind come from? Uneasiness turned his stomach as the whispers began to form words.

Sangre... Sangre mía. [1] The chant was loud in his ears. His hands flew up to cover them, to block the words out, to no avail.

"What the fuck?!" Diego's heart was in his throat, choking him with fear.

Instantly, his skin felt like it was being scalded with boiling water. A burning sensation that traveled from his scalp to his fingers, down his legs, and to his toes. His flesh began rippling before his eyes, like something was moving beneath the skin. That's when it began to stretch, pulling taut like a rubber band about to snap. He cried out, the pain was a blinding, all-consuming pain.

Then his bones began to snap. A snarl ripped from his throat.

---

1. Blood... my blood.

What the fuck?!

His eyes were wild, trying to breathe through the searing pain, and then more bones crunched. His fingers were bending back, elongating at odd angles and he screamed in a mixture of pain and fear.

Sangre... sangre... sangre mía. [2] The whispers circled him, a discordant chorus, a maddening lullaby of unfamiliar voices... all urging. *Que duerme... que despierte.* [3]

Tears clouded his vision as he tried to blink through the sharp, burning pain, struggling to catch his breath. He caught sight of two yellow eyes glaring at him through his rear-view mirror. They glowed with a hungry, animalistic intent. Cold, icy fear slid down his spine. He recognized those eyes. The eyes of a predator. He had seen them in a long-forgotten dream.

Another hot spear of pain shot through him, and his back bowed in his seat, and his voiceless cry was drowned out by a feral growl.

Out of nowhere, his elbows bent forward at an unnatural angle, and he cried out in horror, seeing his arms bent out in front of him, bones poking out from beneath stretched skin. They had to be broken and he gritted his teeth so hard he thought he might crack them, just trying to breathe through the pain.

This was it. This was when he was going to die.

The last thing he thought of was his family, his girls. *Would he ever see them again?* A cold shot of fear hit

---

2. Blood... Blood... My blood.

3. What's sleeping, now awaken.

him low in his belly as he knew with a growing certainty that he would not. He was going to die tonight, right here on the side of the road.

The pain was becoming too much to bear. His entire body bent forward with one violent motion. His spine locked into an abnormally foreign position and his head hit his steering wheel, honking his worn-out horn. It released a pathetic squeak out into the night, not drawing attention.

He succumbed to the numbing blackness and knew no more.

CHAPTER

I

LOST

Los Angeles, California[1] – Almost Two Years Later

"Owwwww," the expression elongated, dripping with over exaggeration and a hint of playful sarcasm. Diego was a big tease.

Jade's laughter peeled out and became higher-pitched as her tiny hands pushed him backwards.

Diego let her push him as he sat with her on the

---

1. El Pueblo de Nuestra Señora la Reina de los Ángeles de Porciúncula – "The Town of Our Lady the Queen of Angels of Porciúncula."

floor, flailing his arms as he did. Mouth open in mock surprise and dark eyes full of humor.

Jade cackled even harder as she shoved her father. The chortle brought a glimmer of joy to Searra's face. Jade's plump cheeks appled as she laughed/screamed. Her tiny mouth filled with little Chiclets. That is what Diego used to say when she first started teething. She had been three months old at the time.

Searra paused the video on her phone and stared at her husband's smiling face. His round eyes were creased with laughter, and white teeth gleamed as he beamed with pure delight.

It had been almost two years since he went missing. Somewhere deep inside, she understood that he was dead, but actual acceptance was a whole other issue...

The last time she saw him, the memory was still sharp. He had been leaving the house to go to the bar where he was the manager. Their daughter, Jade, had been playing in her playpen, and Searra was sitting with her in the pen, scrolling on her phone. Jade didn't mind, though, since she was preoccupied with her Superman Funko Pop and chewing his head into oblivion. Just when they thought Jade was done teething, more kept popping up, making her irritable and clingy, sticking to Searra like Velcro.

"Momma's girl," Diego would say. The corners of her mouth lifted for a moment, and tears threatened to prick her eyes as something still raw beneath the surface cracked open.

She would not cry!

He had kissed them both goodbye, lingering on his kiss to Searra, and then took one last look in the mirror by the front door, double-checking his hair, sharp and close-cropped. His thick brows lifted as his fingers ran through the short, black tresses.

Searra remembered how her own fingers itched, knowing how deceivingly soft it would feel under her caress. When he used to put gel in it to make it spiky, his hair had always been crunchy and Searra begged him to stop so she could rake her hands through it whenever she pleased. So he did.

Diego turned to her, gave them one last bright smile, and headed out the front door to his old black Dodge. It was not the most expensive, but he'd had it since they first met, back when he was still a server and not making much money. She remembered hearing the loud muffler and its familiar popping growl as he took off down the street.

They had found his Dodge by the side of the road the following morning. The keys were still in the ignition and the simple leather upholstery had been demolished, like someone had taken a chainsaw to it. There had been no blood but that didn't mean anything.

Jade had just turned six months old when he disappeared, and now she was already almost two. Walking and talking and everything. The majority of her life without her dad. It was unbelievable.

Searra still expected to see him when she woke up each morning, to be there to help with Jade's eggs, to sit in the playpen with her, to make towering sculptures with Jade and her shape blocks. She wanted him there, to raise their daughter together. Her heart cracked knowing that Jade would grow up and her father wouldn't be there to see it.

Searra lived at home now with her mom and

younger sister. Her mom helped her out, babysitting Jade while Searra trained early mornings. She had taken up self-defense and strength training after Diego disappeared. With it, she regained some semblance of control in her life. It was cathartic to have a routine and something to focus on. Plus, she was a lot stronger now... physically at least.

Searra turned off the screen on her phone and put it in the pocket of her teal leggings.

A voice cut through the early morning silence from deep inside the house.

"Yeah, Ma?" Searra called out.

"Poo Poo!" Her mom warned, hysterical amusement in her tone.

"Okay! I'll be right there!" Searra shouted as she got up from her bench in the far side of the yard and strode into the house.

Her mom was with Jade in the garage. They had converted it into a den ten years back. In the center was a large red love seat covered in blankets. The "leather" had worn down to tissue paper and was flaking off at an alarming rate.

There were overturned tables acting as makeshift barriers, creating a pen for Jade to explore. Her toys were strewn about and a few brown napkin pieces were scattered all over the floor like brown snow. She loved to rip apart paper into itsy bitsy pieces. *Papelita*[2], they called her. Always running around with a piece of paper scrunched in her tiny hands.

Searra grabbed wipes, a mat, and a diaper out of the

---

2. Litte paper (term of endearment)

bag hanging off the end of the small play pen they were using as another make-shift border wall in her larger play area.

Ever since she started walking it was impossible to keep her penned in anything smaller than an actual room. Jade was smart and wanted to explore *everything*.

Lifting her leg over the old painting palette in front of her, yet another makeshift wall, Searra made her way into Jade's play space.

"Hi, my Sweeties!" Searra said in a sing-songy lilt. Trying to coax her daughter into waddling over to where she had laid out the foldable grey mat to change her. Jade's eyes squinted, and a wide toothy smile erupted on her angelic face. Light brown eyes were sparkling with mischief as she walked a couple of steps forward, only to back up another few, laughter peeling out as she did so.

"Come on sweetie pie!" Searra said in her sweetest voice, a big grin breaking out across her face.

Jade was chewing on an empty container of M&M minis; the label had been peeled off, so it was just a bright orange tube.

"Mammamamamamamaaa," Jade said between chews.

"Mama needs to change your diaper Sweetie pie." Hand outstretched and knees digging into the squishy floor tiles beneath her.

Jade hesitated and started to move forward with her little chubby hobbit feet.

As soon as she was in range, Searra grabbed her elbow and pulled her in close. Jade made a squeal of protest, but Searra planted a big kiss on her short mop of light brown hair. It had finally grown long enough to make beautiful, delicate curls at her nape. She could almost make a baby ponytail, instead of the firework tied on the tippy top of her head to keep her hair out of her eyes. Searra closed her eyes and savored the feel of Jade in her arms, her face pressed against her cheek. She began to pant like their dogs would so her breath tickled Jade's face, and Jade erupted into laughter. "Mommy doggy!" She squealed between breaths.

Searra laid her down on the mat mid-giggle and reached for the nearest toy, a blue dragon, to keep her hands busy. But she was still good with chewing on the orange M&M mini container, so Searra put the dragon next to Jade's head, just in case he was needed.

"So Sisi," Searra's mom started while Searra dealt with the dirty diaper.

"What Ma?"

"I just wanted to know... how you were doing?"

"I'm okay Ma." Searra insisted, not sure if it was true, but her go-to move was to fake it until she made it. Pretend like everything is okay... until it isn't.

"I miss him too, you know." Her mom said, her Michigander accent peeking through on the "yah know." Searra looked up at her from her position on the floor, Jade squiggling underneath her as she pulled up her pants after fastening the diaper and making sure her little butt cheeks were fully covered.

Her Mom's eyes were crinkled with concern. Dark brown, glistening with tears that she never showed. As she got older, her eyelids drooped heavily, so her almond eyes appeared even smaller. Her short, bleach-blonde hair was standing up in every which way, like she rolled out of bed and didn't bother with it.

"I know Ma. I do too." Searra sighed, not certain if she was willing to take on her mother's grief on top of her own. She was already cut off from her emotions, like she was underwater and numb, with everyone and everything else on the surface shouting at her but she couldn't hear them. She was focused on Jade and taking care of her. All the other shit was not important. She knew that was probably fucked up, but that was where she was at.

Jade rolled onto her belly and stood back up, pausing while she regained her shaky balance, and then took off in a half run away from Searra and back toward her corner with her toys. Screaming and chewing on the orange M&M mini case.

"You know you can talk to me Sweetie," Searra's mom offered. Her tone was sweet and genuine, a liferaft from the surface. She was holding out her hand, offering to pull Searra in from the numbing depths she was drowning in.

"Ma." Searra breathed, her eyes shut tight, and her fingers pinched the bridge of her nose. A headache was coming on.

"I really don't want to talk about it."Her throat closed a little as a sob threatened to escape, "If I talk about it..." Her breathing was becoming quick and shallow. "..then I'll have to feel it..." A familiar knot pulled taut and began squeezing her chest, a tightness that formed the day Diego had gone missing, clenching around her heart like a vise and had never let go.

"Oh Sisi," her mom got up from her spot on the love seat, leaving a mom-sized shape behind. The rust-red couch did not revert back; her position was engraved on it. She leaned forward, careful to lean the side of her body with her urine bag and tube away from Searra. Her arms pulled her in from behind with hidden strength that surprised her.

Searra's Mom had been diagnosed with stage IV ovarian cancer and stage I breast cancer two years ago. The pee bag was a new addition after the tumor began to press on her mom's urethra. She was still in the fight though, taking chemo like a champ.

They sat on the floor together. Her mom cooed, "It's okay. It's okay," into her ear, squeezing her tight.

Searra felt the tide of tears threaten to consume her, but Jade was burbling less than two feet away. Through stubborn will, she held them back.

No, Mom. Searra thought. *Nothing is okay.* But she didn't say it.

Searra let her mom hold her. Jade giggled at Ms. Rachel on the television singing about big feelings and how it was okay to have them. *Sure.* But what if they were so big that they could swallow her whole?

Chapter 2

Intruder

"Listen to them—the children of the night. What music they make!" -Bram Stoker (1897)

"**I**t's okay sweetie," Searra soothed. "I'm not taking that away from you. I just need to wash your hands so we can go to bed." Jade cooed in response, her pink hands fisted around her Auntie Squee's toothbrush. Jade's favorite thing to do was take her Aunt's things and hide them in random places. One time they found tampons in the bookshelf.

Searra smiled as she grabbed the purple washcloth hanging to the side of the vanity, so she could dry Jade's hands and feet as she sat on the marble rim. Everything in the bathroom was purple, the shower curtain, the linoleum, the bathmat, and even the tub, all courtesy of her mom. Well, not the tub, that was there when they bought the house. And it was less of a purple and more of a mauve, with a sprinkle of mold.

Searra's gaze caught on the mirror. The vibrant girl, full of sparkle and zest, the girl that Diego had fallen in love with was nowhere to be seen. Wiped away like faded chalk beneath a hose. In her place stood someone with worry carved into the skin beneath her deep brown eyes. Her too-large glasses were sliding down her nose and hair piled into a messy bun with a claw clip. It was a careless knot with flyaways that brought to mind an abused Barbie doll. Nothing like the girl Diego met seven years ago.

Goofy, radiant, alive…

At thirty-seven, she felt tired. Bone-deep exhaustion. She was worn down, frayed at the edges. So deeply exhausted by the endlessness of everyday. Raising Jade alone, of being alone… of not knowing what truly happened.

A soul-deep sigh escaped, and she tore her gaze from the mirror, unable to look at the stranger who stared back at her any longer. The sadness in her gaze was too much to bear.

No! She was spiraling.

A smile stretched across her face like a worn tarp as she picked up Jade and nestled her into the indent on her hip, "Time for bed sweetie!" Her sing-songy voice echoed, hollow in the bathroom's acoustics.

A full hour later, Searra tiptoed out of the bedroom, almost tripping on the worn ottoman beside the bedroom door. She bit back a curse and closed the door with a soft click. Holding her breath and listening so hard, praying that Jade was undisturbed and still fast asleep.

Nothing.

Only silence.

Since Searra and Jade shared the primary, she was used to the sneaking. Her king-size bed was on one side, and the crib was on the other.

Breathing a sigh of relief, Searra headed to her couch and plopped down on it. She reached over to the faux marble coffee table and grabbed the baby monitor to turn it on. The red light turned green as she pressed the button and the white noise filtered through from their bedroom. Jade only slept uninterrupted with her white noise monkey that hung in the corner of her crib. It was a lifesaver and the only thing Searra needed to make sure was constantly charged, even more than her phone.

Searra placed the baby monitor back on the coffee table and lay back on the couch, putting her aching feet up and stretching out.

She took a steadying breath, *in and out.*

Then another, *in and out.*

Slowly, her muscles began to relax, and her entire

being started to uncoil. Her breathing deepened and she drifted off. She should be getting ready for bed herself, she had to brush her teeth and wash her face. But she was so comfortable and her body was so exhausted that it just wasn't responding anymore.

Before she finished the thought, she was out.

With a sharp inhale, Searra jolted awake to a dark, silent living room. Of course, her glasses were still on. The nose guards cut deep grooves into the middle of her brow while she slept. She rubbed the sore spot and checked her lenses for smudges. It had become a habit. Before, her husband would remove her glasses for her and place them on the nightstand when she fell asleep in them.

Not anymore.

She looked at the clock on the bookshelf across the room. It was 3:00am.

Damn.

She got up, grabbed the baby monitor, and headed to her bedroom where Jade was sleeping in her crib. Cracking the door open, Searra peeked inside and could see Jade sleeping in her crib, still wrapped in her swaddle but she was horizontal instead of vertical, and her leg was up and propped in between two of the wooden planks.

Searra hated that, because now she'd have to reposition Jade before she went to sleep. Otherwise, her leg might get stuck and she will wake up scared and crying.

Closing the door again with a soft click, Searra headed across the hall into the only bathroom in the house, and it was cramped. In a blind reach, she found the switches on the right-hand side of the doorway, turning on the light. She opened up the first drawer on the vanity to grab her toothbrush.

As she did, she thought she heard tapping in the white noise of the baby monitor.

She listened harder, holding her breath. And the tap came again, no mistaking it.

Oh great.

Jade was either kicking the crib in her sleep or she was awake and standing up, waiting for Momma to come and get her. She hoped it was the former rather than the latter, because Jade would most likely still be asleep if she were just kicking the crib. Searra would just readjust her and hopefully Jade would remain asleep for the rest of the night. But if she was standing, that meant another hour of trying to put her back down, and Searra was so tired.

She sighed deeply and felt the release in her chest.

She was just *so tired.*

Searra headed back across the hall as a sudden unease washed over her, like ice water down her spine.

The darkness in the hallway seemed foreign and more menacing than it had only a moment ago. She peered down the short walkway to her mom and sister's rooms. The doors were shut and neither light was on.

Besides the white noise emanating from the baby monitor clipped to the hip of her pajama bottoms, there were no sounds. The house was still.

Silent. The hairs on the back of her neck prickled as gooseflesh pimpled up her arms like static.

Someone was watching her in the dark.

Watching.

Waiting.

Her mouth went dry, breath stuttering in shaky gasps she tried to control. Then the baby monitor at her hip went silent.

Shit.

In a burst of pure panic, she ran straight to her room and opened the door with a force that may have ripped it off its hinges had her worn brown ottoman not been in the way to absorb the impact. Searra surveyed the room. Nothing was out of place. She could just make out Jade in the light of her night light, which was just a small lamp behind the TV, next to the crib.

She was still asleep.

The room was empty.

Searra took a few steps in, and peered into the darkness. It was silent, but Jade was sleeping and peaceful. Her little belly moved up and down in slow, steady movements.

As she moved closer, Searra saw the fan of long dark lashes resting on Jade's plump pink cheeks and Searra's heart squeezed. She, without a doubt, got those lashes from her father.

Searra turned to make her way out, when it occurred to her that the room was silent because the white noise monkey must have died. She bent over the crib to see if she could get it working again, or maybe she just needed to plug it in to charge. As she reached for it, she paused, seeing that the wire was still plugged in and the light was red. It was still charging. Her fingers slid along the base of the right-hand side of the monkey and flicked the switch. Without delay, white noise filled the room and Searra became even more unnerved.

Someone turned it off.

A cool breath of air hit the back side of her neck and her entire body tensed on high alert. Searra took in a deep breath as time slowed. She knew with a growing certainty that there was an intruder in her house.

Standing right behind her.

Without giving herself too long to think, she pivoted on her left foot as her whole body rotated, surging with speed she had honed over the last two years. Her right elbow came up as she spun and struck a cold, solid mass.

The weight grunted as her elbow hit home.

The impact had been devastating, if not for her attacker, it certainly was for her. It felt like she hit the fucking wall. But she got him with the back of her elbow instead of the tip, so it had a lot of power behind it. It should have been enough to knock him off balance, then she could have grabbed Jade and run. But he was between them and the door, and hadn't moved.

She couldn't discern much in the darkness, but now, facing him with her back to the crib and Jade stirring behind her, she realized just how massive he was.

His dark figure filled the room.

Searra reached behind her to the tall bureau they used as a large TV stand, where there was a pair of old scissors. They weren't the sharpest but they would do. She'd aim for his eyes or bury them in his throat if she had to. As her fingers wrapped around them, her stare never wavered from the menacing, dark figure.

Had he moved closer? He must have... but she hadn't seen him step forward.

Grip tightening, pointed end down, she took another deep breath.

Just then, Jade began to cry! A sharp wail that cut through the darkness of the room. Searra's gaze snapped to the crib behind her. She could just see her standing in the crib in her periphery, gripping the railing, her pumpkin swaddle falling around her like a billowing cape.

Searra steeled herself and lunged toward the dark figure. Arm raised and slashing down, the blade of the scissors glinted. Hoping to land anywhere on the face, get him bleeding and scared so he might run off. Her main objective was to move him out of the room so she could lock it and call the police. As her arm came down, there was no connection as she sliced through empty air.

Searra had missed!

How had she missed!

Using her momentum, she spun around to face where the dark figure now stood over the crib. The intruder was staring at Jade. A type of feral savagery overtook Searra. Her blood began to boil, and she lost all thought, lunging again to strike. All of her concentration focused on protecting her daughter and eliminating this threat, through whatever means necessary.

Jade's cries fueled Searra like gasoline, flooding her with so much anxious energy that she was practically buzzing. With that, she lunged. Knowing her body weight was her best weapon, besides the scissors. Not only was she tall, but she was dense and could use her weight against the intruder.

Her body smacked against the dark figure, knocking the wind from her chest and she struggled to catch her breath. But she had thrown him off balance for a split second, and that was all she needed.

Wrapping her arm around the dark figure's neck, scissors raised high, muscles straining. With a snarl and a viciousness she didn't know she possessed, Searra drove them down.

His arm caught hers as it came down, blocking her attack like a brick wall. Her arm stung with the impact, muscles vibrating. She jumped and wrapped her legs around his waist, throwing her body backwards to knock him down. The dark figure swayed but didn't fall. She tried again, core muscles straining as she swung herself backwards, but this time he didn't even sway.

"Interesting," the intruder whispered into the dark room. His tone was cool and collected but with a hint of something more, a kind of simmering heat that Searra didn't understand. It was nothing like how hers would be, squeaky and cracked with adrenaline. But there was also something otherworldly about it. Like it was coming from both here in the room and all around, with its own celestial echo. It made her uneasy, but she also wanted to listen to it forever. A haunting melody, beautiful and strange.

Like magic.

She blinked and found herself standing on the ground, face to face with the dark intruder. He was so fast... it was disorienting.

How the —?

His large hands gripped her wrists in an impenetrable hold, pinning her arms to her sides. In the dim light Searra caught sight of his face, and Searra's breath froze in her throat. He was beautiful, with the most piercing eyes she had ever seen; it was too dark to discern the exact color, but they might have been green. With tousled brown hair that was long enough in front that it swept across his eyes and a jawline that could cut you. He had a heavy five o'clock shadow and a long, angular nose. Then, her gaze fell on his heart-shaped lips, his cupid's bow was sharp and bottom lip full. Searra wondered how soft they might feel pressed against hers.

What?! Where had that come from?

His glacial gaze bored into hers. "Very interesting." He crooned, his almond eyes crinkling with amusement, those lips had upturned into a sharp smirk that had fear skittering up her spine.

Just then, Jade began to cry again, jolting Searra from her thoughts. Her little hands were above her head, "Mamamamamama!" All one long angry plea for Searra.

Searra looked from Jade to the large man in front of her, pinning her to the spot. He was tall, well over six feet because she was tall as well —five-foot-ten in flats, and she still had to look up to meet his gaze. Her stomach twisted as an ice pick of fear shot down her spine and cleared her head. She wrenched her wrists trying to break the hold to get to Jade, but his grip wouldn't budge.

"Who are you? What do you want?!" She managed to scream at him, her mouth was dry and her lips were sticking to her teeth. Desperation clouding her thoughts. She was helpless and a little nauseous.

"Fear not. I seek only information." He smiled, white teeth sharp in the dark of the room. His smile was disarming and she hated that her stomach was doing flips for the wrong reason. "Mmm...but your scent is far too divine to pretend." He whispered in her ear, it reminded her of a snake's menacing hiss right before it struck.

He loomed over her. His speed unnatural. A blur in the dark. In a single blink, his hand clamped around her jaw and wretched her head aside, baring her throat. The air between them shifted, heavy and charged. The moment before the kill.

Then his face shifted. His eyes went from green to a burning liquid gold, and the muscles on his forehead began to protrude, creating a bumpy ridge along his brow line, revealing the demon beneath. He grew double rows of sharp canines glinting in the light of Jade's nightlight.

Searra tried to scream but only choked on air as fear immobilized her lungs and throat. She wasn't even sure she believed what her own eyes were seeing! Then only sharp, searing pain as his fangs sank into her neck.

Her entire body stilled, frozen in his grip like a fly caught in the web of a spider.

She couldn't move, she was paralyzed.

Pain radiated from her neck, and she gritted her teeth to block it out. A small hiss escaping between her teeth. She was hot and aching all at once as his grip tightened on her. His massive arms wrapped around her waist as he pulled her closer.

He was drinking her blood!

There was an ache deep in her core that she chose to ignore. Her body betraying her by responding to his assault.

The hand tangled in her hair softened, the harsh grip easing until it was almost tender. The messy bun was gone now, strands of dark waves spilling freely down her back. His mouth never ceased his assault on her neck, heat and pressure searing into her skin, while his fingers trailed from her loosened locks to the curve of her cheek.

She shivered. A tingling ripple sweeping from her scalp to her shoulders, down her arms. His finger-tips skimmed the apples of her cheeks before hooking gently around the frames of there glasses. In one unhurried motion, he slid them away, placing them somewhere she couldn't see... couldn't care to.

The tingling faded as Searra began to feel woozy and her eyes closed. Jade was still crying in the back of her mind, but couldn't open her eyes again, her lids were so heavy. A cold slice of fear shot through her at the thought that she wouldn't be there for Jade. That they would probably both die here. She felt his hand cup her face again. The pad of his thumb swept across her bottom lip and she couldn't help her instinctual need to suck his thumb into her mouth. Her tongue tasted something metallic, like pennies. He growled low in his throat, a rough unrestrained sound, as her tongue dragged slowly across his thumb.

As abruptly as it began, the man... or demon.. . wrenched himself from her neck. The sudden loss left her skin aching, the heat of his mouth replaced by the cold kiss of the night air from the ceiling fan above. Her legs were numb, like they had both fallen asleep, only limp weights that she wasn't quite sure how to stand on. Good thing he was still mainly keeping her upright.

Searra managed to look up at him and saw something strange in his eyes. They weren't that other-worldly golden anymore, back to green, with gold flecks she was just now noticing, and his brow looked as normal as her own. She couldn't read her look on his face. *Was that pity?* The realization made her want to roll her eyes; even her intruder felt bad for her.

Wow.

She could barely work her voice, but she croaked, "What are you?"

At that, he let out a low, dry chuckle. "I suspect you already know." The humor didn't reach his eyes, they crinkled at the edges and he suddenly looked much older than he had earlier. The vulnerability caught her off guard and it made her want to reach out.

Instantly, her intruder released her and she crumpled to the ground in a heap. Her eye lids were so heavy, she blinked hard, trying to see through her bleary vision as copper still danced on her tongue.

He stepped over her. Jade had gone quiet in her crib, either from shock, fear or Searra didn't know what. As his footsteps faded away, her eyes closed again as she drifted off into the dark.

CHAPTER
3

MUERTE (DEAD)

"A DEEP SLEEP FELL UPON ME- A
SLEEP LIKE THAT OF DEATH. " -
EDGAR ALLAN POE (1842)

Searra awoke and her head was throbbing. Blinking hard to clear her vision, she tried to make sense of her surroundings.

Searra was in her own bed. She looked straight ahead to the crib where Jade was sitting upright, burbling to herself, as her little fingers tangled in her swaddle. Searra smiled, relieved, but she couldn't remember for why or what. She looked to the floating shelf she used as an end table, and saw her glasses placed with care beside her water bottle and coconut lotion. She grabbed them and put them on, her brows furrowing.

A shard of ice cold dread shot down her spine as the wisp of a vague memory had her hands flying to her neck. Her mouth went dry as the previous night flooded her mind. The man, the dark intruder, the fight, the demon he became... and the bite.

She expected her skin to be tender, but it was all smooth. Hesitant fingers explored, but there was no wound at all, at least what she inspected with her hands.

She got out of bed and crossed to the mirrored closet. The reflection staring back at her appeared... normal. No hair out of place, save for the soft tousling of sleep. Her pajamas hung fine, a bit rumpled, but no cuts or stains. No evidence of the struggle she remembered. Even her neck... healed. Smooth skin. No marks. No blood. Nothing.

Could she have dreamt it all?

A loud thunk came from behind her, and Jade was standing in her crib looking at her with a Chiclets smile and joy filled eyes. "Mammamamamama-mamaaa," she squealed, hands outstretched to be picked up.

"Okay, Sweetie Pie," Searra said as she lifted Jade from her crib to sit her on her hip. "Let's go have breakfast, cuz we really overslept." She glanced over to the digital alarm clock on the dresser beside the TV, the blue light showed it was after 8:00 AM. On a regular day, Searra was lucky if they made it to 6:00 AM, so this was a strange treat. However, Searra still felt the heavy weight of exhaustion, despite the extra sleep.

There was a wet spot on Jade's onesie around her lower back, butt and legs.

"Uh oh!" Searra exclaimed, kissing the top of Jade's head, her light brown hair was soft like down feathers and tickled Searra's nose. "But first, you need a diaper change, Missy!"

After Jade ate her eggs and beans for breakfast, Searra got the baby gates ready to set up in the living room so Jade had the freedom to run around at will. She had started walking several months ago and was an official pro now. Her favorite thing to do was bounce like a ping pong ball onto the couches. Squealing as she did it.

On a normal morning, Searra would ask her mom to babysit Jade while she made her own breakfast, but... she wasn't hungry.

In fact, while she cooked Jade's scrambled eggs, she was growing nauseated. Searra was vegan, going on five years now, but she had never had that kind of visceral reaction to eggs before.

She was a little worried that she might be fighting a cold, and that was the last thing she needed. Searra could not afford to get sick. Not only would she spread it to Jade, a nightmare on its own, but to her mom too, who was immunocompromised.

On cue, her mom rounded the corner, her pee-bag swaying on her hip with each step she took. She had a big smile as she cooed at Jade, her eyes crinkling until they were practically closed. Her eyelids had grown heavier with age and while her cheekbones remained high, her cheeks had sunken in a little, the skin droop-ing below her jaw, swaying in tandem with her pee bag. She still didn't look like she was in her seventies though, despite her cancer. The prior week, she had shaved her head on the sides and dyed it blonde, the long strands on top were pulled into a little bun. She looked like an old hipster who didn't get the memo that man buns were out. Or she was cosplaying as an old lady ninja.

"I'm here, Sisi!" Her mom announced as she shuffled into the living room, fighting with the baby gate longer than usual. Long enough that Searra almost left her spot on the floor to go help her. But she finally heard the latch and her mom trudged through, struggling again to close the gate behind her.

Searra bounded up to go help her but without warning she felt a numbing weirdness wash over her. Her vision became spotty, and she lost control of her legs as they folded beneath her, crumpling to the floor like a puppet without strings. Her breath came in short gasps as she fought to remain calm and force deep lungfuls of air. She tried to blink away the spots, to bring her vision back to clarity, but for the moment, she had gone blind.

"Sisi! Are you okay?" She heard her mom exclaim, but she couldn't answer her, still blinking to refocus her gaze. Her heart seemed to thump slow and hard in her chest, each beat heavy and sluggish.

Searra blinked, her vision clearing. She was able to sit back up; it must have been a couple of minutes.

"Hon!" Her mom's worried voice drifted to her from far away. Jade had run over from her spot in the middle of an avalanche of toys and board books. Her pink Crocs slapping the hardwood floor, and plopped right onto Searra's stomach. Sending a *woosh* from deep inside her, a toddler gut punch.

"I'm okay, I'm okay," Searra repeated, mostly for her own benefit than for her mom.

"How often have you gotten dizzy like that?!" Her mom questioned, but there was more accusation in her tone, like *What did you do?*

"Ayyyy... Ma," Searra said, her voice flat as she rubbed her temples.

"If it happens again, you should make an appointment to see your doctor."

"And what are they going to do, Ma?" Searra asked with an incredulous tone. "They are just going to say stupid shit like stand up slower, or take vitamins... get more sleep... blah, blah blah..." and then added under her breath, "plus, the copay is $65 just to see my GP, and $90 for a specialist. I cannot afford to just throw that much away right now."

Her mom clicked with her tongue, understanding in her eyes. She knew that money had been more than tight since Diego had disappeared. Her mom and sister helped her out, but it still didn't make up the difference. Some months she was lucky to make her share of the mortgage.

"Besides, I bet *I did* get up too fast. Plus, I haven't even had breakfast yet. Low blood sugar and all." Searra managed a small smile, waving her concerns away with her hands as she stood with caution.

Since she wasn't hungry, Searra wanted to take advantage of her mom being there, but her Mom's abilities were limited. Good days and bad days were a coin flip. Searra wanted to get a work out in but she needed to double check, make sure her mom was ready for a Jade session.

"You got her Ma?" Searra asked her mom.

"Yeah, I got her." She cooed to Jade, who was sitting on the floor with her legs spread out and kicking.

Jade's pink Crocs were a blur as she went to town banging her heels on the ground. Searra was shocked it didn't hurt, or leave bruises on her heels.

While Jade was distracted, Searra hopped the baby gate that led from the living room to the office/dining room, and kitchen. Jade was her cute, little velcro baby but Searra made it to the kitchen unnoticed and out the back door.

It was still overcast, even though she woke up a little later than usual. The fall weather was kind to her today. She walked over to her makeshift gym she had set up under a carport tarp.

As she reached from your pink gloves resting on the bench, the metal door slammed and her sister's voice called "Sisi! Help!"

Searra turned and saw her sister trying to carry an old microwave to the trash bins. She ran to her, catching the bottom corner and lifting just as it was about to hit the pavement.

"Jesus Syd!" Searra chided. "You could have hurt yourself."

Syd let out a lout laugh, "I gotta get this bitch out somehow."

"You could have asked me to help *before* almost eating it." She pointed out.

"Yeah, but where is the fun in that?" Syd said grunting as they made their way to the bins.

It didn't feel very heavy to Searra. "Hey, you can let go. I got it."

"You sure? This one is a dinosaur, back when they

made shit out of cement and rocks. So... it is pretty *heavy.*" Syd warned, her lavender hair falling in her face so she had to blow it away.

"Yeah, I got it." Searra assured her. Syd let go and Searra carried the microwave with ease to her bin and tossed it in. It hit the bottom with a loud crash. The impact reverberated in the cement beneath her feet. *Damn, she was pretty strong.* It surprised Searra and her face pinched in confusion.

"I told you it was heavy, but it turns out you are SheHulk." Her face lit in a bright smile before falling again. "Did you see Ma?" Shadows crossed her sister's expression as she said it.

"Yeah, she is watching Jade right now. She seemed in good spirits today. A lot of energy." Searra said, keeping her tone light.

"Yeah, I think today is a good day. But she threw up last night. She didn't have anything in her stomach though." Syd's voice wavered, but her expression stayed impassive, clinical. It was the mask of a nurse, a caregiver.

"Yeah..." Searra didn't know what to say. It had been like this the last two years, their Mom's health steadily growing worse as the treatments continued.

"Okay, I'm gonna go help Ma and then take a nap before work." Syd said before giving Searra a salute and heading inside.

Searra stood there for a moment before heading back to the canopy to start her workout.

Her thoughts drifted from her mom to her dream from last night, and the mysterious demon intruder. Her heart began to beat faster in her chest, like a hummingbird. And his words echoed back to her from her memory, *You already know.* What did he mean by that?

Did she though? She had a sinking suspicion that the most outlandish idea was not far from the truth. Her gut tended to be right, and her gut was screaming at her now that something was *wrong.* The fainting, the crazy strength, that last night might not have been a dream. She wanted to test her theory.

That monster bit her, sucked on her neck like a fucking vampire. And what did vampires hate?

Searra stood next to her workout bench, her dumbbells scattered around her, and decided to go back inside the house. Striding through the back door and into the kitchen, she went straight for the spice cabinet and grabbed the garlic powder. She popped the shaker and took a deep inhale, taking in the aroma into her nose.

The first thing she thought of was pasta, which would have made her hungry had she not already been queasy this morning. She turned it over and shook some out into the palm of her hand, but nothing happened when it touched her skin; no burning sensation or disgust, or she wasn't quite sure what she thought would happen. But so far, it was a whole lot of nothing. With slight hesitation, she brought her hand to her mouth and her tongue stuck out to gingerly explore the mound of garlicky powder.

The taste that hit her tongue was rancid. So sour and abominable that she spat it out into the nearby sink. She reached out, desperate for water, and turned on the faucet. Scooping up the cool water with her other hand and gargling it, trying to purge the putrid flavor from her mouth.

With complete disgust, she turned over the bottle on

the counter to further inspect it. It expired over ten years ago.

Oh my god. Ewwww.

She unscrewed the top of the shaker and took a look inside. It was alive and wriggling. Searra blanched, pretty sure she was going to vomit, she put the cap back on so violently that she ripped right through the plastic threads and ran outside to dump them in the trashbins.

The gloom had vanished and the sun decided to burst through and bring some heat to the day. The thread-bare screen door creaked in its tin frame as it shut behind her, the hinges rusted over.

The sun was more intense than usual as she opened the lid to the dumpster bin and tossed in the container of wiggly garlic worms. Gagging a little as it thunked to the bottom. The stench of old trash wafted to her nose as she let the lid fall closed.

As she turned away, she lost balance for a quick second, but she caught herself. She wiped her brow with the back of her hand and was shocked that a slick sheen of sweat coating her skin. She was sweating, profusely. It really wasn't that kind of hot, but Searra was melting.

There was upper lip sweat! Which was reserved for intense workouts only, not taking out the trash.

Her breath came in shorter and shorter gasps, like she wasn't getting enough air. Her sweat beaded on her top lip. It had been one hundred and fifteen degrees only a few weeks ago, and she hadn't sweat like this.

She must have the flu.

Her stomach began to churn with a nausea so violent, she thought she would puke right there, but she swallowed down the bile building at the back of her throat with sheer force of stubborn will.

Determined to make it to the bathroom, Searra ran inside the house. Her feet were like lead blocks with all the coordination of cooked spaghetti, she half-tripped, half-fell into the kitchen. Her hands out to brace her fall, she bounded up and in one leap was in the dining room with grace she didn't know she had. She was about to hop over the baby gate and into the living room with Jade and her mom to get to the bathroom, but she stopped. The nausea had subsided. In fact, she was fine.

She probably was coming down with something. Or that nasty old garlic powder made her sick. *It did have worms.*

"Hey Ma!" Searra called from behind the barrier, "Do you think you could watch her while I nap a little?"

Her mom nodded with assurance. Syd was sitting next to her on the couch and Searra caught her eye. Her sister dipped her head in a slight nod, assuring Searra that she would watch both the little baby and the big baby.

"Thanks Ma. I'm feeling a little weird and I hope I'm not getting sick."

"I'll set my alarm for thirty minutes okay?" Searra said more for Syd, than her mom.

"Sure sure. Take the time you need. I got the little one." Her mom said, smiling big so Searra could see the gap on the sides where she was missing teeth.

Giving them a thumbs up, Searra hopped the second baby gate and headed to her bedroom. She made it to her bed and flopped down on it like a limp fish.

She was so tired that she succumbed within mere moments, drifting into darkness and was dead to the world.

Chapter
4

Sickly

A high-pitched scream peeled out, and Searra went rigid. Her heart began to thud in her chest and her adrenaline spiked. In an instant, she was out of bed and standing. Through the light of her bedroom window, she noticed it was already dark outside. Her half-dead spider plant peeked at her through the curtains on the window ledge, casting long clawed shadows across the room. Diego had bought it to help keep the air fresh in the room for Jade, but Searra had managed to kill it.

How long had she slept?! Searra thought to herself. *It was only supposed to be thirty minutes!*

She grabbed her phone, resting on the floating shelf

above her headboard, and realized she had slept for ten hours!

What the fuck?!

Searra stormed out of her room, expecting to give her mom an earful and make sure Jade was okay. But as soon as she peeked out of her room, they were both sitting on the couch. Jade was in her lap, content and watching Ms. Rachel on the projector. She was curled into her grandma like she was a plush recliner. Searra's anger melted into nothing but vapor and blew away.

Seeing everything was alright, Searra went into the bathroom to relieve herself and splash some water on her face. She did feel better than she had earlier, but that was with an entire extra day of rest. So she *better* be feeling better. It was rare she would get extra rest like this *...any rest really.*

She was shocked her mom was able to handle Jade for so long; the longest she had gone was three hours before her energy had run out, and she needed to go take a nap. Searra couldn't blame her, though; she was in her seventies and was going through chemo. Her mom helped her out as much as possible, but it was limited. Thank goodness her sister was there as a back up.

The overhead lights in the bathroom were harsh on her eyes, searing them in their sockets. Searra had to turn them off and wash her face in the dark.

In the mirror, she looked so pale. Normally, she had a golden tone to her skin, instead of a pink tone like her sister, but this was the palest she had ever seen herself. Her veins popped from beneath her skin. The green tracks were prominent on her neck and arms. She had never noticed how many veins she could see before. Searra wasn't the most observant, so maybe it was something she had overlooked until now.

It took her months after she gave birth to catch the new thin webs of varicose veins on her thighs.

Maybe she needed more sun? But the idea made her stomach lurch.

Searra washed her face and headed to the living room and plopped down on the couch next to her mom and Jade.

"Sorry, Ma," Searra said with a huff. "I didn't mean to sleep so long." She rubbed her palm against her forehead, "I guess I forgot to set the alarm." Although, she could have sworn she had. Searra let out a heavy sigh. She was still exhausted, but that was nothing new. She consisted of only caffeine and protein powder these days... since Diego.

"How was she?" Searra asked, smiling at Jade. Her voice lilting as she pinched Jade's plump pink cheeks, getting a high-pitched giggle out of her. She still had dry beans on her cheeks from her earlier meal. But she just managed to look cuter with a bean-y grin. Searra couldn't help her own answering smile. Jade's happy disposition never failed to pull Searra out from the depths of her darker thoughts. Her little wiggling ball of sunshine.

"Oh, she was fine." Her mom said, "She was crying for you though. She wanted Mama." Her eyes crinkled with a thin smile that made the apples of her cheeks look extra full, like a chipmunk stashing treats for winter.

"Did she eat?"

"Yeah, she had eggs, beans, and a pouch. She had a

little bit of her bottle, but didn't finish."

"Okay. That's good! I'm surprised she ate with you! What about the dogs?"

"I fed the dogs too. And, she was hungry! Plus, I couldn't wake you up!"

"What?!" Searra was dumbfounded, there was no way she was dead asleep and couldn't be woken up if someone tried. That's coma status, or more like her sister. Syd couldn't be roused if the house was on fire; but not Searra.

"You must not have tried that hard Ma. I'm not Syd." Searra countered, giving her mom a scowl.

Jade giggled at Searra's face and made a scowl of her own. She even crossed her plump arms and made a little huff too, breathing air out of her little nose like a tiny angry dragon. But a loud laugh bubbled up and exploded from her, a high-pitched raptor noise, as she wiggled out from her seat on grandma's lap and onto the floor.

She spun on her heel, slightly unsteady, and took off screaming. Clomping her feet down and arms straight out, a baby Frankenstein's monster. Her tiny Crocs echoed on the hardwood floor as she stomped.

Searra's heart squeezed.

Jade was the most precious thing in her life and she loved her with all her heart. She didn't know what she would do if something happened to her. Searra's thoughts turned dark as she was reminded of last night and how terrified she had been for both her and Jade.

Had that been a dream? Or had all that happened?

Ice cold dread seeped into her veins and her mind began to unravel, dragging her down, down, down to despair, the intrusive "what ifs" creating a black abyss she didn't know how to climb out of.

Searra was pulled from her thoughts as she realized her mom had been talking to her, "...I even kept hitting you! And nothing!" Her mom waved her hands to mimic the smacks she gave earlier. "I was actually about to check on you again. Was getting a little worried since that kind of sleep isn't normal."

"Well, I'm up now." Searra huffed, not quite able to shake off her dread.

"I hope you feel better at least!" Her mom said, "Although, I think you need more rest. You look a little worse."

Searra nodded absent-mindedly; she didn't want to tell her mom she still felt exhausted. It's not like she could do anything about it. If she were sick, the only way out was through.

With every passing moment, her entire body was growing leaden and weighing her down. Moving was becoming more and more of a struggle, like a piece of clay in a kiln; the hotter she got, the less she was able to move. Her body was being stiffened, molded in a forge.

She felt her forehead, and to her icy hands, she did feel hot and a little sticky. She wiped the excess moisture on her pajama pants, getting a little grossed out by her own juices, and bile rose in the back of her throat.

She really was getting sick, it must be the flu or something. It was going to take her out, she could feel it.

Fuuuuuuuck. She did not have time for this.

Jade began to rub her eyes with the backs of her hands, a low whine building in her throat.

"Did she have a nap today?" She was so thirsty, her

tongue stuck to the roof of her mouth as she spoke.

"She fell asleep on me with her bottle earlier, and I let her rest there." Searra's mom gave her a faint smile. Her mom couldn't pick Jade up to put her in the crib, so she had made the best of it.

"How long ago?"

"Around two."

"Awesome. Okay, Ma. Thanks. I really appreciate you watching her." Searra gave her mom a smile that stretched across her face, even though she was starting to feel worse. Searra knew her mom was tapped out, especially since she had a chemo session three days ago, and the fatigue always hit hardest on day three.

"Pee-Paw loves to hang with her little June Bug." Her mom cooed to Jade. Shuffling over to where Jade had laid her head down on the floor sofa —half on, half off.

Her little body hung off and her butt was sticking up in the air, the outline of the little lion stamped on the diaper peeking through her pink pants. Jade began to emit a low keening sound. Her chubby pink hands covered her eyes as her whines began to get louder, the sound made Searra wince and her heart rate increased, but it felt sluggish in her chest. Like it was pumping thick mud through her veins and struggled.

Searra's mom bent over low, hands on her knees as she tried to get down to Jade's level. "I love you cutie pie! Pee-paw is going to go to bed now!" Jade did not look up or acknowledge Grandma, a sure sign she was about done for the day.

Bedtime ASAP!

Searra told Jade as she looked into her big brown eyes framed by long luxurious lashes, spread out like a fan on her pink cheeks, "Okay *mi amor*[1], time for bed! We gotta wash your hands and feet and brush your teeth."

Jade pulled her hands from her face and stopped her whine long enough to ask, "Teeeeee?" Her short, stubby fingers pointed to her bottom row of teeth. Her little finger moved from side to side, mimicking a brushing motion as excitement sparked in her warm, russet eyes.

Searra smiled and confirmed, "Yes sweetie! We are gonna brush your teeth!"

The number of words Jade had picked up was astounding to Searra. Jade was so smart and learned quickly. It made her heart swell with pride. "You are such a smarty pants, *vida!*[2] "Searra murmured as she pressed kisses into Jade's hair on the crown of her head.

Searra held out her hand as she guided Jade to the bathroom sink to help her brush her teeth. As Searra was about to grab Jade's toothbrush from it's drawer, a shadow moved across the large window to the left of the toilet.

---

1. My love (term of endearment)

2. Life (term of endearment)

CHAPTER 5

SOMBRA (SHADOW)

"THE SHADOW OF THYSELF IS ON ME." - LORD BYRON (1817)

The bathroom window overlooked the front porch. It was full of thick, opaque glass blocks that made it impossible to see any details outside, but she did see movement, she was certain.

Maybe it was a delivery driver?

Searra tried to use logic, and didn't want to panic with Jade sitting at her feet.

A late delivery?

She craned her head to listen for the telltale sign of a package hitting her porch, but the sound didn't come. She listened harder, thinking maybe she might hear a knock or the doorbell. But she was only greeted with silence.

"Teeeeeee?" Jade asked again. Her tiny voice was unusually loud in the quiet, tinkling like windchimes in a gathering storm.

The quiet was unnerving. She held her breath, sure someone was there. The hairs on Searra's arms and the back of her neck began to stand up. A cold shiver snaked down her spine as her instincts kicked into overdrive. She definitely felt like she was being watched and her mouth went dry.

Searra picked up Jade, who felt so light and fragile in her arms that it unsettled her. Pure adrenaline coursed through her veins as she clutched Jade to her chest.

Jade giggled in response, unaware of the potential danger.

She wasn't as little as she used to be and her long toddler legs could almost touch behind Searra's back when wrapped around her waist.

Searra rushed out of the bathroom, but instead of heading to their bedroom or the front door, she bolted to the sliding glass door that led out into the backyard, flicking the light switch on as she went.

The backyard was immediately bathed in a warm glow from the hanging tea lights zigzagging across the yard. It was spacious enough that they could fit another house back there if they had the money. But a larger area meant more places to hide. The shadows expanded around her, despite the lights and she clutched Jade to her with even more ferocity.

Her dogs, *Pepito*[1] and Hazel, were sleeping out there on the back covered porch that had been converted into a makeshift mini bar and Searra knew they would act as guards if anyone broke in and followed her out there. They were two large fawn-colored boxers and were pretty intimidating when they were confronted with people they didn't know.

Pepito began pacing when she got outside, his taut muscles flexed as he stalked from one side of the backyard to the other, a low whine in his throat, his expression alert, eyes searching the dark.

Something was wrong. *Pepito* was never this tense. Even Hazel, who had a habit of wiggling her big butt around, was still and cautious. She was an old girl with little patience, but her sugar face was leery and her deep brown eyes were focused. Hazel sensed something was off too.

Searra's adrenaline was spiking with fear as she realized she wasn't imagining the danger. It was becoming all too real and she felt wired and alert for the first time all day.

She stood there in the dark, waiting, hardly breathing. Straining her ears to hear anything. Jade wriggled in her arms, wanting to walk around, a whiny cry was building and Searra was shushing her to keep her quiet as best she could; bouncing her up and down and rubbing her back to keep Jade calm.

A predatory snarl sounded in *Pepito's* throat and the hairs on her shoulders pricked. But *Pepito* was facing Searra and Jade as he growled, his head bowed low

---

1. Little Pepe

and teeth glinting in the hanging tea lights above their heads.

Searra had never seen that expression on *Pepito's* face before, ever. Even when he was nervous or barked at people walking by the house, it was more anxiety-driven. A snarl like this sounded feral and Searra backed up a step.

She used all the command in her voice to hopefully snap him out of it, "Hey! No! *Pepito!* You do NOT growl at us!"

Her words came out stronger than she anticipated and she took another step back. Her heel hit the foot of her exercise bench, pinning her in a corner of weights and machines. If she had to get out of the way, she was limited in her movements, especially with Jade in her arms.

Pepito's expression didn't change. The low growl reverberating from his chest grew stronger, and he began a vicious bark that made her ears ring.

"Pepito? What's wrong boy?" Searra tried again. Her voice wavered, her calm and controlled demeanor evaporated as cold, sticky fear clung to her.

A voice made of velvet and shadow sounded from behind her, "He seems... less than fond of me." He let out a low chuckle that sent shivers down her spine.

Searra's breath caught in her throat as she whirled around to face the man — *the monster* from her dream. Or what she had *thought* was a dream. *Did he have an accent? How had she not clocked that last night? He sounded like fucking Antonio Banderas.*

"The fuck!" Searra screamed before she could compose herself.

His green eyes sparkled as he barked a laugh. His

lips quirked up into a sideways smile that looked semi-genuine, and his white teeth gleamed in the soft light.

"What the fuck do you want?" Searra spat, putting all the fear and anger she felt into it, which was morphing into only anger the longer they stood there.

Jade went still in her arms, dark eyes watchful. *Pepito's* growl quieted as the stranger stared at him. Emerald eyes flashed gold for a moment and Pepito scampered away. His tail was down as he circled his blue fuzzy bed on the porch and curled up as if he was going to sleep.

The stranger's eyes locked on her again, they were back to a simmering green and his beautiful smile fell away. "I'd rather continue this conversation in private," his voice was rich, like red velvet cake as he brought his hand up to examine his nails, nonchalance painted into his very essence as he stood there. His gaze flicked to the door behind her, "Inside, preferably."

What?!

"Why *the fuck* would I want you in my house again?" Searra's eyes were wide in disbelief and more than a little fear. She felt like she was in a bizarro world. Where people broke into your house and acted like it was their right. That they could *bite* you and still expect civility.

Who the hell did he think he was? What the fuck is going on? Had she been drugged? Was she hallucinating?

She had no idea what was going on, or who he was, or even *what* he was. Had he come back to finish what he started last night? Searra knew she would go down fighting to her last breath to keep Jade safe.

"I know things must feel disorienting to you. I'll explain everything — once we are inside." His broad shoulders and chest seemed to relax as he said it, making his giant frame shrink a little, like he was trying to be less intimidating. It wasn't working.

"We are fine out here," Searra stood firm. "There is no one else around."

Jade was now clutching the strap of her razorback tank so hard she thought her shirt might rip. Her little fist was balled up tight, making her knuckles white.

A flash of irritation crossed his features, but it was gone in an instant and his handsome, rugged face smoothed out again. "The night has ears," he breathed, "and you have neighbors." His bright eyes shifted left to right.

Did they glow? They reminded Searra of a jungle cat. Reflective and shifty.

"Anyone or *anything* could overhear." He added.

Anyone could overhear what?! You killing us?!

Searra could not keep her cool any longer and pure exasperation had her spitting out a retort before her brain could stop her, "What if I don't give a *fuck?!* I promise to scream bloody murder if you so much as touch us," Searra gave him a furious point with her finger as she continued, "And you won't have to worry if the neighbors heard, 'cause you will know for certain they did. No matter if we are out here or in the fucking house." She put as much venom and conviction into her tone as she could muster.

Silence hung in the air between them as they stood in her dark backyard, a chill settling into her bones as the temperature dropped. Her breath danced on the night air in whisps of smoke.

His voice cut through in a sudden burst of gruff admission, "I'm a friend of Diego's."

CHAPTER 6

STRANGER

"I AM VERY LOW, I AM THE WORST OF ALL MEN; I HAVE DESTROYED MY LIFE, AND I HAVE NOTHING LEFT BUT THE NIGHTMARE OF

MY OWN EXISTENCE." -ROBERT LOUIS STEVENSON (1886)

Searra's heart dropped into her stomach as she took in what the stranger had just revealed. Her brain had frozen over and nothing was getting through.

Unbidden, she was back there... the last time she saw Diego. She remembered his big smile as he walked out the front door, his goodbye kisses to her and Jade. It dragged her down into a pit of despair, thinking about him and how she would never see him again, that Jade would never see her father again.

Her eyes stung with tears long since dried and she

felt the icy stab of nausea low in her stomach. Bile rose to threaten the back of her throat, it was hard to form words. She had to work to swallow and keep her composure.

"What?" Searra finally said, her voice cracking with grief and tears sprang out and clouded her vision.

Do NOT cry! She screamed to herself, willing everything she had into that one thought.

Jade wriggled in her arms, tearing Searra from her grief for the moment so she could catch her breath. Jade began stretching out her body and let out a loud whine to be put down. Searra tried to shift her so she was more comfortable on her hip, but with Jade's shrill whine growing louder, Searra looked deep into the eyes of the man before her, the depthless green pools were swimming with emotion, but not one she could place or understand. There might have been pain and maybe even sincerity?

She made a snap decision she would most likely regret later, but she was trusting her gut. If she didn't need answers before, she fucking needed them now.

Searra readjusted her daughter on her hip and turned her back on the stranger. With a subtle nod of her head, she motioned for him to follow her inside.

As soon as they crossed the threshold, Searra put Jade down on the ground, and she took off like a wind-up toy. Searra ran and beat her to the hallway to lock the baby gate, and then Searra turned around and crossed to the other side of the room to lock the other one, separating the office from the living room. Searra heard Jade stomping after her in her little Crocs as she tried to escape.

The stranger stood in the threshold of the sliding

glass door, his wide body looking a little too broad to fit in the frame. He took a deep breath, tension between his brows and his lips pursed.

He took one step and then another, moving like he was in pain, or through cement. His shoulders came in one at a time so he didn't hit the sides of the door frame, and he bowed his head to make sure he didn't hit the top. Then he was inside, and the energy in the entire house shifted; the air crackled and Searra couldn't help but hold her breath.

Suddenly, Jade ran straight for the man like he owed her money. Searra's heart leapt into her throat as she tried to intercept her, but Jade made it to him first. Her little arms wrapping around his leg like the trunk of a tree. She squealed with joy as she repeated, "Sit too? Sit too? Sit toooooo!"

Searra caught the expressions as they flashed across the intruder's face— first confusion, then surprise, and finally... warmth? His emerald eyes shimmered as he looked down at Jade, a genuine, gentle smile tugging at the corners of his mouth. He then proceeded to sit down in the middle of the floor with her, his hulking frame comical amidst the field of toddler toys.

The stranger scooted the nearest box of random items next to Jade, who smiled mischievously at him. All it contained was a bunch of different colored blocks and a hairbrush. She shuffled away on her butt and sat on the edge of the floor couch, taking the box of toys with her. In one swift move, she dumped out the entire thing, and everything scattered in an impressive arc around her. Searra fought the urge to tidy up and just stood in the middle of the room, watching this man as he sat on the floor, transfixed by Jade.

Searra cleared her throat, "Okay. Go on."

It took a moment for him to respond as he tore his gaze away from Jade, but his brows slowly lifted and his full mouth twitched upward, "What? Offering no refreshments?"

Searra swore his teeth gleamed and lengthened as he drew out the last word.

Jeeeeesuuuussss. Just when she was comfortable enough to forget the predator he was.

Searra could guess what he was alluding to and she did nothing to hide her irritation. There was no way in hell she would let him bite her again.

Searra gave him the most withering stare, trying to bore holes into his head with her steel will. She was not amused, especially with him sitting so close to her daughter.

A moment of silence passed between them, and only the sounds of Jade playing on the floor permeated the quiet. Her blocks clacked as she enthusiastically tried to push them into each other. Her little brow furrowed as her frustration mounted over pieces that didn't fit together.

The whining would start soon if she didn't distract her. So Searra quickly bent down and handed Jade the hairbrush that was on the floor. Jade gave her a big, open-mouthed smile and accepted the hairbrush with gratitude, and proceeded to bang the head of it on the floor. The *bang, bang, bang* reverberated in Searra's head and gave her a slight tension headache.

Searra was already overstimulated and tried her best to remain calm and level-headed. She pinched her nose under the pads of her glasses, massaging away the pressure, and readjusted them. Her vision seemed more blurred than usual, and she guessed the most likely culprit to be exhaustion.

Searra knelt down again and pried the hairbrush from Jade's vice-like grip, saying "Thank you, Sweetie!" And switched it for her rubber remote lying in the box on the coffee table.

Jade hesitated a moment, scrutinizing the rubber toy, but soon she smiled and put it in her mouth to chew. Her eyes crinkled with pure joy and a giggle escaped her. She shook her head like a dog, making the remote flop from side to side, reminding Searra of a limp noodle. Jade was burbling to herself and began to chew it like gum. Time was limited before Jade realized she was tired again and needed to be put down.

"Okay, I've only got so long before she needs to go down for the night." Searra pointed with her chin at Jade, hands on her hips. "I need to know who you are and what the hell is going on?"

Searra looked down at her dirty and worn Crocs, not quite able to maintain eye contact when she at last asked, "And how do you know Diego?" She didn't need him to witness her pain. Clearing her throat, she sighed and looked up to meet his eyes, which were already locked on her.

The stranger's posssive gaze swept over her and sparkled.

Searra felt the heat in his expression and was suddenly very aware that she was in her flannel pajama bottoms and racerback tank with no bra. She chided herself for not having her sweater. As if on cue, her nipples hardened under his piercing stare. Searra crossed her arms against her chest to cover them up, and her cheeks flushed a little.

Completely mortifying.

The corner of his mouth lifted for a second, almost looking smug, like embarrassment was stamped on her face. Then his gaze landed on Jade. A muscle ticked in his jaw, and he looked at Searra again. Saddness emanated from his stare for a fleeting moment, before it evaporated like smoke.

"My name is Juan. I've been sent to protect you. Both of you." He nodded to Jade. His voice was hypnotic, his words a melody on his tongue.

There was a beat of silence while Searra tried to process what he just said even though she was half distracted by the way his lips formed words.

"You're serious?" Searra's tone was dripping with incredulity. She almost laughed if it wasn't for his grave expression. "What are you even talking about?" Searra's hands raked through her long dark hair, her frustration evident and she wished she had her claw clip handy to pin her hair up. When it was down, it annoyed the shit out of her.

"Diego got involved with some..." Juan paused, seeming to search for the words, "very bad people."

"What do you mean? Like illegal shit?" Searra questioned, though she doubted Diego would have gotten involved with criminals. He wasn't a saint by any stretch of the imagination, but that would have put Jade at risk and Searra wasn't sure he'd do that.

"Very," Juan confirmed, as he stepped closer to her, eyes flashing with something close to hunger.

Searra felt the heat as the space between their bodies narrowed. She took a step back. "So, what was last night then? That didn't feel like protection."

"I had to see what you already knew, and make you

stronger to stand against what is coming."

"And what is coming?" Searra asked, worry lacing her tone.

"More like me."

CHAPTER 7

PODEROSO (STRENGTH)

"THE ONLY WAY TO GET RID OF A
TEMPTATION IS TO YIELD TO IT."
-OSCAR WILDE (1890)

His words were smooth, like silk but the warning in them was clear.

More like him? What did that mean? A gang of sexy demons that break into people's bedrooms and drink their blood? That was insane!

Amusement flashed across his face, making her cheeks heat but Searra shook it off, trying to focus.

"What do you mean, *make me stronger?*" Searra wasn't sure she heard him right, but her stomach sank to the floor and her heart began to race with dread. Her mouth went dry and she would have killed for a drink of water. She was so thirsty that her tongue stuck to the roof of her mouth.

"You already know what I mean. *No te hagas.*[1]" He gave a soft smile but it didn't reach his eyes. "I can already see 'the change' in you. It's only a matter of time now."

A matter of time?! Searra felt like she was being spoken to in a foreign language. Nothing was getting through and her frustration was mounting. "What did you do to me?!" She wailed. Searra began to back up, fear coating her veins; it was fear and disbelief. *The change?!* Was she turning into a monster too? The realization hit her like a ton of bricks. She had the strongest urge to grab Jade and run, but where would they go? They were trapped in the house with a *monster.*

What if Jade wasn't safe with her? The thought was like ice water in her veins. *What if she were the monster now? Would she hurt her own child?*

Searra shook her head, there was no possibility— she would take her own life first. She couldn't think like that. Those kind of intrusive thoughts were all too familiar, and she refused to entertain them again.

"I gave my word that I would protect you, and that's what I've done." Juan took a step towards them, green eyes lit from within. His gaze searched hers, an almost desperate gleam to them.

"What *the fuck* are you?" Searra hissed through her teeth. She couldn't stand him saying Diego's name or whatever promises he *claimed* to have made to him.

---

1. Don't pretend.

Juan's gaze remained on hers, "I am what your myths and legends would call a vampire, or the undead... nosferatu." His face was deadly serious as his tongue seemed to roll languidly over each syllable of 'nosferatu,' like a song. But there was not a hint of playfulness on his beautiful face. He went on, "But 'undead' is not accurate."

Searra's mouth fell open, speechless. Her brain came up blank.

Vampire.

He was a vampire.

She couldn't deny that she had skirted around the idea earlier, but she wasn't able to label it in her thoughts. She kept edging around it, never quite leaving the outer reaches of her mind.

Vampire. That would have been ridiculous! Vampires weren't real.

But, he *had* bitten her last night. It wasn't a dream no matter how much she wanted it to be. He had drunk her blood and even displayed crazy speed and strength, where she had been no match for him, like swatting a fly. She remembered how quick he had been, seeming to appear behind her out of thin air. And yet, it was still on a whole other level to actually say it out loud.

It became so much more.

It made it real.

And he had said he *changed* her. So, she was becoming a vampire too.

She felt sick.

Her brain was filled with so many questions that they overwhelmed her and the only thing she could ask was "How long?" Her voice came out threadbare, a whisper.

Wet heat stung the corners of her eyes and she looked at Jade. She was lying down, almost out of gas. She chewed on her squishy fingers as her eyelids fluttered.

Searra's heart squeezed as she looked down at her daughter, and she couldn't hold back the tears. Twin trails of wetness tracked down her cheeks and she didn't even care that Juan was watching her.

He had turned her into a *fucking demon.* She remembered Juan's glowing golden eyes and ridged forehead... the double rows of canines reminiscent of some kind of mutant shark. Searra shivered, disgust clogging her throat making her almost choke.

Her thoughts came back to Jade. *What if she couldn't control herself?* Searra didn't know, but couldn't imagine her life without Jade. Of potentially giving her over to someone else? *No.* Everything in her recoiled at the notion. She couldn't imagine her life without Jade. Her sadness was giving way to anger.

Anger at him, at the world... at Diego.

It was a white hot rage that made her face flush and her heart thud in her chest. Her face was so hot, she was surprised the tears didn't evaporate straight off her skin. This kind of anger felt foreign. Searra was never an angry person, so this rage was new to her and she wasn't quite sure how to handle it. It was all-consuming, like she *was* the tempest.

Juan had moved closer, looking on full alert, waiting for Searra to make the first move.

Searra took a deep breath and, again, looked to Jade where she was lying on the floor. Her eyes had closed. Her *pancita*[2] moved up and down as she breathed. She was all little pink cheeks and beautiful, shaggy, light brown hair. It was pulled up into a little firework on top of her head, or at least as much as Searra could gather in the hair tie. Jade's little arms and legs twitched as she fell deeper into sleep.

"I need to put her in her crib, and then we can finish this." She said it as calm as she could through the red haze of rage.

She breathed in and out. Through the nose and out through the mouth. Imagining her anger passing through, like smoke in the wind. Telling herself that emotions were temporary, even intense ones.

She bent down to pick up Jade, careful to get under her legs first, then her shoulders, and cradled Jade against her chest. Searra moved inch by inch so as not to wake her, turning and walking from the room and careful not to jostle Jade.

There was a prick of awareness when she turned her back on Juan. It was probably something he wasn't used to. You shouldn't turn your back on a predator. She'd heard that on a documentary somewhere.

Searra made it through the hallway and turned into the open bedroom striding toward the crib at the back of the room. With gentle hands, Searra lowered Jade down and rested her head on the pillow, then lowered her legs onto the rest of the bed.

---

2. Little belly

Once Searra withdrew her hands, Jade began to stir, turned a little, and moaned. She then scrunched a little more into a tight fetal position and didn't stir again.

Searra turned on the white noise monkey, increasing volume until it was at the max, and began to back away. She moved silent as a shadow through the room and back out the door, holding her breath as she went.

When the latch clicked on the door handle and she was safely outside the bedroom, Searra let herself breathe out a long gust of air, shoulders slumped as she leaned with her back against the hallway wall.

She turned her head and her gaze collided with Juan's. Searra had almost forgotten he was there. His green eyes were observant, watching her, but his expression was unreadable. She wasn't sure what he saw when he looked at her like that, but she was so tired she didn't care anymore. Maybe it was because Jade was finally asleep for the night, but all the strength and energy left her body. She practically crawled back to the living room and plopped down on the couch in a big heap.

Searra was quiet for a long moment, and the air between them began to grow thick with tension. She wasn't sure which of them would speak first, but she didn't know what to say anymore. Her brain was mush and all the questions she had escaped her.

The silence grew heavy.

She let out a long sigh and got up from the couch, unable to sit in the silence any longer.

"Did you want something to drink?" Searra had every intention of heading to the kitchen to grab her bottle of Moscato from the fridge and pour herself a hefty glass.

Surprise flickered in Juan's expression, which then turned mischievous and a small smile played across his lips.

As her words sank in, Searra bit back a harsh laugh. "I meant alcohol, you leech." But there was surprisingly little hostility in her tone, just exhaustion. She absent-mindedly rubbed the spot on her neck where he had bitten her the night before. Her pulse quickened at the memory and a throb of pleasure began deep in her core that she ignored.

She cleared her throat and looked down at her feet, hoping he couldn't tell how flustered she was. "I have reposado tequila or white wine." She offered, her face flicked up to his, and she raised her dark eyebrows in invitation and waited for an answer, even though she really didn't feel like sharing her wine. She did have a bunch of whiskey and vodka too in the bar Diego had stocked, but she didn't like those options, so she didn't feel like offering them. Plus, they were probably dusty as fuck and she didn't want to have to clean.

"White wine."His voice smooth as he moved to the side of the couch with the attached ottoman and put his feet up, careful to keep his shoes from touching the fabric. He was the picture of comfort. His body language was casual, looking like he belonged there.

When Searra raised her eyebrow in surprise at his choice, Juan said, "I prefer sweet."

She couldn't help her answering smile. It was refreshing for a man to admit to liking white wine. All the guys she had known or dated would have rather choked on the nastiest rubbing alcohol than drink a dessert wine. *Machismo*[3] *at it's finest.*

Juan gave a sly smile back that lit up his eyes.

"I do too," Searra replied.

Before she went to grab the wine, Searra remembered she needed to turn on the baby monitor. She walked over to Juan and bent over. Reaching into the little hole made between the couch, fireplace, and the coffee table. It was where the extension cord was that had all the electronics plugged into it, like her phone charger, the baby monitor, and the charger for the vacuum. It was the only place Jade couldn't get to, so stuff she wasn't supposed to play with tended to find its way into that hole.

Searra had to reach over Juan's legs to get to any one of those things. Trying her best to ignore how close he was, she could feel the heat of his proximity buzzing in her veins. Her breasts brushed the top of his thighs as she reached to grab the monitor, sending a zing of pleasure right to her core, and her nipples hardened beneath her thin tank. She tried to shake the feeling off, but she felt her face get hot with embarrassment and her skin prickled with gooseflesh up her arms and down the back of her neck.

Her pulse began to race as her fingers reached haphazardly and finally brushed against the monitor as she scrambled to grab it. She pulled the baby moni-

---

3. In Mexican culture, it is a traditional ideal of masculinity rooted in hyper-masculinity, male pride, and authority, often reinforcing gender inequality and emotional suppression, while also carrying expectations of honor, protection, and family duty.

tor out of the hole and held down the button to turn it on, and waited for the satisfying *chhhhhhhh.*

She clipped the monitor to the waistband of her pajama bottoms and tried to sneak another look at Juan. Her dark eyes met his and there was heat in his gaze. She quickly slid her eyes away and hustled out of the living room, through the office and into the kitchen.

She grabbed the wine that was chilling on the bottom shelf of the refrigerator and headed back to the office. Lifting up the door on the top shelf of the large metal cabinet and pulled out two wine glasses, or they might have been champagne flutes or whiskey tumblers for all Searra knew. But they were the fancy glasses, and she decided wine deserved a fancy glass.

With the wine and glasses, Searra made her way back to the living room. She set the glasses down on the coffee table and unscrewed the cap from the wine bottle. She heard the satisfying crack of the plastic seal breaking and poured the wine until it was almost to the brim of each one. The bubbles fizzed inside the thin glasses, traveling up from the bottom to the surface to break against the lip. The site made her mouth water, and she could not remember the last time she wanted a drink so bad.

She grabbed the full glass and handed it over to Juan, their fingers touched and it sent a spark of awareness through her. Searra cleared her throat, "Okaaaaaay." Drawing out the word as she sat down on the opposite end of the couch with her wine, legs curled up under her as she took her seat.

His expression was unreadable as she stared at him.

"What were you doing here last night?" Searra asked before taking a big mouthful of Moscato. The sweetness coated her tongue as the bubbles burned her throat and a delicious warmth spread in her belly. She didn't quite have her thoughts gathered enough for a full interrogation, but she thought if they started in order, she could at least keep shit straight.

Juan swirled the wine in his glass and took a sip. "This reminds me of something from long ago." His expression turned wistful as he looked, lost in his thoughts for a minute. "I needed to know that you were who I was looking for."

"Last night, you said you needed information." Searra prodded, one of her brows raising. She was already starting to feel a little tipsy from the alcohol. Her tolerance was in the gutter nowadays.

Juan nodded, but he didn't speak. The white noise from the baby monitor echoed in her ears making the quiet between them all the more pointed. "Yes, it's my gift," Juan said, breaking the silence. He took another swig of his wine and smiled. "The blood, you see. It tells me things."

Searra's brows knitted together, trying to stay focused on the conversation, but his mouth was so distracting and her head was swimming. "What do you mean?" Juan's bottom lip looked so soft, like she should bite it.

No. Lordy, she shouldn't consume alcohol ever again.

"When I drink from someone, I can see thoughts, images. Sometimes a single memory, with others I get impressions. It's different with everyone."

Searra almost spit out her drink in a scoff but tried to cover it with a cough. "What did you see when you drank from me?" She croaked a little as wine went down the wrong pipe.

Even though she didn't believe what he was saying, she was still curious where this conversation was going. And the warmth from the wine had begun to spread, relaxing her entire body, including her brain—making her a little bolder than she would have been. Plus, he was just so pretty to look at.

Juan's jaw muscle ticked, bringing her attention from his mouth to the sharp line of his jaw. Her eyes traveled down his strong neck to his broad shoulders and chest, her pulse began to race as she starred, tilting her head as she did.

Juan cleared his throat, a knowing smile on his perfect lips. His eyes looked molten for a quick second but Searra blinked and it was gone.

On a normal day, she would have been embarrassed to have been caught staring, but she didn't have the energy for it and the wine was doing wonders for her confidence. Her tolerance was definitely shot, and she was buzzing.

Juan's voice was a little gruff and his eyes darkened, "I mainly got emotions from you." He paused and took a breath, "But I was able to see Diego in your memories. So I was confident it was you."

At the mention of Diego, Searra immediately went frigid. It was like a bucket of ice water had been dumped on her, the warmth and relaxation from the wine was gone and she was left cold and vulnerable. Searra tried to track down her buzz but she had withdrawn back behind her walls.

Searra didn't have the words, other than violation, like Juan had violated the sanctity of her thoughts, her experiences, the core of who she was as a person. Now shame was like an invisible oil coating her entire body like a second skin and she felt dirty.

What had he seen? What memories had he pilfered?

Maybe he saw when they first started dating, and they wound up having sex outside on the pier in Long Beach and got caught by a teenager on a skateboard? Even though Diego swore he was an unhoused man. *Because that somehow made it better? Less embarrassing? Maybe in Diego's mind.*

Or when they got so high in San Pedro that they were tripping balls and hiding from the wind? It would have been funny had the weather not freaked them out so much. Searra was pretty sure the joint they had smoked had been laced.

Or maybe he saw the time when Diego proposed to her outside in their backyard under their avocado tree? She had been so worried about spiders since it had already gotten dark and she couldn't see the webs. But he had lit the tree up with beautiful tiny lights and she had bawled like a baby.

Or did Juan see the day that Jade was born? Searra had been so scared. Jade was a scheduled c-section because she was a breech baby. During their entire three night stay, Diego had slept in the chair next to her, never leaving her side.

She had never been so afraid as she was when she first became a mom. She was never the type to worry, especially about shit that was out of her control. Yet, there were so many intrusive thoughts, all of Jade getting hurt. From rolling out of the hospital bassinet, to someone stealing her from the nursery, or getting into an accident on the drive home from the hospital. Searra and Diego had been so tired and delirious those first few days... first few weeks, it was a blur of anxiety and nerves.

The pure panic of motherhood was debilitating.

Those thoughts continued after they got home. She couldn't watch scary movies anymore because it invited that shit into her mind and made her anxiety worse. Like she was asking for something horrible to happen. It got so bad that she never left the house.

She had lost herself for a little bit.

That made her feel like a bad mom, and a horrible wife. Then Diego went missing.

The horrible shit she was worried about... had happened.

Did Juan see all of that?

Humiliation burned in her cheeks.

"I didn't see anything specific, just impressions and the sense of Diego. But no actual memories." Juan explained in an even tone that felt so far away.

Searra had to pull herself from deep in her own head to pay any attention to what he said. She locked her eyes on his, searching for the truth or if he was sparing her feelings, but she only saw an earnestness there.

Searra swallowed hard.

"Okay," She said slowly, struggling to ground out each syllable. "What does all this have to do with Diego?" Her voice cracked a little on his name. Her throat felt thick and her eyes pricked. But she would not cry.

She would not cry!

Juan seemed to wince at her tone. Searra knew her eyes were glistening with tears, but she would not let them fall. She would hold them back with all her will. Her gaze did not leave his stormy green one as she dared him to tell her the truth.

"Diego got involved with the people I work for and it did get messy," Juan's gaze shifted to the floor, "I promised I would protect you and Jade. He has important information..." It sounded like Juan was being very careful with his wording. "...But they couldn't get it out of him." He looked back up at her, the gravity of what he said taking root in Searra's heart, tugging at her soul with the weight of it.

"He was *tortured?*" She could barely get the words out. And her heart was breaking all over again.

"Yes, but he didn't break." Juan's words were meant to console, to offer some solace... And possibly admiration in his expression.

"By the people you work for?" Searra didn't want to know anymore. She felt physically sick, like she might throw up right in front of Juan. If she did though, she decided she would aim the spew right at him.

His mouth was pinched in a tight line, and his eyes were guarded. It was like he was holding something back but Searra couldn't figure out why.

"Just say it." Searra said, her tone flat. She had tried to put more feeling into it, but it was like her insides had iced over and she couldn't thaw herself out.

"Yes." His answer was short and matter of fact. Like that was just the way it was, like people were tortured all the time. *She guessed in his world, they were.*

"And they are va–vampires too?" She stuttered on the word. It was just too surreal and stupid to say out loud.

"*Sí.*[4]"

"I don't understand."

"What don't you understand?" Juan's perfect face was creasing with frustration the longer their conversation dragged on. The lines between his brows deepened and his green eyes glowed with faint irritation.

"I don't understand why are you here? Why are you protecting us? It doesn't make any sense." Searra ran her hands through her long dark hair in frustration. Her legs were tucked underneath her on the couch and the long dark strands of her hair brushed her thighs as she sat. "If they are your bosses, and they *tortured* and *killed* Diego, why *the fuck* are you protecting his widow and kid?" Searra almost choked on the word *widow.* She had never used it before because she never accepted that Diego was dead. He was just gone. But now, the word felt wrong and vile in her mouth. It made her want to spit.

A light seemed to dim in his gaze as he looked at her. Juan sat so still that for the first time she saw the otherworldly vampire in front of her, an apex predator just lounging on her couch.

A jolt of genuine fear skittered down her spine as some primitive instinct recognized him for what he was... a monster.

This entire situation was ludicrous, but it was happening. Crazy shit was happening and she needed to make sure that herself and Jade were far, far away when the shit storm landed at her door.

---

4. Yes.

Although, she was starting to think it was too late. The crazy shit was already inside and sitting on her couch.

As Juan sipped the last of his glass of wine he reminded Searra of an old world king, someone who would sit at long tables full of gluttonous amounts of food and toast to the pilfering of another country.

His eyes flicked to hers and there was a jolt of electricity when their gazes met. She felt warm and tingly and decided to chalk that up to the wine making its way through her system. He set down his glass on the coffee table and the base made a small clink on the faux marble.

It drew her eyes to her own glass that was still half full. Searra rarely drank anymore and just wanted to drown in the soothing warmth of the alcohol a little bit longer. She reached for her glass but Juan's hands got there first, his fingers brushed against hers in the process and heat began to pool in her core and her entire face flamed. She was surprised her glasses didn't fog up. If he noticed, she hoped he thought it was from indignance, or the wine and not bald-faced desire.

She just couldn't take any more embarrassment.

Juan smirked at her, his full bottom lip looked so tantalizing that she bit her own in response, and he tipped her wine glass back, downing the whole thing in one go. It took a moment to register as she was in a daze, hypnotized by his ruefully handsome face.

"What the—!" Searra protested.

The mischief left Juan's expression as he said, "You need to feed." There was a sincerity in his voice that she couldn't help but believe despite herself, even if she had no idea what he meant.

"Feed?" Searra asked dumbfounded. "What are you talking about?"

"You haven't fed since I turned you last night."

Searra starred at him, not quite sure what to say. She was remembering back through her day, but she couldn't recall eating anything. To be fair, she slept through most of it and hadn't been feeling well.

His green eyes were lit again, bright and full of heat and frustration. "If you don't feed, you will do the same thing that you would if you were starving without human food, you weaken and your body turns inward for sustenance. You would become more desperate and act on that desperation. People will get hurt that way and it will draw unwanted attention."

Searra shook her head, there was no way any of this was real. "It's not your fucking business what and when I eat."

Juan frowned, "Yes it is. I sired you. Which means I'm responsible for you. There is a code I must abide by." His tone was stern. "You are a lot stronger and faster than you realize, and you WILL hurt someone if you don't feed and it will be messy." His lips met in a tight line and his jaw locked as past storms swam in his eyes. "Unless that is what you want?"

Searra bristled at his tone. He was talking to her like she was a child and it really rubbed her the wrong way.

"This is bullshit." Searra spat, jumping to her feet. She swayed a little as the room spun around her and her eyes struggled to find a focal point that wasn't him. Pure frustration was making her face hot and her skin buzz. She had too much energy and too little patience to listen to this shit. "I can't…" she mumbled under her breath as she turned to leave the room. she needed air, or space, or a moment to think.

This was crazy.

There was no way she could trust this random guy, no matter how hot he was.

Wait, what?! Her own thoughts were betraying her.

In an instant, Juan was no longer on the couch, but standing directly in front of her. She was face to face with his broad chest, only inches separated them. The hair on top of her head fluttered with his steady breaths and the faint scent of cedarwood and citrus wafted to her. He smelled bright and clean, like lime, and it made her want to lean in and take him deep into her lungs, despite herself.

She hadn't truly registered his height until now. Searra was tall herself… 5'10 and eye level with most men. But with Juan, she had to tilt her chin up to meet his gaze. They were glowing green fire at her and she flinched at the intensity.

"I realize the learning curve is going to be sharp and quick, but I need you to listen to what I'm telling you." His strong hands reached out and grabbed her by the shoulders, not hard enough to hurt, but she couldn't move if she tried.

Every point of contact was a spark that spread like wild fire beneath her flesh. His thumb swept languidly over her clavicle. A slow, revenant stroke that felt both tender and claiming. Liquid heat coiled low in her belly, pulsing outward until even her heartbeat was loud in her ears… A wild drum that matched the chaos in her chest.

She wanted to shake him off, to break the contact

but that devilish diget made it so hard to concentrate on anything else.

Juan tightened his grip on her and jostled her slightly. It was like he thought he could get her to listen if he shook the explanation into her.

He leaned his head down to lock eyes and they sparked green fire at her, "You can drink from me. I fed earlier, enough for both of us." Juan's voice came out raspy and his mouth quirked up in a sensuous smile. She saw his canines elongate and press against the corners of his delicious bottom lip.

Searra watched, completely transfixed as he applied more and more pressure into his own lip with his fangs until twin beads pooled on his lips, coating them in his own dark red blood. He looked like something out of an old CW TV show, the type that only hired the hottest actors. The thought made her pulse skip.

The heat in his gaze held her own captive. Her mouth was suddenly so dry, she was so... so... so thirsty. She needed, she needed... *what?*

Searra was parched but water couldn't sate this particular thirst. Her tongue lapped at her own bottom lip as she concentrated on the red beads lazily making their way down the corners of Juan's mouth and onto his chin. She was overwhelmed by the metallic scent of copper, but there was a sweetness to it too, like warm honey. And she wanted a taste. She wanted it more than anything.

Searra was *starving* —hungrier than she had ever been in her life. And she *needed* him. She had never need anyone like that. Not even Diego

This was different.

Every inch of her body hummed with it, buzzing and

frantic. Desire burned through her veins, so hot she thought she might combust if she didn't find relief.

Her eyes locked on his... That impossible green fire ... and she drowned in their depths. She couldn't look away. Ccouldn't stop herself. She was falling.

Before she even realized what she was doing, her hands moved. A blur of inhuman speed, guided by instincts that weren't her own. She seized his face with strength she didn't know she possessed and pulled him towards her. His eyes widened. Surprise flashing green for only a heartbeat, before he lowered his head to hers. Then, in a wild, reckless frenzy, her mouth claimed his.

CHAPTER
8

FAMISHED

Searra thought his lips were soft yet crushing as they parted for hers. Her tongue lapped at the blood on his lips and made her way to explore the inside of his mouth.

He groaned as she did and that spurred her on to taste more. Tasting and touching. Sparks ignited in her blood as their tongues mingled. He was like warm honey and moonlit nights and he moaned into her mouth as his desperation rose to match her own.

That sound awoke an animal in her, as a possessive growl reverberated from deep in her chest, she deepened the kiss and they collided like two merging storms, a new tempest unleashed from their joined desire.

Their kiss was full of desperation and unbridled need as they both let go of all inhibitions and leaned into it. His arms wrapped around her in a tight embrace, pulling her closer, so her body was flush against his. She needed to be closer, needed it with everything she was. Searra lifted her leg to wrap around his waist, almost losing her balance in the process, and tried to pull him into her.

Juan's hands were greedy, grabbing her ass and lifting her up so she straddled him. Her hands fisted in his thick brown hair as he deepened their kiss and pulled them closer together, until they were practically one person, one inferno, one desperate need.

The strength of his desire pushed against her heated center and a throbbing began deep inside. It built to the point where she needed friction, was desperate for it. She ground her hips against him trying to alleviate the pressure that was building, but because of her pajama bottoms and panties, she couldn't get the relief she wanted.

She wanted him skin on skin, needed his flesh pounding into hers, and the need was going to burn her up from the inside out.

Seeming to read her thoughts, Juan's hand lifted from her ass. It made its way to tease the front waistband of her pajamas, and then his hand explored, skin on skin, going lower and lower, until he was at the apex of her thighs, rubbing her mound with his fingers, teasing her, pushing against the thin fabric of her panties. Searra whimpered at his touch, and her hips bucked against him, trying to get his fingers deeper.

His breathing grew more ragged as he began to grind against her, needing the friction as much as she did.

He hooked her panties to the side in one deft movement and his fingers plunged into her slick heat, and he released a moan that morphed into a seductive growl.

First one finger, and she clenched around him, wanting him deeper. He sucked in a sharp breath, like he was trying to maintain control of himself. His finger was gentle as it pressed into her and went in and out, in and out, in tantalizingly slow strokes, going deeper and deeper each time. And then he pushed in two fingers and groaned against her swollen lips as he continued to kiss her, sucking on her full bottom lip. Searra let out a gasp at the pressure of his two fingers inside of her. She threw her head back and her dark hair cascaded around her; her entire body shuddered at the fine hairs brushing against her ultra-sensitive skin.

The friction began to build to an entirely new height. He began to leave a fiery trail of kisses from her ear, down the side of her neck.

Each kiss was like liquid fire as he licked and sucked his way down, her skin tingling with gooseflesh until he hit the top swell of her right breast, and her nipples pebbled in response. Since she wasn't wearing a bra, he instantly caught them in his heated gaze.

He grabbed the neckline of her tank and yanked it down to expose her full, sensitive breast and hardened nipple. A sharp flash of excitement skittered up her spine as the cool air kissed her flesh. And then his hot breath teased her, making her nipples tighten more, and his tongue flicked out to taste the tight peak. The sensation was like being shocked by lightning and she moaned, feeling the slickness build between her thighs around his fingers as he pumped them in and out, in and out. His mouth was hot and wet as he suckled at her breast, intensifying the throb in her core and winding her tighter and tighter, so close to release.

Her nipples had tightened into small diamonds, and her breasts were swollen and heavy as they demanded more attention. Searra yanked at her tank with such force that it ripped, and the forgotten garment floated to the floor as she freed her other breast. Her body burned. A wildfire of need as she rocked her hips against his hand, pure animal need driving her toward relief.

Juan lifted his head from her breast and gave her a sexy smile. Searra couldn't stop herself; she was so tightly coiled and close to release. Her instincts screamed at her to bite. His thick neck looked so tantalizing, his arteries showing through his skin like a delicious road map. She leaned in for another kiss, her bare breasts skimmed against his chest, sending little sumptuous shockwaves through her body. Her tongue dragged slowly along the sharp edge of his jaw, deliberate and claiming. Her entire being went still for half a heartbeat... then she bit down, teeth breaking skin. Copper flooded her tongue, metallic and electric... and sweet.

His hiss of pain melted into a guttural groan of pleasure, and her own pulse roared in her ears. All her focus narrowed onto one thing... the bite, the taste, the surrender to a hunger she couldn't hold back.

For a moment, there was nothing.

Only her.

Only Juan.

Only his blood.

It filled her mouth and cascaded down her throat

like molten honey. She swallowed greedy gulps as more spilled from the bite of his powerful artery than it had from their earlier kiss.

They both panted in ragged unison, breath mingling in the fevered air. The ecstasy of his blood on her tongue was indescribable... the most dangerous candy, decadent and addictive. She could never get enough, would never get enough.

He reveled in her feeding from him, as evidenced by his hard, pulsing length pressed between her thighs; twitching against her sensitive bud.

She tightened her grip on him and drank deep. Power crackled through her veins, wild and intoxicating. A rush so sharp it bordered on pain as her strength increased. Her entire body was buzzing.

His deft fingers continued to explore her velvet heat, massaging the bud at her apex. She was ready for him... aching, drenched, every nerve screaming for more. So wet. So open. So desperate to be filled she could barely breathe. She was still grinding on his hand when he withdrew his fingers.

The sudden loss tore a whimper from her; she needed him inside her or she was going to burn up from the inside out.

She released his neck with a low, possessive growl as his wet blood dribbled down her chin.

Lifting his slick fingers to his lips, tongue dragging slowly over them, Juan tasted her, his eyes locked on her dark, burning ones. His green gaze was lit with seductive promises as he savored the taste of her. In an instant, they spun, becoming a blur of preternatural speed and wound up on the far side of the living room. Juan moved so fast that she barely registered it.

Her back hit the wall but she barely felt the impact as he maintained his hold on her, legs still straddling him. With dizzying speed, Juan ripped her pajama pants and then her panties to get full access to her slick heat. She was in his arms, naked, and she didn't care. Searra didn't even see when his pants hit the floor, but she heard the clanging of his belt buckle as they did.

She licked her lips in anticipation, still tasting his blood on them. The honeyed sweetness made her moan with pleasure. She couldn't help but squeeze her own breasts to relieve the tension. As she pinched the taut peaks, it sent lightning skittering down her spine and intensified the ache between her thighs.

Juan skimmed his hand over her body, with feather-light touches. He pressed himself against her as he traced a tingling trail down her side, past her waist, and over the lush curve of her hips. His thumb found its way to her throbbing core, and began flicking her most sensitive spot, fast, relentless... circling so fast he was vibrating. He wound her tighter and tighter, driving her higher and higher until she couldn't take anymore. Just as she teetered, ready to fall off the edge of oblivion and fall apart around him, Juan stopped and withdrew his thumb, leaving her wrecked and gasping. Pressed between the wall and his solid body, she ached with need, grinding against his hard length in a desperate, urgent plea.

His eyes found hers, searching for something in them. There was desperation, a plea in his molten gaze.

His voice came out low and raspy, dripping with need, "Is this what you want?" He hissed through his teeth. His breathing sounded stifled, like the very air was locked inside his lungs as he held his breath.

She let out a strangled, "Yes!" She did not have to say anything more, as the hard length of him twitched in response against her thigh. She licked her lips in anticipation and in one powerful thrust, he was inside her. Searra let out a cry as he filled her, the delicious stretching coiling her tighter until she thought she couldn't handle the pressure. He set a slow rhythm, thrusting in and out, holding her up with his immense strength. Each push eased him deeper until she molded around him, until he was sure she had adjusted to his size. Then he drove forward in one savage surge, burying himself to the hilt.

She sobbed with pleasure, gripping his back, her nails digging into his flesh, as she tried to hold onto something, anything, to maintain her sanity. He moved faster and harder, burying himself deep in her slick heat, filling her completely. Searra was so high on ecstasy that it bordered on pain. She clutched him hard, her fangs sinking deep into his neck while he drove forward. Hunger and desire and pleasure all melting into one ravenous need.

"Fuuuuuuck." He moaned into her ear, and it was her undoing. The warm sweetness of his blood coated her tongue, colliding with his raw, animal need. The pressure inside her snapped. A wave crested, the dam breaking wide as her walls clamped down around him so tight that it tore a cry from his throat. Together, they shattered, spiraling over the cliff and into blissful oblivion.

Chapter 9

Sire

Searra's body trembled with the aftershocks of her release, muscles twitching as she slumped against Juan. Pleasure hummed through her limbs, numbing and sweet.

He stayed buried inside her, pinning her to the wall, one arm braced as it shook with the effort. His breathing was ragged, and she felt the muscles on his back flex and contract beneath her palms.

"Jeeeee— zuuuuussss," Searra breathed when she was finally able to make sense of her thoughts, and they weren't spilled all over in a puddle on the floor. "What the fuck was that?" Her voice was a lot hoarser than it had been an hour ago, like she had gotten home from a concert and exhausted it screaming all night. She let out a little laugh of astonishment and couldn't help but smile into his neck.

With a burst of speed, Juan placed her on the couch, her clothes next to her. She blinked and he stood across the room, fully dressed. He'd moved so fast that Searra didn't see when he put his own clothes on.

His large arms were crossed over his broad chest. Searra tried not to stare at him as she dressed, but she kept sneaking glances that she hoped were subtle from under her lashes. His eyes were guarded now, but she still saw the flickers of desire as he watched her, his gaze burning her skin.

"That was..." Juan hesitated a moment, like he wasn't sure what that was either. "... the blood-lust." His face was impassive as his hands moved to rest in his pockets.

Searra scoffed. "There was no way that was just bloodlust!" Anger was rising before the post-coital bliss fully ebbed away from her body. "So you're telling me I'm going to want to *fuck* anyone I feed on?" Searra stared daggers at him while arching a skeptical brow, indignation coloring her tone.

Talk about killing her afterglow.

On instinct, she touched her teeth with her tongue, feeling only flat, regular canines. She figured they must retract when you weren't feeding, or turned on, at least. Unless vampires were uncontrollably fuck-ing all the time, she doubted that Juan was telling her the truth about what they had just done. And it stung a little, even though she knew she shouldn't care that much. She just met this man and knew noth-ing about him. She couldn't catch feelings this quick, she was a grown ass woman who knew better. Although she hadn't been intimate with someone in so long, she wasn't sure she remembered how.

Well, that was one way to do it.

And now there was a pit in her stomach the size of a boulder. This is why she had no interest in dating, or sleeping around, or whatever the fuck this was; and she sighed inwardly. Shame reared it's ugly head as one name flooded her mind, *Diego.*

Guilt became a pit in her stomach as she tried not to think about the betrayal she had just committed. Searra waved the thoughts away, she would beat herself up later.

The silence between them stretched, and the only sound between them was the white noise emitting from the baby monitor sitting on the coffee table.

At least Jade was still asleep, thank God. That would have sucked had she woken up in the middle of... that. The idea made her cringe.

"Whatever. Don't answer me then." Searra waved him off, voice dripping with the most attitude she could muster, because she was too tired to muster much. If he wasn't going to care, she'd mirror that energy.

Juan's eyes shifted, like he really wanted to say something, but was holding back, "Our sire bond is.... particularly intense right now." Juan said slowly, cherry-picking his words.

"Okay," Searra said, trying to keep her voice casual and schooling her face into the picture of nonchalance while also feeling like a tired, clueless idiot. It was a tightrope to walk, for sure. "And a 'sire bond' is?" She asked as she raked her hand through her dark hair with nervous energy.

"It's the connection between a vampire and any

vampire they create."

"What kind of connection?" Searra asked, genuine curiosity making her sit up straighter and listen despite her exhaustion... and bruised ego.

"It's different for every sire bond." He said, letting the words sit with her, an odd heaviness to his tone. He continued, "They have a psychic bond ranging from reading each other's thoughts to knowing where the other is at all times. Depending on how strong their abilities are on both ends of the bond."

"Why did you turn me?" Searra waved her hands at him, effectively silencing him, needing to add, "I know you said protection, but I don't see how that makes sense. Now I'm *undead?*" Her body shivered at the word. "How is that protecting me and my daughter?"

Juan's eyes darkened. Searra figured he wasn't keen on having his decisions or logic questioned. "In my experience, the best way to protect someone is to make them stronger." His mouth was set in a tight line and a muscle in his square jaw ticked. "And you aren't *undead*. I detest that word, it's imprecise. We aren't zombies." He added dryly. "Zombies are mindless, we are not."

"Then what word would you use?" Searra challenged.

Juan's expression was set with solemnity and utmost seriousness when he offered, "Immortal or just vampire would be fine."

Searra fought the urge to roll her eyes, "Okay, *just vampire*." Sarcasm coated her words because she couldn't help herself.

His mouth quirked up at that, like he was trying not to smile, and his green eyes went molten again.

Searra had to fight from becoming hypnotized by him, so she let her gaze settle on the floor by his feet. She knew it was awkward as fuck, but she was not about to get lost in his eyes again and look like the stupid one. So Searra was going to do what she always did to sabotage.

"Alright, *sire*," Searra said with saccharine sweetness on her tongue, hoping she might get a little rise out of him. She was feeling a little frisky and couldn't help the sarcasm, it soothed her own wounded pride. She flipped her long hair over her shoulder, it cascaded down along her back in dark waves and she watched as Juan's gaze followed them. Feeling a little smug, she continued, but genuine curiosity bubbled to the forefront as she looked back up at him. "What do I need to know?"

Juan's head lulled back and hit the wall he was leaning against with a soft thud. His eyes were closed and he suddenly looked tired.

Searra wanted to reach out to him, massage the tension from his shoulders, and erase the exhaustion from the lines of his face. But she stayed where she was on the couch and crossed her legs. Her eyes never wavered from him. She refused to give in to her people-pleasing tendencies and wondered if it was the sire bond making the impulse feel like they were intensified.

People-pleasing on steroids.

She would have rather peeled off her fingernails one by one than let him know she was feeling those kinds of urges.

Juan pushed himself from the wall, his expression determined and his green eyes dulled a little, like he was already resigned.

"First, you and your daughter will have to go into hiding."

Searra couldn't believe what she was hearing and she sat up straight, "What! ...What do you mean?! Where are we supposed to go?" Panic was rising in her chest at the prospect of leaving their home. "What about my mom and sister?"

"Your mom and sister are not on *their* radar. YOU are." Juan huffed, his eyes full of fire.

That look sent a chill down her spine, but she knew it wasn't just from fear as heat began to pool in her core again.

Searra straightened her shoulders and held her head a little higher, refusing to cower or acknowledge the way he affected her.

"So, they are safe," Searra said, uncertainty coating her words.

Juan confirmed with a curt nod, his jaw tight. "For now."

Relief flooded her system at the knowledge that no one would be looking for her family. At least that was one good thing right now.

Juan continued, "I will need your help."

Searra's brow furrowed. "Help with what?"

"I'll need your help to find what my employers are looking for."

The crease in her brow deepened. *How would she do that? What about Jade?* She wasn't going to leave her. Panic began to swell in her chest and up her throat before she could stop it, and she was starting to struggle to breathe, her anxiety running rampant as her thoughts began to spiral to worst-case scenarios.

She felt two strong hands on her shoulders, their warmth burning through her and slowing her racing heart. The warmth seemed to spread as her breathing returned to a slow, steady pace, citrus cloying her nose... it was oddly comforting.

He gave her a little shake and said "If I bring that item back, the search ends and no one will need to come looking for you and your daughter. It will be over."

He sounded so reassuring that Searra found herself wanting to trust him. And it made sense... at least, as much as it could. The little she knew about the situation was finally starting to come together —finally.

Sort of.

Except it would never make sense why Diego got himself tangled up in this shit in the first place. She had the sinking feeling in her gut that *this* is what got him killed. She was hyperaware that Juan was keeping information from her. Either to keep her in the dark on purpose or because he didn't think she warranted the full explanation. Both options made her blood heat with rage, the last thing she wanted was to be used. Searra felt her cheeks flush as her anger flared, but she didn't give voice to it.

"What is the plan then? I don't have anyone else to stay with and I don't have money for a hotel." There was more bite in her voice than she intended, but she could only do so much to stifle her temper. She didn't have anyone she felt comfortable turning to with a baby in tow.

She'd lost contact with her in-laws after Diego disappeared. As soon as Diego went missing, they all dropped off the face of the earth. She had been especially close with his sisters: Lety and Lissette but not even they stuck around, not even for Jade, their niece. It infuriated Searra. It was one thing to cut her out, but Jade was their blood. So yeah, she wouldn't be reaching out to them anytime soon.

Her best friend lived in another state and was also eight months pregnant. Literally about to pop. Searra couldn't to add to their stress.

"You can stay with me." Juan said, his expression flickered with what looked like confusion, but was quickly replaced by a slow, wide smile.

"I can't stay with you. I don't even know you." Searra protested, but her pulse quickened at the thought of spending more time with him, staying with him. But then, she thought about Jade and her rosy bubble popped. There was no way she could stay at his place with her. The effort and work of packing everything and then baby proofing seemed so overwhelming that it made her stomach clench and she sucked her breath in through her teeth, hissing at the idea.

"I don't think that will work. I have too much to bring for Jade. I would have to hijack your place and I—" she sighed, "I don't think you would like that." Searra said. "It's a huge imposition to take someone in with a kid. Especially, if you have never had kids." Searra raised her brows at him, questioning him with that last statement.

Seeming to get the hint, Juan confirmed, "A long time ago, I was once a parent." There was a deep sadness in his eyes that Searra wanted to wipe away. He raked both his large hands through his light brown hair in frustration.

Searra noticed the muscles on his arms and chest flex beneath the thin layer of his white tee. She bit her lip as she felt the heat of desire pulse through her and she found it hard to listen to anything he said.

He continued, "But I know it's been much too long to truly remember."

"Are they... gone?" Searra swallowed thickly, not wanting to say the actual word, but was pretty sure Juan knew what she meant. Searra couldn't even comprehend the pain of that. If Jade was no longer in this world, there would be nothing for her anymore. She could not bear it, she would not bear it. So his pain would be beyond comprehension for her. Maybe that made her weak, but it was the truth. Jade changed her world. Everything revolved around her.

One look at his pained expression gave her the answer. He looked broken. "Were they still human?" She asked, the question tumbled out before she could stuff the words back in. *Was that offensive to ask a vampire?* She didn't know, but too late now.

He took a beat before he answered, like he was gauging what he should say to her. It was beginning to annoy her. She wasn't the type to hedge around shit, truthful and blunt but never mean spirited and didn't have time for games like this.

He cleared his throat and swallowed hard, "They were. It was another lifetime ago." All the life drained from his eyes, and a vast emptiness gazed back at her.

Searra's heart squeezed at that and she felt tears prick the edges of her vision but she blinked them away.

Juan didn't look inclined to elaborate and she let the subject drop. There was nothing she could say to make it better, or make it right. So she felt it was better not to give useless platitudes that didn't mean anything to anyone.

The silence between them stretched as the white noise hummed in the background from the baby monitor.

The lids of Searra's eyes grew heavy, and she curled up on the couch so that her legs folded beneath her like a cat. She knew that Juan stood across the room, but she was so tired, she didn't feel like talking anymore. She just wanted to rest.

After a while, Juan cleared his throat, the noise jolted Searra awake as she felt herself nodding off, her neck jerked as her head lolled backwards. Exhaustion draped over her like a heavy blanket. She yawned, "Do vampires get sleepy?"

She heard a throaty chuckle and a *"Sí."*[1]

The idea made her smile, but she refused to open her eyes.

"I'm rather fond of sleeping." Juan added, his voice was as soothing as a lullaby. But even with her eyes closed, she could sense his amusement.

"Oh yeah?" Searra mused through a wide yawn. Her eyelids were much too heavy to lift. So she hummed agreement along to whatever Juan said in response. Soon, she was gone on the tide of sleep.

---

1. Yes.

Chapter
10

Visions

The muscled flank of a large gray wolf approached her. Its shoulder blades bobbed up and down with its slow and steady stride. Its eyes made contact with hers, intelligence deep in its amber gaze. They glowed with power in the dark and pinned her down, keeping her locked in place.

She knew him, yet she didn't, and her heart ached. Something inside her whispered to look deeper, but she was unsure what that meant.

They stood together, on the edge of a cliff, the waves pounded against the sharp rocks below and the stones were cold against her bare feet. He bayed at the moon that seemed too close to be real, like she might reach out from her spot on the cliff and pluck it from the sky.

She was wearing a flowing white lace gown that caught the wind as she stood, basking in the light of the moon. Her face was sprayed with droplets of water as the waves crashed against the rocks beneath her feet, bare toes curled against the cold stone. An immense weight dangled between her breasts, from a thick, silver chain around her neck. It throbbed hot with power, almost burning where it touched her skin. She raised her hand up to the moon in supplication, her wrists covered in silver bangles that glinted at her in the moonlight. They clinked against each other with a metallic hum that echoed in her ears.

Swirling tattoos covered both her forearms in intricate, beautiful patterns. Recognition flitted through the back of her mind, but it was gone as soon as she reached for it.

Voices were speaking to her on the wind, but Searra couldn't quite make out what they were saying. They sounded like an ethereal choir, but the tune was foreign to her ears. They whispered over her skin, causing her to prickle with gooseflesh. She flexed her fingers and felt the power, the energy building inside of her, a heady sensation that made her heart begin to race.

Her voice bellowed out and back into the wind, singing in worship alongside the chorus of voices, speaking a language she didn't fully understand but recognized... like a long lost home.

Luna arriba, mar abajo,[1]

---

1. Moon above, sea below

muéstrame por dónde va su paso.[2]

Her dark hair was unbound and whipped around her face as the wind picked up in strength. Voice echoing onto itself, multiplying until it didn't even sound like her voice anymore, if it had been at all.

The wolf at her side howled again, his voice tangling with hers in the air, creating a majestic duet that fed the power building inside of her. A storm of torrential winds that built a delicious pressure just beneath her skin, and the scent of starlight and gardenias filled air.

Jaspe de tierra, mar de poder;[3]

guíame ahora al anochecer.[4]

As she looked up toward the heavens, her left hand clutched the hot jewel dangling between her breasts and held it up in offering to the moon.

The sky broke and the heavy clouds let loose a torrential downpour. Fat droplets pelted her face, her arms, her chest, until she was practically soaked and the lace gown she was wearing had gone see-through.

With her right hand she pulled something from a hidden pocket in her bra and held it up in tandem with the red jewel. It wasn't paper, the texture was more slick and thicker.

A photograph.

Searra squinted for a better look in the moonlight and she froze.

It was a photograph of her and Jade.

---

2. Show me where their footsteps go.

3. Jasper of earth, ocean of power

4. Guide me now in this moonlit hour.

Searra stared at their smiling faces, unable to comprehend what this meant.

She couldn't think. Rain pelted her face, but her chanting didn't falter. The same words repeating in an endless loop. *Luna arriba...*[5] The power rising and building within her *...mar abajo...*[6] the pressure of it, her ears were going to pop *...muéstrame por dónde...*[7] the stone in her hand was so hot the steam rose in thick tendrils only to be carried off by the wind. *...va su paso.*[8]

Lightning cracked the sky in a sudden flash, and the rolling thunder slowly followed. *...Jaspe de tierra...*[9] the thunder rumbled deep in her bones, *...mar de poder...*[10] and the ground bucked beneath her feet with the intensity.

The lightning began to intensify, *...guíame ahora...*[11] coming in more and more frequent bursts until they were right overhead, the thunder shaking her to her

---

5. Moon above

6. Sea below

7. Show me where...

8. ...their footsteps go.

9. Jasper of earth

10. Ocean of power.

11. Guide me now...

core. .....*al anochecer.*[12]

For a moment, everything grew still. The chanting stopped.

Not a sound could be heard beyond her own heavy breathing and a high-pitched ringing.

The wind and rain had ceased in the stillness.

Then, the hairs on her arms and the back of her neck began to rise, and static tingling along her skin. Even her wet, heavy hair began to frizz with the rising energy in the air.

She felt the crack before she heard it; and then a sudden, sharp burning in her left hand traveled to her chest as she realized the lightning had struck the jewel in her hand. It was the sharpest, most delicious pain and her lips parted in a scream, but she heard no sound.

Her eyes snapped open. Searra was in bed, sweat coating her brow. Breathing hard, confusion scattering her thoughts, her dream faded into the recesses of her mind where she couldn't grasp it.

She couldn't remember what had frightened her, there were only remnants. A dull pain in her chest and a soreness in her left hand. She rubbed her palm, swearing there should have been a burn or a bruise

---

12. ...in this moonlit hour.

but couldn't remember why.

There was nothing, her skin wasn't even warm.

Searra felt her forehead for a potential fever, but her skin was cool to the touch, almost too cool. No fever. So, she wasn't sick anymore, at least. She looked around and she wasn't in her room, or in any room in her house, or one she recognized. Everything was high end, cream and wood.

And clean?

Her adrenaline began to spike as she slipped into panic mode.

Where the fuck was she and where was Jade?!

Searra jumped from the bed, the honey brown hardwood warm to her bare feet. Her Crocs were within reach on the floor, and she slipped into them.

She began to move through the room in a frenzy, only finding Jade on her mind.

Crossing the center of the room, she drifted past a sleek, double-sided fireplace standing to the left of the cream-colored bed she'd just rolled out of. Its modern lines caught the light, illuminating the marble it was carved from. The surface veined in taupes and deep browns that mimicked wood grain. Near the floor, a narrow rectangular slot held crystal pebbles, glowing where flames flickered to life.

Searra thought it was crazy fancy, and no doubt expensive but her anxiety couldn't let her fully appreciate it.

She had to find Jade.

The fireplace served as a divider between the sleeping side of the room and the sitting area. On the far wall, a massive TV was mounted above a pair of cream-colored chairs and a matching crib, the soft tones tying the two halves of the space together.

It was then the comforting *chhhhhhh* of the white nose monkey reached her ears. She hadn't recognize it at first because it wasn't at the loudest level, which is where she would always set it.

As she got closer, Jade's sleeping face came into view from inside the crib. Relief washed over Searra as she gazed down at Jade. Her pink cheeks looked plump and her light brown hair was extra fluffy, like it did right after she had a bath. Jade looked every bit the idyllic angel.

Searra knew better, depending on her mood, she could be a *traviesita*, [13] just like her dad.

The thought made her smile, and her eyes burned.

Diego... The name haunted her mind and caused a confusing pang of grief and guilt in her chest. It had all become one horrible and tangled knot in her head. She didn't know where the grief stopped and the guilt started and that seemed to make everything feel worse.

Searra pushed the thoughts away as she crept backwards from the crib, muscles bunched with caution, afraid to wake her with the slightest noise or disturbance. She realized, however, the floor made no noise beneath her feet. Not like the creaky boards at her house, where if you breathed wrong the boards themselves would sigh.

She made her way back to her side of the room, which had large sliding doors that opened out to the backyard. The glass panes were darker than typi-

---

13. Little trouble maker

cal windows, so there must have been a tint, but still enough light to see.

Searra felt a little exposed. There were no blinds, no curtains... just naked windows.

It looked like early evening based on the waning sunlight outside. The property looked isolated as well. Only vacant hills for as far as the eye could see. Lush greens and browns coated the landscape. There were acres and acres of untouched land, something she didn't know still existed in California.

If they still were in California.

She snuck out of the room and down the hall, hoping to find a bathroom. Her prayers were answered as she peered through the next open door down the hall and took in the huge space. It was the largest bathroom she had ever seen. In the center of the room was a huge window looking out to the wilderness, and right in front of it was a huge white ceramic garden tub. On either end of the room stood a large mirrored wall, each with its own vanity and sink. Push-to-open storage drawers stretched from wall to wall. All in cool wood tones and creams. It gave the space an overall soothing appeal, a very clean aesthetic. Not one that Searra was comfortable in. Lived in and cluttered was where she felt most at home.

Searra strode over to one of the drawers, curiosity getting the best of her... along with the simple urge to at least attempt to brush her teeth. She hoped for a tube of toothpaste. If there wasn't a toothbrush, well, her finger would do for now.

She pressed the top right drawer and the latch released with a gentle click. Inside were her and Jade's toothbrushes. Her's being pink with a black brush head, Jade's was green with little elephant ears on the sides. Searra scrunched her face in confusion.

How did her stuff get here? How did she and Jade get here? Where was here?

Her first guess was Juan's place. She couldn't explain it, but she felt him all over. And with that feeling came an overall sense of safety that she couldn't reason through.

Brushing her teeth, Searra began rifling through the drawers. All of her bathroom essentials were there—her vani cream and castor oil she used for daily skincare, and Jade's coconut cream soap, the little bathtub, and bucket with her aquatic-themed bath toys.

It was a little unsettling, but to her surprise, she wasn't afraid. She was afraid of a lot, but not of Juan. Searra wasn't sure if that made her a little unbalanced and reckless, or too trusting and stupid.

Probably stupid, for sure.

Searra stepped out of the bathroom and walked through the rest of the house. There were so many rooms and even more bathrooms. It was ridiculous. One man did not need this much space.

Unless he wasn't alone.

The thought came unbidden and out of nowhere. Bitterness coated her tongue and a little bile rose in the back of her throat at the idea. Jealousy wasn't something she was too familiar with; she wasn't a jealous person and Searra wondered if it had anything to do with their sire bond. If it got worse, she would have to ask him about it, but until then, push forward and deny, deny, deny.

That's healthy...

Eventually, Searra made her way into the kitchen,

which was also massive. Two gray marble waterfall islands centered the room along with a pristine white eight-seater dining table, with matching chairs.

Just beyond the table stretched a full wall of accordion doors that opened into another seating area in the backyard. The entire left wall was lined with countertops and storage, while the right side housed more storage and built-in appliances. Cool, light wood tones blended with white and cream. Very clean, very modern, *very* gorgeous.

Why would a vampire need a kitchen anyway?

Searra got the impression that Juan didn't cook and never used this kitchen, so that was probably why it still looked so pristine. Although, the entire house looked pristine. He may never actually stay here in this house.

The fridge door was ajar, and a jean clad butt was sticking out the other end. The hips swayed back and forth like they were jamming out to a beat. Her sharpened hearing picked up a familiar guitar riff.

Was that Metallica?

Stepping closer, Searra tapped him lightly on the back. He let out a loud, cat-like shriek before spinning around, losing his balance and landing flat on his ass. From the floor, his wide, dark eyes stared up at her in shock. His short pink hair stuck up in messy tufts, framed by thick black eyebrows, a mustache, and a soul patch. The combination reminding her of an anime pirate.

"Oh shit!" He said, yanking his headphones down to rest on his neck. "I'm sorry. I didn't know you were awake yet. Normally, Juan doesn't rise until sunset." His voice was friendly and he wore a nervous smile.

"Hi!" Searra said, her hands up in a surrender. "I didin't mean to scare you." She smiled down at him and her new senses caught his scent.

Human. His heart pounded like a hammer in her ears.

"Ummm... Where are we?" She asked, "Oh yeah, and I'm Searra." She held out her hand to shake.

He looked at her outstretched hand, considering it a moment before a wide grin spread across his face. Then he clasped her hand in his, giving it a firm shake. The heat of his hand startled her — it was almost burning compared to her own cool touch.

"I'm Pichi."

"Pichi?" She said, her brow raised. The name was unusual.

"Oh, my name is Prichard, after my dad. But I just go by Pichi."

"Nice to meet you, Pichi." Searra said, and waited a beat before she repeated,"Where are we?"

"Oh sorry," he said, a sheepish grin on his face. "And yeah, we are at Juan's. I was just stocking the fridge before I left for the day."

"Oh! Okay. Are you like Juan's assistant or something?" Searra asked, genuinely curious.

"Something like that." Pichi said, his dark eyes flashing. "Juan is my *primo*[14]. And he just pays me to do odd jobs here and there. Yah know, stock his fridge. Move his car. ...Watch a random baby." He chuckled as he

---

14. Cousin (term of endearment), could also be a close friend.

looked at her from beneath his fan of dark lashes. He was handsome like Juan, it wasn't surprising that they were related.

Model status for sure, and late twenties maybe? Very James Dean... but with pink hair... and a moustache.

"Oh shit!" It had just dawned on her that Jade would have been awake all day while she had been sleeping.

"You watched Jade today?" Searra asked, her anxiety building. The lack of control was making her head spin.

"Oh yeah. She is a good baby. Don't worry. All good today. We mainly watched TV. I had just put her down and then went to get provisions for the fridge." Pichi's smile was soft and his expression was genuine. A long patch of pink hair had fallen in front of his eyes, and he let out a breath to blow it away from his face.

"I was told that you and Jade share a room at your house, so I put the crib on the other side of your room, that way when you woke up you would see her."

Any anxiety Searra had melted away, she didn't trust people often, but there was something about Pichi. He was definitely likeable, and thoughtful.

"Thank you." Searra said, trying not to cry. "It means a lot that you took care of her and I appreciate it. She is everything to me." Her voice cracked and she tried to cover it with a throat clear. It had been so long since she had help with Jade, outside of her mom and sister. She was truly grateful.

"Oh! No problem. She is pretty cool, for a baby." Pichi's grin was wide and warm as he shook his head.

Her temples were beginning to throb. "Is there any coffee?" Searra asked, her caffeine dependency rearing its ugly head.

Pichi nodded his head to the counter, "Oh yeah, I just started a pot. It should be done in a few. It's a fancy percolator." He waved his fingers for effect and rolled his eyes.

Searra spotted the percolator and walked over. A deep gurgle filled the room as the coffee brewed. The air was rich with Colombian bean, and her mouth salivated. Her entire body was jonesing for it.

"Smells good." Searra admitted.

"Yeah, it's Juan's favorite. I have to go to a special coffee shop in East LA for the beans and then grind it on the spot so it is fresh as fuck." Pichi said with a shrug of his wide shoulders. "Feel free to sit. Juan should be up in a few and I'll get out of your hair." He waved and placed his headphones on as he went, so she only waved goodbye in response.

Although, she wished he would have stayed a little longer. He seemed easier to talk to than Juan, more open at least. And Searra wasn't sure how to approach the subject of her kidnapping... with her kidnapper.

The silence was more empty and yawning now that she was alone. The kitchen was too massive, the marble too blinding. She decided to sit in the middle, so the room felt smaller. She picked one of the silver bar stools that were tucked beneath. To her surprise, it was oddly comfortable for a stool and the upholstery was buttery soft.

Searra stared at the percolator, watching the brown liquid burble in the clear crystal top. Her fingers began to drum on the countertop. The marble was cool against her skin and sent a little chill through her. She wished she had a hoodie and not just her tank and flannel PJ bottoms. She would check the closet after she had coffee to see if Juan packed some of her clothes.

As the percolator finished brewing, Searra jumped up to grab a mug from the cabinets. They were full of all sorts of cups, plates, and glasses. Everything looked so old and mismatched, like they had been collected over many, many years and from every corner of the world.

She found a grey mug that looked like a rustic cartoon honey pot with an "S" written in delicate calligraphy. It reminded her of Winnie the Pooh, which was Jade's favorite at the moment. She grabbed that one, plus, it was the perfect size for coffee… huge.

As soon as her fingers grazed the handle of the mug, a sudden heat flushed beneath her fingers and she became lightheaded, like she was about to have another fainting spell.

CHAPTER II

CONDENADO (CURSED)

"THE HAND OF FATE IS ON ME,—THE PAST IS IN MY VEINS,—THE FUTURE IN MY SOUL: I CANNOT ESCAPE THE WEIGHT OF DESTINY." - LORD BYRON (1817)

B lack spots flickered in the corners of her vision and her blood slogged through her veins, an eternity between beats.

She tried to blink away the spots as she braced her body for the collapse as best she could, but the knobby-kneed feeling never came; only a bottomless pit of guilt and grief seemed to overtake her. But the feelings were foreign and not her own. Like she was wearing a too tight dress, and it was squeezing her in all the wrong places. The feelings were so uncomfortable and intense. They didn't fit right at all and the weight of carrying them threatened to flatten her.

As her vision began to clear, Searra realized she was standing in the same kitchen, but Juan was there. She knew on instinct she was seeing something that had already happened. This *had* to be a vision or a hallucination.

Or a psychotic break?

Honestly, she couldn't rule it out. This was happening to her more and more the last few days.

Time felt stretched, like she was looking through a thin fabric. The farther back in time, the more stretched that fabric felt.

This was recent.

Juan looked... disheveled, his clothes were filthy, like he had been wearing them through a mud run and his golden brown hair was caked in crusted dirt and debris. Anger was coming off him in waves and the energy in the room was rich with contempt.

A long, double bladed sword lay in front of him on the marble island. The emerald jewel set in the pommel of the blade seemed to wink at her. She had the oddest desire to touch it, to feel the cold steel against her skin, and she reached her hand out. Heat building in her chest and traveling down her fingers, needing to touch the blade. It was so strange, this warmth that felt so much apart of her and yet, more. Then she blinked and pulled her hand back, the heat receded, and her fingers became chilled once more.

Searra tasted remnants of magic's spicy tang on her tongue, sweet and tropical... like warm, sun kissed skin on a summer evening. It reminded her of the delicate fragrance of plumerias. They had three trees at her house but never experienced their scent as strong as she did now. But none of that made any sense to her.

"I can't do it anymore," Juan said quietly. His voice was flat and desperate and caused something in Searra's gut to twist. She did not like him sounding so broken.

"What do you mean? There is no other option." A lilting feminine voice sounded from the hallway. "We have always hunted them, this time is no different." Her voice bounded off the walls, the sound amplifying inside Searra's head.

She watched as a small redhead came into view. She was short, but her wiry copper hair added to her stature so she appeared larger than she was. Her ice blue eyes shifted back and forth, scanning the room. She had a light smattering of freckles across her nose, like someone had taken a paintbrush and flicked brown paint across her face. Her red mouth was set in a severe line as her hands rested on her generous hips.

"I know, but I can't do it anymore, Liv." Juan's face was in his hands and Searra noticed dirt had crusted beneath his nails. "I can't explain it! Liv—!" His voice was broken and trembled a little as he said it. "The things I've done. I didn't— I didn't want to."

The one that Juan called 'Liv' bent down to where he sat on the island, placing her hands gently on his shoulders in an attempt to comfort. But the gesture looked stiff, almost statue-like. Her expression remained cold and unreadable.

"Something is wrong!" Juan let loose a savage snarl, his eyes growing dark. "I'm feeling EVERYTHING. I can't stand it! This curse." He spat those last words, like it was a jinx to even say it aloud.

Juan shook his head and stared down at the surface of the marble island. The naked pain on his face made something tug in Searra's heart and she wanted to reach out to him.

A mug was steeping on the counter, the same one Searra had just grabbed. It was Liv's tea Searra realized as Liv picked it up and took a quick sip, placing it back down. Searra saw tendrils of steam wafting from the cup with the heat, the condensation built a ring around the base of the marble.

Liv leaned in and spoke barely above a whisper, "Once we've spoken wi' Ambrose, he'll see to it. The man's got the birds on his tether. He'll set it right." There was still a trace of an accent in her voice. *Was that Scottish?* Her cadence brought an old world musicality to her words, so much so that Searra found herself leaning in, transfixed. The conviction in which Liv spoke was strong, and even Searra was inclined to believe her.

What did she mean by birds?

Juan's face looked gaunt as he shook his head in agreement. His strong hands were shaking as they raked through his hair. Flecks of dried dirt rained down onto the countertop and floor around him. The metallic decay from the rich earth wafted to her nose as it fell away from him.

Juan's gaze quickly flicked up, emerald eyes full of raw pain and storming, and they locked with Searra's.

Could he see her?

His head tilted, confusion and recognition on his face.

Without warning, there was a tug in her temple, so

quick it was almost painful, and then she was falling away. Away from the scene in the kitchen. Away from Juan and Liv. Growing ever distant and fading to blackness.

She felt herself return to her body, jerking to attention as though waking from a dream. But thankfully, she caught herself on the verge of falling face first onto the kitchen tile.

Her heart felt sluggish in her chest, adrenaline peaking. She tried to catch her breath, to blink her vision back. Sensation began to return to her limbs and she felt more grounded, more inside her body than she had been only moments ago.

A large hand braced the small of her back, keeping her upright. She was led back to her seat with shaky steps and her gut fluttered at the contact. It made her cheeks flush.

Searra shook her head and looked up, then froze. Those burning green eyes, dull and broken only seconds ago, now blazed back at her. Her heart twisted, tight with sudden relief.

Juan's brow furrowed, his lips pressed into a tight line, concern etched into every feature. Yet, there was a brightness in his gaze that he hadn't had before in that vision with Liv. That man was a different person, frantic and empty. Not the confident and sarcastic demon she had only just begun to know.

"Are you alright?" Juan asked.

Her hands were still clamped around the coffee mug she had been reaching for earlier; locked in a death grip, muscles frozen mid-cramp. It took effort, concentration, to force her fingers to obey. Slowly, she pried them open and set the empty mug on the countertop.

Her fists bunched in her lap as she tried to massage her weary fingers. Attempting to loosen the joints, they were like rusted hinges on an old door, and if she listened, they might even creak.

Her eyes snagged on the baby monitor clipped to the collar of Juan's white t-shirt. The soft *chhhhhhhh* was familiar and comforting. Searra relaxed a little, her shoulders loosened and her jaw unclenched. She hadn't realized she had been grinding her teeth, biting down so hard her jaw was aching.

"Yeah." Searra breathed. "Ummmm, I don't really know what that was. I'm probably just tired." She wasn't sure she wanted to tell him exactly what happened yet.

Did she trust him enough to be open? How would she ever learn from him if she didn't ask questions? Were visions a vampire thing? Was that a vision? How did the visions work? Could she control them?

Right now, he was the only one who could answer these questions for her.

Was Pichi still there? Maybe she could ask him instead?

She was a horrible liar with no poker face. A fact that never bothered her until now, when it could be used against her. She bit the inside of her cheek, trying not to meet his probing gaze again, sure she would give herself away.

Juan was still staring at her. Searching her face like he was reading a book and he crossed his arms. His shoulders and biceps bulged as he did, his muscles on full display. Searra tried not to stare, but her gaze kept creeping back up his body and she wanted to slap herself.

Juan gave her a suspicious side eye, the expression would have made Searra laugh if she wasn't concentrating so hard on avoiding direct eye contact. Her coffee cup was suddenly very interesting as she stared so hard she thought it might combust into flames.

He clicked his tongue before he said, "Out with it. Now." His tone was demanding, no hint of teasing, only exasperation. He raised his eyebrows as he waited, and Searra made the mistake of looking up from her seat at the kitchen island into his gorgeous face. His eyelashes were so long and thick it made her jealous. It was infuriating because he had no business having lashes that luscious.

"I was jonesing for caffeine." She managed to piece that sentence together with loose threads and spit while her brain was currently restarting like an old computer. Searra looked down again, trying not to fall into his thrall, but her gaze got snagged on his pouty bottom lip. She remembered how they crushed against hers when they kissed. Soft, yet demanding. So full of passion it ignited a fire inside her. Heat crawled up her cheeks and a renewed throbbing pulsed through her core. She fidgeted in her seat trying to give herself a little relief, but his eyes were on her, catching that little movement. Searra raised her gaze and Juan's expression became clouded and dark with desire. That look made her breathing hitch.

"What do you need to tell me?" Juan breathed, his voice sounded rough as he stepped closer. His eyes were burning molten green and locked on hers.

"Uhhhhhh..." Searra couldn't think. Her brain was like pudding. There were no thoughts except how nice it would be to be crushed in his strong arms again. The crisp scent of bergamot and cedarwood filled her senses, and she fought the urge to breathe him in deeper.

Juan was too close.

She watched as his broad chest rose and fell. His breathing quickened, and his pecs twitched under her perusal.

Searra couldn't get distracted. *Important and weird shit had just happened and this was the last thing she should be thinking about!* She had questions that needed answers and she wasn't some horny teenager. She was a grown woman, a *mom*, someone who thought shit through. Although, this *was* one way to distract them both for now.

She needed to think of something, *anything* that would pour cold water over the tension building between them before she lost all sense. *Was that only last night?* Searra realized that she didn't even know, the days were blurring together.

Before she could stop it, the words tumbled out of her, like water over rocks. "Who is Liv?" As soon as she asked, she wanted to take the question back. It was not her business who Liv was. She also didn't know how she was going to explain how she knew about Liv without telling him about her visions.

Juan went very still and he was looking at her with an expression she couldn't read. Was it anger? Confusion? Fear? And then possibly suspicion? No sooner did the emotions flicker across his face that a solid wall came up, shutting her out. His expression was now a cold and impassive mask. It was a side of him she had never seen, except the night they met.

The night he turned her.

The green of his eyes went icy, reminding Searra of the look in Liv's gaze. Those frosty, blue eyes. Cold and calculating. A shiver snaked up her spine.

"How do you know about Liv?" Juan asked, his voice quiet and cold. The tension he exuded was so sharp it could cut glass.

Searra didn't know how to answer, except with the truth. She needed to come clean, though logically she wasn't so sure it was the smart thing to do. Juan was in control, they were in his house, and everything was on his terms. Searra opened her mouth to speak, but then a loud peeling cry rang out through the white noise on the speaker and bounced off the walls in the kitchen.

Jade was awake and not happy.

Juan's eyes widened and then he took off running toward the bedroom where Jade was sleeping. He was a blur of vampiric speed and Searra struggled to keep up. But she was moving faster than she realized because her right shoulder hit the end of the hallway where the linen closets were. The wood groaned with the impact as she scrambled to make the turn into the bedroom with too much speed. Her body was moving faster than her brain could comprehend.

Once she bounded into the room, her eyes landed on Juan and Jade. He was holding her daughter on his hip, half wrapped in her favorite swaddle blanket with her name in delicate script amongst pink *mariposas*.[1] Jade's light brown hair was big and flying every-

---

1. Butterflies

where. Her plump cheeks were as pink as her pouty pursed lips. She looked *mad.* Little brow furrowed, almost like she woke up confused and in a strange place and did not like it. Searra could sympathize. She was also probably hungry and needed a diaper change. The new surroundings and strange man carrying her, weren't helping either.

Juan looked like he didn't mind in the slightest. A genuine grin on his face that brought light and warmth to his features. It made Searra want to smile too as he bounced Jade up and down, trying to keep her soothed. The bicep muscles on his arms bulged with the movement, but Searra tried not to focus on that too hard. *Maybe just in her periphery?*

Something thawed in her chest as she gazed at them, a tender smile she couldn't control played across her lips. Juan *was* a different person from the man in her vision.

It took a few moments, but as soon as Jade spotted her, her arms outstretched, "MaMa! MaMaaaa!" Grunting with the effort to circumvent Juan's hold and get to Searra. She straightened her legs and squirmed with all her might and her call devolved into a whine.

Searra held out her arms for Jade and Juan handed her over. Jade started cooing once she got to her comfortable spot on Momma's right hip. A big smile bloomed within her eyes, until her whole face was lit with it. Like she was getting away with something, being sneaky. A little *traviesa.*[2] Her squishy legs were

---

2. Troublemaker

strong and flexed as she was nestled in place on her side.

If Searra tried to put Jade down now, she would float above the ground in utter refusal. Throwing out Searra's back in the process... which had happened before. The memory had her cringing and absent-mindedly, she rubbed the sensitive spot on her spine.

A vampire with chronic backpain. Not something you would want to deal with for a eternity.

Jade began to whine in her arms and straighten her legs. She demanded, "Dooow! Dooooow!"

"*Oh pues*,"3 Searra grunted. "I need to change you first Sweetie Pie! And then Mommy will get you mook? It is past bed time *vida*.4" Searra asked Jade in a singsong baby voice she saved for only her daughter. Nuzzling her head and placing a quick kiss on her cheek... and then another.

She looked up at Juan, eyes locking over Jade's head, "We will talk later, yeah?"

Juan looked at her and gave a nod. The light remained in his eyes as he headed out of the room, which Searra took as a good sign. That icy look earlier had chilled her to the bone. She never wanted to see that look again.

---

3. Oh, fine then. (Whatever)

4. Life (term of endearment)

CHAPTER
12

BRUJA (WITCH)

"THERE ARE DARKNESSES IN LIFE,
AND THERE ARE LIGHTS, AND YOU
ARE ONE OF THE LIGHTS, THE
LIGHT OF ALL LIGHTS." - BRAM
STOKER (1897)

Searra checked the wooden dresser by the crib, which was filled with diapers, wipes, and clothes from Jade's drawers at home. There was something meticulous about how everything was folded and put in its place. It reminded her of Diego, and her heart hurt at the thought. He had been fussy like that. It had annoyed the shit out of her all the time, but it was one of the many things he did that she hadn't appreciated until it was gone. Her eyes stung as she held back the tears that threatened to fall.

She didn't want to cry.

She was always crying now.

Searra glanced at the nightstand by the bed and spotted her glasses. She hadn't realized she wasn't wearing them, and went to put them on but stopped in her tracks... because she could see without them.

Everything looked clear, no blurry or hazy objects, and stretched lights.

Searra took one last look at them on the nightstand and turned around to change Jade, leaving them behind.

After changing Jade's diaper, Searra dressed her in a fresh outfit. A long-sleeved yellow shirt with tiny ruffles at the shoulders and pants patterned with sunflowers with a little bow stitched into the waistband. Yellow was Jade's favorite color. She loved yellow ducks, yellow chicks, yellow birds of any kind, along with her yellow blocks and yellow balls. Bright and happy, just like Jade. It was no surprise yellow spoke to her.

Unsurprisingly, Jade didn't want to be held once she had woken up. She was eager to run around and explore.

Searra wasn't too keen on how they had miraculously woken up there and how little agency Juan allowed. It was unsettling, and Searra hadn't quite decided whether they would go back home on principle or try to find someone else to crash with.

Jade's little purple Crocs squeaked with each step on the hardwood floors as she scampered through the house, taking off down the hallway, Searra on her heels.

She made a quick turn into another large bedroom. It looked similar to the one they were in, also with a sleek fireplace dividing the sleeping and sitting parts of the room, but all the furnishings here were a light gray with black trim. Searra assumed this one was Juan's room. It had a clean, masculine energy.

Jade strode straight in like she owned the place, touching everything from the thick black bed posts to the silver handles on the end tables. She tried to open them but in a desperate lunge, Searra pushed them closed, the entire dresser clanking against the wall with the force. She did NOT want to know what was in those drawers, some things needed to be left unseen.

Hell knew what a centuries-old vampire had in his bedside drawers.

Jade began to whine in protest. Her little fingers stubbornly curled in a viselike grip around the handle of the end table. She was confident that not only did it open, but whatever was inside was special and meant for her. Searra did not move her hand, keeping the drawer closed, even though the whining grew louder and louder the longer they stood there.

A standoff.

She heard the squeak of pipes as Searra realized the shower in the adjoining bathroom had just turned off. Her face flushed as she got down to Jade's level, eye to eye. They had to get out of there, *now.*

"Sweetie Pie," Searra whispered in a vain attempt

at staying undiscovered. Juan was a vampire, and there was no way he hadn't heard them. But denial is one hell of a thing, and something Searra was especially good at powering through with.

Jade was still letting out long whines and pulling on the handle, while her other hand scratched at the black wooden corners of the end table, trying to pry it apart with her tiny nails.

"Sweetie, that's not yours. We don't go through other people's things. Okay?" Jade's mouth was still set in a sob shape, but she started to quiet down. Brow furrowed in question.

Searra changed tactics, "Are you hungry?" She asked while mimicking putting food in her mouth and adding a heaping amount of excitement to her tone. Distraction worked maybe sixty percent of the time with Jade, but Searra was feeling lucky.

Jade's brow smoothed out and she started to open and close her mouth in a mock chewing motion. "Ooooood!" Jade exclaimed and stamped her feet.

It was late already, and Jade should be asleep, but with Searra's weird, nocturnal sleep schedule, it was getting harder and harder to keep Jade on one too.

The door to the bathroom swung open and Searra's entire body seized up with anxious energy. She was caught, crouched on the floor of his room and he was naked.

Embarrassing.

The scent of clean laundry and citrus cloyed at her nose and she became intensely aware of him, of every curve and ripple of muscle. His broad, beefy shoulders. The sheer breath of him. Juan was dripping wet, his towel was wrapped just low enough to show off his muscled "v".

Did he even use the towel? Isn't the point to actually get dry?

Searra fought the instinct to facepalm. He glittered as droplets gathered on his chest hair, down his chiseled abs, and along his happy trail.

Searra's face was burning and she bit her lip so hard she might have split it with her teeth.

She had, tasting her own metallic and honeyed blood on her tongue.

Juan's focus jumped to her mouth, and an intense, dark hunger clouded his expression. Although, she knew he wasn't hungry for food.

Searra forced herself to stand from her awkward position crouched on the floor, and took Jade's little hand.

Jade tried to snake her hand away and lunged for the side table now that Momma was distracted.

She was too quick for Searra and her little hands yanked open the drawer. Searra caught the sparkling of gemstones through the crack of the drawer.

"Soooo cute!" Jade exclaimed, her smile wide and hands reaching out for them.

Juan was in front of Jade in a blur of droplets and wind that misted Searra's face. He had moved impossibly fast and now stood between them and his bedside table completely dry.

He knelt down, smiling at Jade and slowly closed the

drawer. *"Pequeña,* [1] those are not for you." His words were a soft velvet as his tongue rolled over the syllables.

Searra kept her grip on Jade and began to back away, guiding her through the room toward the door.

"Oops, sorry," Searra exclaimed and the words just started spilling out. "She was exploring." She shrugged as she tried to look at everything except for him, trying to keep her voice casual, but it somehow came out high and squeaky. "We are going to the kitchen to make her some food, right baby?"

Jade was still struggling in Searra's grip, but she did repeat, "ooooood?" Which was a good sign she might actually eat solid food.

They were almost at the door when another sudden gust of wind blew her hair back and made her stagger on her feet. Juan was standing in front of them in the doorway, creating his own wake vortex with his vampire speed.

"Whoa. You gotta show me how to do that!" Searra was impressed and didn't try to hide it.

Jade let out an excited squeal and then laughed, showing all her teeth, and clapped her hands with so much enthusiasm that Searra was sure her palms were stinging.

Juan reached out to Searra, his hand going to her mouth, and the pad of his thumb slowly swiped at the blood staining her lips, the cut already healed over. He brought his thumb to his mouth and sucked it clean. Heat pooled in her core and made her breath

---

1. Little one

hitch.

"Oooooood!" Jade bellowed. She started to smack Searra's thigh with more and more force.

Searra's gaze tore away from Juan's, a ghost of a smirk on his lips. "Okay, Sweetie Pie! We are going to the kitchen now." Putting her hand down to protect her leg. "No hitting, Sweetie. Let's go check out the food. Okay, my love?" Searra asked and Jade burbled a reply as they walked, the entire time she felt Juan's gaze burning into her back until she rounded the corner and they were out of his sight.

When they got to the kitchen, Searra led Jade to the gigantic, four-door, stainless steel fridge.

"Let's see what we got, *mi amore*,[2]" Searra said as she opened one of the hefty doors to check the contents inside. She was just praying there would be eggs so she could make a quick scramble.

At first, she didn't register what she was seeing. As soon as the lip of the air-tight seal broke, a line of red light spilled from the gap of the door.

She swung it wider, and the entire section was glowing red, like someone decided to put some mood lighting —an idea Searra wasn't *opposed* to. Late night snacks would get a lot more interesting.

Then her frozen brain registered she was looking at... rows and rows *and rows* of blood bags.

This was what Pichi meant by 'provisions'? Searra blanched.

The fridge light was refracting off the deep red inside the bags and cast that entire section of

---

2. My love

the fridge as a vintage burlesque club. The bags all had barcodes and writing on them, like they came from hospitals or donation centers.

The bottom fruit drawer was filled with limes. The pull-out drawer was clear, so the bright green popped. It was like Christmas, red and green.

A very demented Christmas.

Searra pursed her lips and closed the door. She was a little queasy at the flavor combination of blood and limes.

"Let's try a different door, Sweetie," Searra said, looking down at Jade. She had her finger in her mouth, probing her back gums. She was teething. She was *always* teething. Searra let out a sigh and braced herself for what she might find as she opened the second door.

Searra was still closing her eyes, as the lip of the fridge detached with a soft *woosh* and cold air tickled her face. Peeking out through one, she saw a carton of eggs, milk, tortillas, and a steel pot of something with a ladle sticking out.

This was something at least.

After the food was ready, they made their way back to their room.

Searra closed the door and gathered herself and Jade to sit on the floor by her crib on the coral colored fuzzy mat. They didn't have Jade's high chair as far as she knew, but eating on the floor should be safe for now.

Jade sat down next to her with a *plunk*. Searra placed the plate of eggs in between them and picked up a little chunk and held it up to Jade's mouth. Jade looked at it with bright eyes and smiled, all her teeth on display. She crinkled her eyes and opened her mouth for the egg.

Searra plopped it in, and Jade squealed with delight as she chewed with a full, open mouth. Searra pushed the plate toward Jade, inviting her to dig in for herself while Momma watched. Jade proceeded to pick up the tiniest speck of egg between her thumb and forefinger and giggled once she ate it.

"Good job *vida!*"[3] Searra encouraged with a little clap. Jade continued to eat her eggs by the handful, but what constituted a handful was only known to Jade.

Searra found herself jonesing again for coffee. She realized she hadn't drunk any earlier, before she was plagued by that strange vision of Juan and Liv. Searra would have to wait for coffee until after Jade was done. No way would she disrupt her when she was in a good flow and eating on her own.

There was a soft knock at the door. She turned to look over her shoulder to see Juan standing in the doorway.

He was dry and dressed, in another tight white tee and jeans, with two coffee cups in his hands. Searra saw the steam and her mouth watered. Her eyes flicked to his in question, and his burning green gaze made her stomach flip.

"I had a feeling you might be... *jonesing.*" He said, elongating the last word like he was testing it out, sounding awkward and foreign on his tongue, like everyone's *tio*[4] who tried to use the latest slang words.

---

3. Life (term of endearment)

4. Uncle

Searra looked back to Jade, who was smiling at Juan with her fingers and bits of egg in her mouth, and in her hair.

Searra reached back for the coffee cup without looking at him again. The warmth of the cup grazed her finger tips and she grabbed the sturdy handle, but before she pulled it into her grasp, a strong hand wrapped around hers, and she felt the electric jolt on her skin at the contact.

"Searra." It was a plea. Her name sounded rough, with an edge of desperation she didn't expect from him.

She looked at Juan and he was staring at her with such intensity she almost wanted to look away, but she didn't.

"How do you know about Liv?" His tone was measured and calm, belying his intense reaction earlier.

Searra didn't want to lie to him. So, she didn't.

"I saw her." She admitted, trying to keep her tone casual. Searra wanted to trust him. She was so tired of people letting her down. First Diego when he disappeared, then his family when they ghosted her, and even her Mom by getting sick. It was selfish to think like that, she knew that... logically. But she was so exhausted and wanted someone to lean on. To share the load.

Juan's bright eyes widened, the shock evident by the whites of his eyes. "What do you mean?" His tone was still calm, but there was an edge in the question Searra bristled at.

She glanced at Jade, making sure she was still eating her eggs, most of it was now enmeshed in the fluffy carpet, but some still made the treacherous journey to her mouth, so Searra let her be.

"I mean I *saw* her. And you. In your kitchen." Searra was waving her hands for emphasis, though it made her feel crazier now she was saying it all out loud. Explaining her vision was going to be harder than she anticipated.

Juan's confusion deepened in his creased brow and Searra went on, "You were talking. And you were covered in mud and really shaken up. It happened when I touched one of your mugs. I— I think—" The words were trapped on her tongue. It was like pushing them though concrete. "I think I had a... vision, or something..." Her voice petered out like a deflated balloon.

The air stilled around them and only the sound was of Jade smashing her eggs into the floor, first a wet squish and then her unbridled squeal about it.

"Is that normal for a vampire?" Searra asked, a little sheepish at the question, at the fact that she even had to ask it. And at the fact that Juan still hadn't said anything.

Juan starred at her for a long time, the shocked expression on his face receding, replaced with one of contemplation; like he was working out a puzzle in his head. A puzzle it seemed, he had no plans to share as he continued to say... *nothing.*

"I take your silence for a 'no', then?" Searra scoffed. She raked her hands through her dark brown hair, frustration giving way to anger, heating the very blood in her veins like a pot set on the stove to boil.

"I feel like I'm flailing in the freaking dark here!" Searra flung that blatant truth at him, careful not to raise her voice too loud and be more

choosy with her colorful language since Jade was eating only a few feet away. "I need your help. Otherwise
what is the point of all this?" Searra said with a little
bite to her tone, waving to their surroundings. "Then
why are we even here?"

Even to her own ears, she sounded so lost and angry, so unlike herself. She was always sure of what
to do next, of where she was going and nothing
could keep her down.

A hole had been punched straight through her when
she lost Diego. A wound so deep in her soul she'd
thought it had finally scarred over after almost two
years without him. But now, it tore open at the seams,
leaking that same raw, debilitating pain back into her
chest. Searra fought to keep it buried, to hold herself
together but her features tightened and her eyes burn
ed... the grief bleeding through.

Juan stood over her, watching where she sat cross-
legged beside Jade, her face mostly hidden behind a
curtain of dark hair. Through the strands, she peeked
up at him and caught the fire in his gaze. He let out a
loud sigh, something resolute settling in his exasperated expression.

"It is not common." Juan admitted while he strode
closer and took a seat on the floor beside her. He
sat cross legged like she did and their knees brushed.

Juan had a contemplative look on his face and continued, "Among vampiric gifts, that one is very rare
and highly coveted. It suggests that you have witch ancestry, since older witch covens tended to cultivate
seers with strong psychic abilities." Juan explained
with a slight grin, he was practically salivating with
the possibility and he wet his full bottom lip with his

tongue, excitement alight in his eyes.

Searra's focus lingered far too long on his glistening mouth. She gave her head a quick shake, desperate to pull herself back and gather her scattered thoughts.

She couldn't believe what she was hearing, *first vampires, now witches?*

What next? Leprechauns?

The idea sent a shiver down her spine. There was something extremely creepy about real life Leprechauns, and Searra didn't want to find out if those existed too. For some reason, she was certain if they did exist, they would bite. *...with small, green teeth.*

Juan continued, "I haven't come across a seer in a long time. Forgive me if I seem... overly excited."

"Well, now I feel all kinds of special." Searra barbed. It came out more deadpan than she meant, but she didn't care.

"You should!" Juan was adamant, leaning into her personal space. "If my suspicions are correct, you may be the last of a coven thought long dead, forgotten by history."

"So that's a good thing?" Searra asked, not quite understanding the gravity. "You're making me feel like a long lost dinosaur or something. Like one of those birds they just found out was *technically* prehistoric, so now it's an important dinosaur instead of just a giant, ugly bird."

"I make you feel like a big... bird?" Juan asked, uncertainty in his tone as his left eyebrow arched. His bottom lip looked extra full while he pouted in contemplation.

Searra's mouth fell open, and a laugh bubbled up from her chest. It was ridiculous, vampires couldn't be this out of touch.

"Yes, you make me feel like Big Bird." Her tone was sarcastic, and she threw in a bit of an eye roll, but amusement colored her words and a wide smile broke out on her face.

Juan's answering smile was bright with a hint of confusion, and that made it all the more funny to Searra, and she began to laugh harder until her eyes teared up and a snort escaped.

She clapped a hand over her mouth, her eyes wide with mortification and her cheeks pinked.

Juan's expression was alight with devilish amusement as he stared at her. He opened his mouth to say something, but he was cut off by Jade, who began to chant, "'Nana, 'nana, 'nana, 'nana, 'nana, 'NANA!" The crescendo of noise building until Searra couldn't think straight and there was only the sound of Jade's voice and nothing else. The longer it went, the more it frayed at her nerves.

"Sweeeeeetie, shuuuuuush!" Searra tried to interject between "'Nanas," hoping to calm her down, and keep her voice in a soothing tone. "It's okay sweetie pie! Mommy is looking for your 'nana!"

Searra got up from her seat on the floor, her knees bumping Juan's as she did. She leapt to the diaper bag slumped in the corner by the crib, moving faster than what should be possible.

Desperate fingers found the zipper and tugged at it with such force she broke it, it opened like an exploded bag of chips, the teeth ripped from each other and bent in haphazard directions. Searra didn't give herself the time to analyze it as she single mindedly looked for Jade's 'nana.

To her surprise, she still had a handful of pouches left, which would have to do for now. Although, two of them were green. The dreaded apple, banana, mango and avocado mix. Jade hated that one. At least, the last time she tried it, she hated it. But her taste was so fickle, it could become her favorite at the turn of a dime. For now, Searra would try the pink one, a raspberry, banana and apple mix and cross her fingers it was still her favorite.

"Here you go Sweetie!" Searra said as she unscrewed the cap and held the pouch up to Jade's mouth. Jade looked at it with suspicion, her little brow crinkling before she announced, "Pink!" with a big, toothy grin. And lowered her head to drink from the little spout on the pouch.

"*Sí, mi amore!* ⁵ It is pink! Your favorite one!" Searra smiled back at her, holding the pouch steady so Jade couldn't squeeze it all out in one shot and get the sticky fruit goo all over Juan's pristine coral rug, which was now coated in bits of egg. Searra took a seat on the floor right next to Jade, putting more distance between her and Juan. It wasn't much, but at least she could breathe easier now.

Juan's eyes were on her while she fed Jade, his gaze burning a hole in the side of her face. Searra refused to turn to look at him though, keeping her concentration on Jade and finishing her pouch. But she could still make out his shape in her periphery.

"Okay..." Searra started, still keeping her eyes on Jade. "Soooo," she clicked her tongue, not quite sure

---

5. Yes, my love!

how to finish that sentence. "I'm a vampire now."

Smoooooth.

"*Sí.*"[6] Juan said.

She snuck a quick glance at him and his whole body had gone ridged on the floor.

"Why don't I feel different?" Searra asked, eyes sliding back to Jade as she smiled and offered Searra some of her pouch. "No sweetie, that's for you!" Not satisfied, Jade continued to push the pouch up to Searra to take a sip, eyes determined and mouth set in a stubborn line. Searra mimed it with some convincing slurping sounds and turned the spout back to Jade to drink, "Your turn!" Jade proceeded to lower her head and downed the rest of the fruit goo.

Searra was both relieved and a little worried nothing had changed since she was turned, at least nothing she had noticed.

Except the heightened senses, and the strength... and the speed.

"You are." Juan's deep voice rang out, steady and sure, his back was ramrod straight as he remained sitting cross legged on the floor.

"Do all vampires have impeccable posture or something?" She asked, adding with a wicked smile, "Or, did you just sit on a pole that you never bothered to get removed?" Searra was half serious, because she imagined most vampires just stood stiff and straight, like from old classic movies when they would rise from coffins from hidden platforms, arms crossed

---

6. Yes.

over their chests with long fingernails and rat teeth.

Juan's sandy brow raised, amusement in his eyes and the corner of his mouth ticked up. "I'm unsure," He leaned in, and she felt his breath on her skin, "No one has ever tried to remove it." With that, he gave a feral smile, his sharp canines glinted in the light and his green eyes blazed.

He looked... dangerous. Something deep inside her lifted its head to meet the challenge in his eyes. Something in her, something primal. A part of herself she didn't recognize.

"It's harder for you to notice the differences because you are you and in your body. The change starts subtly and tends to take about five days." Juan paused, watching Searra to make sure she was listening.

To assure him, she waved her hand, "Five days. Uh huh, got it." For emphasis, she punctuated it with a firm thumbs up and a nod of her head.

He continued, but his eyes squinted at her with suspicion, "In that time, you will get stronger, faster, your senses will become much more keen and you will also be more sensitive to sunlight. Aaaaand," he paused again, it was like he knew the next six words would make her wince, "you will begin to crave blood."

Juan stared at her so intently she was sure he saw through her like a sheet of tissue paper, so intimate, so probing. She shifted in her seat, but she didn't flinch away. The atmosphere between them pulled taut as she searched for her words.

Searra had the intense desire to do a Count impersonation from Sesame Street just to cut the tension.

You   will crave bloooood   in   one,   two,

three, four. Four more days! Muahaha!

But, the reference might go over his head and he was already giving her squinty side eye.

He was trying to read her reactions but she wasn't processing everything he was telling her. Searra was slow to process and digest information and could not take shit too serious. But, she may come back in a week and be quite pissed about this conversation, and she reserved the right to, even if he didn't know about that particular detail yet. And then, maybe, she might bust out her flawless Count impression.

Searra thought back over recent events and realized she had gotten sick yesterday when she'd gone outside.

But that was a crazy sudden flu, not vampirism. Vampires burned in the sun, right? And when was the last time she ate?

She couldn't remember. *When was the last time she was hungry?*

As if he had read her mind, Juan said, "It's not what you think. We don't burn in the sun like in cinema," He rolled his eyes, "Or sparkle," he added, a little vitriol in his tone.

Searra couldn't help her smile at his expression, a put upon vampire had a certain charm she couldn't resist. It was absurd.

"So, you do keep up to date on pop culture and trendy shit, then?" She asked. The smugness oozed from her like syrup from a sapling, grinning wide like The Cheshire cat.

Juan's expression lit up and he gave a broad grin. His teeth were so white it blinded her. "Honestly, I fade in and out. Sometimes I go whole decades without checking in and then..." His voice went low and deep, and was as rough as gravel, he leaned into her space, his nose mear inches from her own, "Something catches my attention." He breathed and his lips parted, "Then, it becomes my obsession."

Searra found herself transfixed and leaning towards him, caught in his gravitational pull. She didn't have the words or motivation to escape. She wasn't certain she was breathing.

"What does the sun do then?" Searra sputtered out, but she was more than a little disappointed she wouldn't sparkle. She would have saved so much on highlighter and glittery lotion if she did. She wasn't one to shy away from the glistening look. The more shine and glitter the better.

"The sun affects us like it does everyone else, but exponentially faster. Sunstroke can happen in minutes to a vampire. But everyone is different. You can become nauseated and start vomiting. You may get dizzy, terrible headaches or sunburned. And heatstroke too; the list goes on and on... so you should avoid direct sunlight at all cost. It could leave you weakened and get you killed." Juan's voice was grave as he explained. His full bottom lip was pouty as his mouth set in a tight line.

Her stare lingered a little too long on his mouth to not go unnoticed, so she quickly looked away, determined not to get distracted but her face heated with girlish embarrassment.

It was then the realization clicked, the dizzy spell she had yesterday morning was because of the sun. The sick feeling had come on so strong, Searra should have known something else was wrong. She had never been sick like that before, or as quick, where she was so debilitated she almost didn't make it back inside the house. A shudder went through her as she contemplated that possibility. It all could have ended in her own backyard.

He must have been reading her face, because Juan's voice sliced though her thoughts, her stream of consciousness leaking out into a puddle she couldn't make sense of.

"You've already experienced the sun's effects though, haven't you?" His tone was harsh, but not accusatory. His anger was evident, and it gave an edge to his words.

Searra's gaze flicked to Jade, who was playing with the empty pouch next to her on the floor, waving it around and banging it against the hardwood. Jade had folded the shaggy coral carpet back so the hardwood beneath was exposed. She shouted, "Teeeewwwww, teeeewww!" All while pointing tiny fingers to the light wooden planks beneath, counting them with a wide smile on her face that lit up her big brown eyes. She was learning to count, up to three sometimes. But she definitely had two down.

"Yeah. I didn't know I couldn't go outside." Searra admitted, her tone measured. Her dark brown eyes flicked up to his molten green ones again. All chaos in his gaze, so much emotion swirling there, it should have made her dizzy.

There was anger for sure, and guilt, such overwhelming guilt. Her heart cracked. His broad shoulders caved in as she starred. He raked his hand through his sandy hair, tousling it even more after his shower, frustration evident in the crease of his brow and the tautness of his muscles.

"I apologize." He said in a low gruff voice she barely heard. "After turning you, I — I should have stayed, to guide you. To help." His eyes were on the floor now, he didn't want to look at her, like he was ashamed.

Searra leaned back in her seat, giving the small of her back a reprieve from sitting hunched over, keeping herself propped up with her hands. She nudged his knee with her foot with a playfulness she hadn't felt in so long.

"It's ohhhh-kaaaay." Searra smiled at him drawing out the syllables. "I was pretty much asleep all day. I only went outside to work out and came back inside quick, so it wasn't even that serious."

She kept nudging him with her foot, but a dark cloud had descended on him, swallowing him up. His gaze was empty and thousands of miles away, no longer there in the room with her. In some distant time and place where she could not follow. If it was possible, he looked smaller somehow, for a moment. He was a rather large man and he took up space wherever he was, but right now he had sunk into himself, like a dying star becoming a black hole.

"I'm not sure of vampire etiquette but I think you made up for it by showing up later that night." She shrugged, "It's not like you didn't come back." Searra wasn't sure what the big deal was, but it upset him and something inside her wanted to soothe it away. "And now we are here." Waving her hands around.

Juan growled in frustration. "Newly sired vampires need to be taught. They need to be guided. Leaving—" he paused and shook his head, still not looking at her. His mop of sandy brown hair hung in his eyes as he brooded. Emerald eyes smoldering.

Searra stared at him a moment, but then she leaned forward and grabbed him by the shoulder, his muscles rippled and were hard as stone beneath her grip. She tried not to dwell too long on that, and he looked up at her, his green eyes a sea of emotion peaking through the tendrils of hair as she said. "Then *teach* me."

CHAPTER
13

YIELD

A few hours later, Searra put Jade down for the night and went to the living room to collapse onto the massive cream couch. It was the type of couch you just wanted to sink into. She wouldn't have minded sleeping on it since it was more comfortable than most beds she had slept in. The cushions were deep which meant Searra could curl her long legs up beneath her and get cozy without feeling like a crazy pretzel. All she needed now was a blanket and a book, or maybe an episode of *Real Housewives*.

Instead, an awareness prickled up her spine and she

went tense. The singing of metal hit her ears and she had the intense desire to move. Pushing off the couch with her all her strength, she dove to the floor. Her hands smacked against the hardwood and the impact reverberated up her arms. She turned her head back to the couch and saw a long shinning sword sticking out of the cushion her ass had just been sitting in. The grip was wrapped in a dark brown leather and the pommel had a massive emerald. Searra recognized the blade. It was the same one she saw in her vision.

"The fuck?!" Searra screamed, scrambling away and to her feet. Juan was standing across the room, amusement on his handsome face.

"Retrieve the sword before I can." Juan said evenly, she felt the compulsion woven between his words and her body began to move. Out of the corner of her eye, he became a blur as he made his way to his sword.

All Searra could hear was the sound of her own breathing as she pumped her legs, thighs burning with immense strength as they pushed against the floor beneath her, creating her own moving walkway.

Her hand was on the hilt and she pulled, but before the sword could dislodge, his hand enveloped hers sending sparks skittering over her skin. She tried to pull again, but he was too strong. A small smile played about his lips, showing off the glint of his fangs.

"Duck." His eyes sparkled at her as his other hand came across at dizzying speed, swiping at her face.

Searra ducked, only a hair's breath away from being slashed to ribbons.

"What are you doing?!" Searra gasped, dodging as his arm came back around to swipe low and she let go of the sword.

"Training." Juan instructed.

Jesssssuuuuus Christ. Talk about just throwing the baby in the pool and calling it a swim lesson...

"A little warning would have been nice." Searra barbed, bringing her fists to eye level, protecting her face.

Juan pulled the sword from the couch in one swift movement, the metal ringing.

To Searra, he held that sword out like a warrior on the battlefield, steel resolve in his emerald gaze, "Take my sword." It was a challenge. He quirked a brow at her, his voice echoing in the recesses of her mind. *Don't hold back.*

He charged at her and Searra let out a small yip of surprise before she used her speed to turn on her heel and run to the kitchen.

How the fuck was she supposed to do that? They never had medieval day in her self-defense class. *People don't run around with fucking swords anymore!*

She sped around one of the kitchen islands, putting the full stone block between them so she could have a chance to think. But fear was clogging her thoughts. A sweet scent began to cloy at her senses and saliva built in her mouth — her fangs erupted as a growl of challenge bubbled from her throat. *Fuck... What was that?*

Juan leapt over the island in one fluid motion and Searra did the same, clearing the stone block in one movement, the marble continuing to act as a barrier between them.

Searra needed a weapon, something to even the playing field and spotted the frying pan she had used earlier to make Jade's eggs. It was still in the sink

Chapter 14

Clarity

Searra relaxed her stance, letting her shoulders slump and her knees bend. She sauntered past Juan, a little high on her win and a small smirk on her lips. Placing her pan next to Juan's sword, she then headed straight for the couch. It was calling her name as the adrenaline rush began to dissipate. She wanted a nap *ASAP.*

Juan's expression was lit from within with a wide grin, his handsome face becoming something beautiful, an eternal beauty that she wanted to study. Something went molten in Searra's chest at the sight. She loved making him smile like that and couldn't help the answering goofy grin that stretched across her own face.

She beat Juan to the couch and plopped down. Her entire body sagged, a melted puddle of a person and right next to the giant hole left by the sword. That couch had to be expensive and Searra cringed at the thought of having to replace it. At how easily he ruined something that probably cost a fortune.

Juan was silent as he sat down beside her. His leg brushed against hers which sent a hot jolt up her spine.

"There is a lot of couch to choose from, yah know." Searra snarked at him, but there was no venom in her voice, which was surprising given the battle they had just waged.

She did ask for it though...

"It is my couch, I shall sit where I want." A smug expression on his face.

Searra rolled her eyes, "Losers shouldn't get to choose," and sighed, resigning herself. "Sooo... you're a sword man, huh?" Her tone was dry.

Juan let out a big belly laugh, the sound was magical, pure baritone "I suppose so. If that is what you want to call it." He was still smiling, his fangs winked at her in the light of the living room. "It is my good luck charm. I —," He was suddenly very serious, his smile wiped away, gaze locked on hers. "I never enter a battle without it. Which seems to have worked out in my favor. I haven't lost a fight in over six hundred years." His lips curved into what would have been a smile, but there was no humor behind it. Flecks of onyx invaded his emerald gaze as the shadows overtook his expression.

Searra wanted to comfort him and she nudged him with her knee. "Hey." She said softly. "You look good for an old man." Her grin was inviting and mischevious.

Juan chuckled, some of the earlier light reentering his eyes. He cleared his throat,"What else do you remember from your vision?" His voice was stern and matter-of-fact as he changed the subject.

"Just that you were pissed." There was a chill to her voice that hadn't been their a minute ago, with a bit of bite she regretted the second she spat it out. She started again, abandoning the forced chill in her words, "Sorry, it's just that Liv was comforting you." She tried to soften her voice, "It — It looked like something, something... horrible had just happened." Searra offered a small understanding smile, trying to take back the earlier judgment she had dished out.

If that information rang any bells, Juan didn't let on. His face remained impassive as he crossed his arms over his chest, the only sign he was on the defensive. His pecs twitched and he shifted in his seat on the couch. "What else?" His mouth had set in a slight sneer. A muscle in his jaw ticked.

Searra watched him for a long time and it dawned on her that he didn't want to give anything away. He wanted to know what *she knew.* That pissed her off and her face heated with it.

To Searra, trust meant giving up *all* the information, not picking and choosing.

A lie of omission is still a lie. A breach of trust.

Juan still hadn't spoken, so Searra closed her eyes and narrowed her thoughts to Juan and Liv. To that moment in her vision. Juan was covered in mud, his hair a mess, everything was caked into a hair and mud helmet. But she still caught a glimpse of his sandy colored hair through the dirt. Liv was inches away as she whispered, "Once we've spoken wi' Ambrose, he'll see to it. The man's got witches on his tether. He'll set it right." The soft rise and fall of the Highands on her tongue sent a chill down Searra's spine and her eyes snapped open. *Yeah, definitely Scottish.*

Juan was now sitting inches away, leaning into her personal space. His gaze was a forrest in a storm as they searched hers. "What is it? What are you afraid of?" His tone was stern, but a little bit of hurt frayed his tone.

Did he think she was afraid of him? She was, but that was beside the point. She didn't want him to know that.

Searra took a deep breath, steely resolve in her heart soothing her nerves. "Who is Ambrose? Liv said he could 'fix' you. What is wrong with you?"

Juan's mouth hung open as he froze. It felt like all the oxygen had been sucked from the room. The white noise from the baby monitor echoed like rolling thunder in the quiet. Juan was so still, she wasn't sure he was breathing.

Did vampires breathe?

Searra could see the whites all the way around his eyes as they popped out of his head in shock.

"Us working together... me helping you, the training... It only works if we are honest. And you are holding shit back and I don't fuck with that." Searra was stern. "Where do I fit in... in all of this? Why do you need *my* help?" If Liv said Ambrose could help Juan, what could he possibly need from her?

Juan's gaze never wavered from her as he shifted

and leaned back on the couch. He was assessing her, Searra felt his stare and gave him one of her own. Refusing to speak more.

Juan pursed his lips and sucked air through his teeth. His jaw set in steel. Then, it was like a switch flipped and his shoulders relaxed. The tension in his body had lifted like a vapor, and he leaned farther back with his arms wide, cradling the backrests of the couch as he just ignored the giant hole in the upholstery that was now in the crook of his arm. He had a long wingspan Searra realized, as she lingered a little too long on the sinewy muscles on his arms; head tilting during her perusal.

"I need your help finding someone. A *brujita*[1] stole something of mine, and I want it back."

"I doubt that I know any witches or *brujas*,[2]" Searra scoffed, but Juan gave her a knowing smile. "What did they steal?" Searra continued.

"Just an heirloom. I've had it for centuries and I want it back." There was no room for argument in Juan's tone.

"Well, why would they steal it from you? Is it worth a lot? Or is it powerful? I can't imagine a witch would steal from a vampire, just cause."

"It doesn't matter why she stole it. It is mine, and I want it back." Juan's gaze was icy as he looked down at his nails, "Plus, vampires and witches have been at war for centries, so that would be reason enough to

---

1. Little witch

2. witches

steal from me." The bite in his tone didn't go unnoticed. His green gaze was full of intense focus, his lips were pressed tight and his jaw was tense.

"Okay, what does it look like?" Searra was starting to feel tired, her temples began to pound.

Searra's smile fell away and a gnarled pit began to form in her stomach. "War? What do you mean? What war?" She said between quickened breaths, panic beginning to bloom in her chest like a hot poker to a block of ice. "Between vampires and witches? Where did that leave humans?" Searra's anxiety was already on track to make her hyperventilate. It was getting hard to control her breathing.

In and out. Breathe. In and out. Breathe. Focus on breathing. In and out.

The air whistled through her teeth as her breath came out fast and shaky. Pushing things down to process later only worked for so long. Once she reached the final boss level of overstimulated... she woud be done, and easy prey for a full on, earth shattering panic attack.

Juan's deep voice cut through her thickening fog of apprehension, "Searra." He sounded gruffer than usual and Searra risked a glance at his face while she continued to breathe through her gritted teeth.

His eyes were tempests and flashed with their own power and lightning. But beneath that outer layer of brute strength... he looked concerned?

Was he worried about her?

Distress was coming off of him in waves. His brow had furrowed and his jaw was tight.

But she couldnt tear her gaze away from those eyes, Searra could drown in them and her breathing began to even out the longer she stared. They became cool, green and soothing pools of emerald, reminding her of thick, untouched forests or a soft meadow full of lush grass.

Peaceful. Her anxiety began to ebb away.

Juan continued, keeping his tone soft, "Humans are unaware of our war." His fangs caught the light for a moment and their sharpness glinted, "Vampires thrive on secrecy." His smile was a tight line that didn't reach his eyes. "But we are at war."

Searra felt a bit better knowing vampires were not planning on human involvement in their war. Her breathing had almost returned to normal, but the question was nagging at her, "What would this witch gain from stealing from you? How would it help her? It's gotta hold some power then, because otherwise all she did was piss off an old and powerful vampire."

Juan remained quiet, but his eyes were lit. She knew he was debating on what to tell her. Searra's jaw tightened, and she said, "If you want my help at all, I need you to let me in." She began pointing, using her fingers as weapons to aid her words, "*You* got me involved in this shit. And it's not just *my* life on the line here, my *daughter* is involved now too." Searra took another deep breath, "I need to know what is going on *now!*" Her voice rang out in the quiet room, exuding more strength than she felt. The white noise coming from the baby monitor clipped to her collar cut out for a moment and then resumed its monotonous drone like she hadn't spoken.

Juan's handsome face stared at her; she couldn't read his expression. He sat so still on the couch, it was as if he'd stopped breathing. His broad chest remained motionless. Searra found herself holding her own breath waiting, almost afraid for him to respond.

"It is a Jasper pendant. It has the power to amplify magic and spells. So a *bruja astuta*[3] would be very inclined to take it," Juan said through his teeth, as though Searra pulled the information from him like splinters from a wound.

Juan stared at her, the green of his eyes had gone mossy and soft. The corner of his lips curved up into a cunning smile. "Witch blood runs through your veins." He pointed to Searra as he leaned forward.

He had strong hands.

"And I suspect that you know the thief."

Searra was so focused on his large palms, she didn't catch what he said. She could only think of the way he gripped her the other night. The way his hands felt on her body. The way he made her climax with those same fingers.

Her gaze flicked back to his face, and he was still smiling at her, but his features had darkened, had gone molten. As though he knew what she was thinking about and it had stoked his own desire.

She bit her lip in anticipation, not realizing when her fangs broke through the full curve of her bottom lip, a thin ribbon of blood blooming where they pierced.

Jesus...that was beginning to become a hazard. Stupid, sharp-ass fangs.

She hissed at the pain blossoming on her lip as her tongue slid along the edge of her teeth. Searra inspected her newly formed fang with the tip of her tongue

---

3. Smart witch

and then began to gingerly probe the wound. Her attention was seized by the taste of her own blood. The pull was more potent than it had been only a day ago.

All thoughts of Juan and his deft hands had flown from her mind, and she was consumed with a bloodlust she didn't understand. Her world narrowed, and she no longer saw Juan sitting next to her on the couch; she didn't see anything. Her eyes were open, but she couldn't process what was in front of her. She only had thoughts of blood. The sweet, honeyed liquid bathed her tongue and filled her mind with dark promises of moonlit nights, of sweet caresses, nights reminiscent of candles, steam, and satin sheets. Of hunger... of pl easure... of need.

Something warm was shoved in her mouth, and she heard Juan's deep voice call her name, but he sounded so far away.

"Searra! Searra! *¡Escúchame, por favor!*[4] Bite down!" His voice was getting louder but remained firm.

She obeyed without thinking and warm blood coated her tongue. She gulped it down like Jade and a pouch of applesauce. It was only then that it dawned on her... she was sucking on one of the blood bags from the fridge.

She braced herself for the disgust, for her stomach to turn at the thought of drinking blood like baby food... but it never came. Instead, a shiver of ecstasy rippled through her as the sweet warmth slid down her throat. She drank in greedy swallows, like someone

---

4. Listen to me, please!

parched and hungover, desperate to quench a craving she hadn't known she had.

Searra closed her eyes, surrendering to the pull. She didn't open them again until the bag was sucked flat in her hands, her own vacuum seal.

A contented hum slipped from her throat, low and rumbling. When she opened her eyes, Juan was watching her. He had an empty blood bag gripped in his hand too, satisfaction oozing from him.

Her gaze flicked from the bag in his hand to his face, then down to the one flattened in her own.

"You made me hungry." Juan said, in a rather sticky voice, the thick blood still coating his throat.

He shrugged his shoulders with a half smile that lit his eyes up like sapphires, his shoulder muscles rippling through his thin white tee.

The veins bulged in his arms from the new blood, like something out of *Pumping Iron*.

"Is this how vampires eat now?" She waved her flattened blood bag in the space between them, brows raised. "Because this is toddler status." She couldn't help her accompanying smirk.

"Heh, not all." Juan said with a smile dripping with sarcasm. His fangs were still glinting from having just fed and the spark was reflected in his darkened gaze. "It's more like fast food, super convenient. But, not everyone can afford it, or even cares to prepare ahead."

"Kind of like living on food delivery," Searra said absent-mindedly, her fingers played with the tube used to hook the bag up to smaller tubes and administer it into people's veins.

Searra cringed. She just ate something that could

have saved a life somewhere. She had given blood many times in her life and she would have been pissed if she thought her blood went to some vampire with a Postmates account.

"Do you notice anything different?" Juan questioned, a little earnestness in his tone, shaking her from her thoughts.

Searra started, "Ummmm..." she was trying to think what he meant by that.

Different how?

Searra's brows knitted together in confusion.

"Do you feel any different? How are your senses? Your reflexes?"

Now that he mentioned it, everything looked clearer. Colors were brighter, more rich despite the hour and lack of light. She saw clear through the kitchen and down the hall from her spot on the sofa. The hallway was dark, all the lights were off. It was late night, but she could see all the way down to the end of the hall where her and Jade's room was.

They're was something odd with the door. A red light was permeating through the wood and when she squinted, the light took shape. It was a small body, asleep in a crib.

Searra's mouth fell open, not comprehending what she was looking at. The little body moved, shifting from one side to the other, little chubby legs kicking at the blanket around them before finally settling back to a sleepy stillness.

Searra's heart dropped into her stomach and it felt like her gastric acid began to devour it. Was she somehow seeing Jade sleeping through the closed door?

"H-H-How..." Searra's voice was stuck in her

throat, the words clogged in the blood soaking it, knowing she was seeing her infant daughter differently, *like
prey.*

Searra looked down at Juan. He was still sitting on
the couch and she hadn't realized she was on her feet.

His eyes were flecks of obsidian staring back at her,
not a trace of green to be seen. His fangs pierced the
dark of the room and it made the hairs on the back of
her neck stand on end. It seemed as though all sound
had been sucked out of the room until the only thing
she heard was her own labored breathing.

"You are seeing her body heat." Juan's voice rumbled
from deep in his chest with an almost animalistic
growl. There was something dangerous in that sound
and she found the hairs on the back of her neck had
prickled to attention.

Searra looked at Juan, and she couldn't see any
light around him at all. Besides the slight flush in his
cheeks, there was nothing.

"Why can't I see anything around you?" Searra
asked, although she was pretty sure she figured it out
already, but didn't want to voice it.

"Because I don't have any body heat. I'm room
temperature." The corner of his mouth quirked up,
the points of his fangs peeking out from his lips.
They seemed to wink at her in the soft living room
light.

"We don't emit body heat." Searra whispered, the
words not making sense or sinking in. Everything
was upside down. Even talking with her fangs poking
her was tripping her out.

Did she have a lisp?

It wasn't like she knew how to retract them. She

was pretty sure she was going to cut her tongue talking.

In that moment, there was something, a taste on the air around her, it was both tart and cloying at the same time. She found herself drawn to it and tried to open her mouth and breath in more. Searra had tasted this scent before.

Juan was watching her like a jungle cat, and a growl tore its way up her own throat in challenge before she could stop it.

Predator sensing predator. Slowly, she stood from the couch. Instincts compelling her, muscles tensing, readying for a fight.

Juan put his hands up in mock surrender, and casually crossed one leg over the other so his ankle was resting on his knee. "I apologize. We should have eaten right after our training session. It would have helped with the ...animal urges."

Searra grabbed her own throat, thinking she could stifle the involuntary growling. "What is that in the air? It's like sweet and sour sauce or something. I —I keep smelling it." Searra asked, trying to distract herself and hoping her question didn't sound insane.

The corner of Juan's mouth quirked up in a sideways smile and he let out a breathy chuckle; amusement painted on his darkened face. "That is your fear you taste."

Chapter

15

Ache

Searra felt like all of the air had been sucked out of the room and her head was swimming. *My fear?*

One second, Juan was sitting on the couch, looking up at her with flint in his blackened gaze; the next, he was right in front of her, almost nose to nose, invading her personal space.

Searra did not flinch, she did not back down.

She stood, with him in her face, their breaths comingling. All of her senses felt heightened, an otherworldly electricity permeating the air. She thought her hair might stand on end with the strength of it.

Juan closed his eyes and took a long, deep inhale through his nose, his full lips pursed and his nostrils flared.

"Your scent is exquisite, meant for kings." He growled out. They were so close she felt the vibration in his muscled chest.

Searra didn't know what to say. The green had returned to his eyes and they were now glowing hot with desire. His gaze raked over her body, like shadowy fingers stroking over her skin. A shiver raced down her spine and her gooseflesh rose with the pleasure of it.

She was still in the same pajama bottoms and tank top she had been wearing when he had dropped into her backyard last night. She could remember how he had pushed those very same pajama bottoms aside to explore her. His fingers had caressed the innermost part of her body and shattered her into oblivion and still... she had wanted more.

It didn't matter that nothing made sense anymore, that her entire world had been thrown out the window. Thrown by *this man*, this *demon*.

The crux of it was she was *feeling* again, and it was intoxicating. Searra hadn't realized how withdrawn she had become until Juan crashed into her life, fangs and all.

His scent of cool, spicy citrus enveloped her, peppered with an apple-sweet cedar. He smelled so good, like a cool night in an orchard, making her think of clear, moonlit nights and crisp cider.

She just wanted to lean into him, to feel his hard

body against hers. For him to pin her against the wall again and drive into her with all his strength.

Oh Lordy...

The memory made her breath hitch and liquid heat pool in her core. She wasn't smelling fear in the air anymore, now she could smell her arousal, and she was confident Juan could smell it too.

His pupils dilated as he took in another long, deep inhale. Searra's eyes grew hooded as she stared into his handsome, rugged face, his stubble only drawing attention to the sharp square cut of his jaw, and her breathing began to quicken.

Juan bent his head down, and the closer he got, the more the air between them seemed to vibrate with need.

Searra held so still, she wasn't sure she was breathing. He was now so close to her that the tip of his nose was almost grazing the delicate skin at the crook of her neck. Searra didn't dare move or flinch away. She even held her breath as he inhaled her in deep.

"You still carry my scent, even now." Juan's voice was no more than a growl. "How deliciously loyal your body is." Pure possession in his tone.

The idea had Searra's adrenaline spiking, and heat rise to her cheeks. She let herself lean into him. Her breasts brushed against his hard chest, making her nipples peak. She felt fire in her veins and she began to throb between her thighs. She couldn't help the soft, breathy moan that escaped her lips.

A sound she was sure Juan didn't miss.

She needed more friction and leaned in closer, so close that their bodies were practically tangled as her hips began to slowly grind against his.

He let out a growl that surrendered into a deep moan. Juan was all raw hunger and pleasure and she was melting in the heat of his jewel toned gaze.

Searra liked that she still had Juan's scent on her from last night, but that didn't mean she wanted him to know how much she did.

"I haven't had a chance to shower." Searra whispered, her telltale obstinacy rearing it's head. Although, she couldn't help the small smile playing against her lips or that her voice was a little lower and rougher.

"Don't," Juan whispered, his breath teasing the skin on her neck, sending shivers down her spine. "You should always smell like me." He growled into her neck, teeth nipping at her skin but not hard enough to draw blood, although she was silently wishing he had. Her insides clenched at the contact from his mouth and sent sparks of pleasure throughout her body. His hands made their way to wrap around her waist, sending shadowy tendrils of pleasure coursing through her.

She felt it then, a new darkness growing within her. Darkness in her soul. A monster that reared its head when her most primal desires claimed her senses. Searra was being dragged under like a rip tide out into deep, endless water and she was drowning... drowning in feeling, in touch, drowning in hunger.

She couldn't escape or get enough.

It had been so long since she felt like that. Searra *hungered* for him. She craved Juan's mouth on hers. She ached to have him inside her; his fingers playing with her most sensitive spot. She was so wet and ready and throbbing for him. Searra needed to grind against him harder and harder just to find relief.

Juan leaned back to look down at her, his face a mixture of so many emotions it was impossible to read.

Even though she was only half a foot shorter, he towered over her with his otherworldly presence. Even his fangs had a savage, surreal glint to them and she wanted to feel their vicious sting again.

She licked her lips in anticipation, and looked into Juan's eyes, finding a vast wilderness in their forest green depths... a dark desperation, a need that only devoured and was never sated.

A yearning that matched her own.

A twin to her own ravenous beast.

Before she could react, Juan grabbed her. His large hand tangled in her long dark hair as he pulled her mouth to his. His lips crashed into hers with a force that shook her down to her toes, literal worlds colliding in sparks and flames, in heat and desire. It was a kiss that would burn her from the inside out, a passion she had never known before. So strong, it felt like pain.

His fangs nicked her lips and tongue as he explored her mouth, the hot stinging sparking fire though her body. Her innermost walls clenched in response. His tongue lapped at the blood before the wounds could mend. Juan tugged on her hair to pull her head back and take a good look at her. Her scalp tingled with the force. The sharp pain intermixed with a heady desire that pulsed in her core like a heartbeat. She yearned for more.

All thought flew from Searra's mind until she was only a bundle of raw nerves.

As he looked down at her, Juan's emerald eyes burned with unholy fire, searing her from the inside out. Juan bit his own lush bottom lip and gave her a smug smile.

"You are *mine*." His words were gruff with possessive command.

On instinct, she used vampiric speed and her immense strength to loosen his hold on her hair by gripping his wrist and wrenching it back. She heard his surprised grunt and his lips pulled into a wicked grin, eyes lit with surprise and his fangs on full display.

Searra barreled into him with the force of a freight train, and they both went crashing into the side wall together. The dishes clacked against each other in the nearby cabinet from the impact.

She grabbed a chunk of Juan's sandy brown locks and dragged his head to the side, exposing his thick, strong neck. She could see the green veins popping from beneath his burnished bronze skin and heard the blood rushing through them.

Searra licked her lips, anticipation wetting her mouth as she salivated with a profound longing she had never felt before. And like a snake, she struck. Fangs sinking deep.

Juan groaned as she drank. Blood and power poured from him into her, a voracious need blossoming in her chest. The honeyed taste of his blood was addictive. It bathed her tongue and cascaded down her throat in thick, sticky gulps. She moaned at the delicious pleasure of it all.

She ached to be closer, craved the heat of his skin on hers. One moment her fists clutched his white shirt as she fed; the next, it shredded like tissue in her hands, falling away in ribbons. His perfectly carved chest and abs lay bare before her, and still she drank, deeper and deeper.

Juan's strong hands gripped her tank and tore it from her in one fluid motion, exposing her bare breasts to the cool air. She pressed herself against him as she drank, a throaty moan escaping her lips. Every inch of her skin tingled where it met his. Her right leg lifted, curling around his waist, drawing him closer as she leaned in, her sex pressing hard against him. They were still halfway clothed, but Searra could feel his length grinding against her. Only mere fabric acted as the barrier that kept him from being inside her.

Searra unlatched her teeth from Juan's neck and leaned back. She could feel the wet blood drip from the corners of her mouth and down her chin. She watched as Juan's ravenous gaze tracked the blood trail as it dripped even lower onto her bare breasts. Her nipples were taut under his hot stare and he licked his lips.

Juan's possessive stare devoured every inch of her body, and she felt it against her skin, lightly caressing her with tendrils of cool air.

Her cheeks flushed hot and she shivered with antici-pation as his eyes locked on his target —her left nipple. The corner of his mouth lifted and a mischievous light lit his lethal emerald eyes. He scooped Searra by the small of her waist and pulled her closer. Her soft flesh was pressed against his, and he began a slow, enticing assault of kisses, starting at her clavicle and making his way down to her breast, nipping and teasing as he made a fiery trail down her skin.

She shivered with pleasure. As he got to her nip-ple, she felt him pause for only a moment, and she braced herself.

Pleading.

His fangs sunk deep as he bit her breast.

Searra was overwhelmed by the most exquisite pain. Her muscles clenched so tight, she couldn't help the moan that escaped from deep in her throat, animalistic to even her own ears.

I'm going to make you scream my name.

The words came unbidden from the air. Dark and full of promises.

Cedar and bergamot flooded her senses, heady and warm, as if Juan himself had slipped inside her mind. His very presence enveloped her. Searra wanted to yell or react in *any* way, but the noise in her head had gone quiet. Drowning in sensation.

She was wound up so tight, she needed release. Searra was so close, and Juan knew it; the slightest bit of friction could send her plummeting. And as if on cue, Juan's other hand crept inside her pajama bottoms, exploring her most sensitive spot.

Oh god... the tension inside Searra coiled impossibly tighter. She was on the edge of shattering into a million tiny fragments, pieces so small she might never find them all.

Then a wolf's baying howl sounded somewhere outside and Juan went ridged.

CHAPTER
16

ESPANTO
(GHOST)

The wolf's howl sounded again, closer this time.

Searra could have sworn it sounded mournful; there was something so familiar about it. Almost like deja vu.

Juan released her breast from his mouth. He licked the wounds delicately, which caused another involuntary shiver down her spine. Then, he released her waist and unwrapped her leg from his.

She felt the sudden chill at the loss of contact.

His eyes were locked, looking past her, on the front

door, unblinking. "I'm sorry." Juan's voice was quiet and full of regret. And then he was gone, his vampiric speed making him too quick to see.

Her sex-tousled hair wooshed around her with the wind of his departure. The dark ends tickled her breasts as they did. She was suddenly very aware of how naked she was and covered herself with crossed arms.

Her tank was gone, in pieces on the floor and she stared down at the ruined fabric. Trying to will the pieces back together.

In a flash, Juan was back, standing in front of her, with a new white shirt on and another in his hand outstretched for her to take.

Searra stared at it with icy eyes.

She had been so in the moment only a minute ago, so ready to have sex with Juan again, she chided herself. She had needed it. Now... she was embarrassed.

What the fuck happened? She didn't know.

"Where are my clothes? I'll wear one of my shirts." Searra said with a clipped tone, eyes still trained on the scraps of fabric on the floor.

She could sense Juan's stare, and his arm remained outstretched, "There isn't time. We are about to have company and you will want to be dressed for it." He paused, the hesitation in his voice made her want to finally look up, "Plus, I want you in my clothes." His voice was raw with what might have been vulnerability and she looked at him.

His green eyes were wary instead of the playful ones she had grown accustomed to, like he wasn't sure if Searra would bite his head off.

Maybe she should!

Searra let out a disgruntled huff and snatched the shirt from Juan. Not meeting his eyes in the process. Her pride was wounded, but she would have time to nurse it later when she was alone.

Rushing to put on the shirt, which to her surprise, fit her well and showed off her curvy figure. In the past, she had never been able to wear a man's clothes comfortably before. They were always too tight in the thighs or baggy in the wrong places, or too tight. She was not a 'boyfriend look' girl, but this shirt was trying to change her mind.

Juan closed the gap between them and grabbed her face by the chin, but Searra flinched back. Not wanting him to touch her. Her defenses were already firmly in place.

"Hey." Juan pleaded. "Don't do that." And he grabbed her chin again, his eyes searched hers for a moment, but Searra wasn't sure what he was looking for.

She refused to meet his gaze.

"I'm sorry. I didn't want it to happen like this. I thought I had more time." The pad of his thumb rubbed at the corner of her mouth, and then he brought his thumb to his lips and sucked it.

Her insides clenched and she did her best to ignore it. Apparently, she still had a little blood on her.

Who knew she was a messy eater?

The front door slammed open with a loud cracking sound, like something barreling into it with the force of a fucking bulldozer. She almost jumped out of her skin, letting out a short, surprised yelp.

Searra spotted the claws first, black elongated talons protruding from muscled hands and veined forearms that were covered in patches of grey hair.

Dark eyes were glowing amber with untamed rage. It was a yellow she had never seen before on a human, something more akin to what wild animal eyes might look like. Like a dog or a cat...

Or a wolf?

Its mouth was misshapen and resembled more of a muzzle than a human face, like it was stuck mid-shift.

Its teeth were sharp and dripping with drool. A growl emanated from deep within its chest as she stared, and the ground she stood upon shook.

Yet, she wasn't afraid.

Chapter
17

Savage

A mournful howl pealed out from between the savage maw of the creature standing before them, and her heart twisted at its cry. Something inside her wanted to reach out and comfort the beast but Juan casually stepped in front of her, blocking her path. She wanted to challenge him, but she didn't. She had no logical argument for getting closer to the pissed off creature with sharp ass fangs and claws, so she stayed behind Juan's protective stance and didn't protest.

Before her eyes, the thing standing in the doorway lunged straight for Juan. It's long claws glinting at her in the light.

Juan ducked out of the way with dizzying speed,

pulling Searra along with him.

The wolf-like creature growled deep and menacing, turning on a dime to follow them. Swiping the air in long arcs to snag Juan's flesh with its razor sharp nails.

Juan pushed Searra behind one of the marble islands in the kitchen and tried to herd the creature into the living room.

The beast's fiery amber eyes locked on Juan — only Juan — tracking his every move as it lunged in quick, snapping strides. Claws slashed, teeth gnashed, each strike a savage attempt to land a devastating blow.

Juan was too fast for the creature and it's labored breathing echoed off the walls in the quiet.

Suddenly, the creature froze and sniffed the air, it's muzzle tasting the air like a hunting dog. It's yellowed eyes widened, and the beast's whole head snapped toward the hallway beyond the kitchen.

The creatures eyes flashed, narrowing to slits. A loud howl ripped from it's throat, so piercing that Searra's ears rang. In an instant, it bolted toward the bedrooms.

Toward Jade.

No.

Searra sped toward the creature, her leg muscles pumping with all their strength to catch the beast. She pushed herself faster than she ever had before and reached out. Leaping into the air, she seized the creature by the back legs, they were somewhere between human and hound, knees bent at sickening angles that would make any stomach turn.

They both tumbled to the floor mid-run, her elbow smacking against the ground so hard she heard a cracking sound. A hiss escaped Searra's lips as pain exploded through her. Spots danced in her vision but she did not loosen her grip. Instead, she managed to yank the beast backwards. It's body squeaking on the wooden floor as it skidded to a stop.

Searra jumped on top of the gigantic creature, her own hands contorting into claws as she swiped at the monster's face.

She raked all her fingers deep in the flesh of the beast. Her nails carved through meat and sinew. Fresh blood bubbled to the surface to coat the matted gray fur.

Searra was rabid.

The scent of the creature's blood on the air triggered a frenzy in her, spiking her adrenaline. She could only think.... *more.*

"Searra! Stop!" The command came from behind her, from Juan, but she couldn't hear him.

"*Stop!*" This time, his voice was laced with something else. A need to listen, a compulsion? The scent of magic hit the air and she tasted it on her tongue. His clean scent of citrus zested the air and she found herself lowering her hand. Blood and bits of skin coated her fingers and under her nails. Gray hairs had gotten stuck in her frayed nail plates.

Looking down, straddling the beast, it began to shift. The gigantic claws retracted, shrinking back until they looked like normal human hands. The eyes, lost in the wild, beastly yellow began to fade until only familiar dark brown eyes were staring back at her.

Eyes full of pain, pain she did not recognize or understand.

The muzzle and teeth shrank back, bones cracking

and shifting beneath his skin, until a set of the most dazzling white teeth she had ever seen emerged. She had never seen such teeth, all except for...

His lips pressed tight, his features still, they're was something in his gaze. The echo of something so intrinsic, but it was all gone now. Like a habit he had long forgotten, the ghost of a smile she thought she would only see again in her dreams. A smile she thought was lost to her forever, but it wasn't a smile on his face now. It was an expression she had never seen, and never directed at her, full of anger and pain and sadness.

Straddled beneath her, with five deep gashes carved from his temple to his lip— marks she had made— lay Diego.

CHAPTER 18

CONFESSIONS

Searra was struck dumb. Her brain couldn't form words.

Diego.

Not dead.

Not dead.

Alive.

Alive.

She jumped off of him, like his mere touch burned her.

Tears stung Searra's eyes as she looked at her husband. She couldn't speak. Hot grief clogged her throat as she stood there. Her knees were weak and she thought she would pass out. Searra reached out and grabbed the nearest thing to steady herself, and it happened to be Juan's forearm.

"Please take a seat," Juan asked as he looked back from her to Diego. "Both of you."

Diego grunted from the floor and spat, "Fuck you! Bloodfucker!"

Juan shook his head and locked eyes with Searra, "The dead have risen and have come calling." Juan's voice was hard and accusation dripped in his tone as his focus landed back on Diego.

Diego lay there on his back, muscles straining with the urge to fight, but his body refused to obey. Dark eyes whirling with raw emotion.

With hesitant steps, Searra backed away until the backs of her legs hit the couch. There she collapsed into the cushions, sinking deep wishing she could curl into herself and disappear... never to surface again.

Was she going into shock?

"Searra..?" His voice was a question, a plea. She heard Diego grunt as he rose from the floor.

Diego. That voice.

She knew it so well and yet it was so foreign to her now. A living ghost from her memory.

"Fucking bloodsucking motherfucker..." Diego trailed off under his breath while he gingerly touched the wounds on his face and hissed.

He was alive.

Where had he been all this time?! Why didn't he come home? Why did he leave?

Anger flooded her system like an avalanche, an all-consuming force. The words came unbidden from her mind like poison.

He... left... us...

He was alive and he just left?

He left... Jade.

How could he? The thought ripped a hole through her chest, the stark pain awakening something feral within her.

This couldn't be the man she loved. He would never!

Searra was on her feet in a blur of preternatural speed. A wild, vengeful roar ripped from her throat as she bore down on Diego.

All the worrying, the grieving, and the sleepless nights flooded her mind. How much she had missed him, that their daughter was in the next room and could see her dad again. She thought about how lonely she had been, and how scared... to raise Jade alone.

Yet here he was, safe. *Fucking safe.*

He abandoned them. The words sank in her stomach like a stone and bile rose to the back of her throat. She swallowed it down with her sheer force of will. Pure hatred burned in her eyes and all tears evaporated into nothing but steam.

She launched herself at Diego. Teeth biting, jaws snapping. She was a rabid animal. Diego's eyes were wide with shock and maybe even a hint of fear. He went to grab her arms to restrain her, but she dodged his grip with ease thanks to her newfound speed.

In an instant, she was behind him, her right arm snaking around his throat. Her left hand clamped over her own wrist, locking the hold as the crook of her elbow crushed against his windpipe. Then she squeezed.

Tighter... Tighter...

Just like she had been taught, she had him in a full choke hold. Her bicep and forearm were leveraged against the spots that cut off his airway.

Diego went still beneath her. He didn't struggle or try to get out of the hold. With a gentleness she didn't expect, his hand laid on her elbow and he squeezed it.

He wasn't even fighting her. Just gave her a squeeze to let her know that he surrendered.

Her mind flashed with memories of him doing the same gentle squeeze on her knees when they were cuddling on the couch and watching a movie. He'd do the same to Jade, spinning her round and round until they collapsed into a tickle fight on the floor; making her chortle so hard she would forget how to breathe. Jade's laughter would devolve into shrieks so high-pitched it felt like it should've shattered eardrums.

That subtle touch pulled her back to herself, and she drew in his scent; blueberry and warm, woody amber. Now intoxicatingly sharp through her new heightened vampiric senses. She could also detect the slightest hint of dog. Similar to when Pepito and Hazel went too long without a bath, and the whole house would stink with it.

Searra's grip loosened, but before she let go, she bent toward his ear and whispered with all the venom she had, "Fuck you." Her protruding fangs gave a little extra emphasis on the "f" sound, and she wasn't mad at it. "You're lucky I'm not a violent person."

Even though she let him go, her fury was still burning through her veins and the sting of betrayal was sharp in her chest. Searra backed away from him and made her way to where Juan was standing.

"How did you get on the property?" Juan's voice was cold and clinical as he stared Diego down.

"Fuck you! *Pinche pendejo...*[1] Fucking leech." Diego hissed at Juan through his teeth.

Gold glowed in the emerald of Juan's gaze as he tilted his head to listen. Understanding dawned on his face. "Ahhhh, the *brujita*[2] ... She *is* clever."

"What do you mean?" Searra asked, not following.

"They used magic to break my wards and bypass my security. Very advanced magic. I'm impressed." Juan lauded their prowess, but Searra knew his grin could still cut like a blade.

Diego didn't even acknowledge Juan's words and began to rub at his neck. Red marks were already forming on his skin where Searra had put the most pressure. The gashes on his face had begun to heal but the blood was still dripping down his face and onto the hardwood floors. "I suppose I shouldn't be surprised you would try to kill me too?" Diego said to Searra, bitterness coating his words.

A spiteful laugh escaped Searra, "What do you mean 'too'? Juan wasn't even fighting back earlier. If he had, you would be dead... *again.*" Searra barbed with an eyeroll.

"I *mean*, this bloodsucker has been hunting me and my family..." He paused, gesturing to Searra, "*Our* family, the past two years!" Diego screamed, spit flying and face turning red. "I don't know what the fuck he

---

1. Fucking idiot

2. Little witch

told you, but this fucker almost killed me. And I've been doing everything in my power to find you and Jade since you disappeared last night." His eyes flicked to the hallway for a quick moment before his dark eyes found Searra's, sincerity in their blackened depths.

"How? How would you have even known we left?" Searra asked.

Diego did not break contact with her gaze, "I've been keeping tabs. Not close enough to be noticed, but... I've been watching." Torment and aching loss cracked his voice as he stared her down. He laid himself bare before her and the grief she saw in him, mirrored what she knew was in herself... and she didn't know how to feel about it.

Searra glanced at Juan, she needed confirmation. She could not believe what she was hearing. His hands were loose at his sides, but Searra caught the slight fist flex as he maintained his casual stance.

"What does he mean? You said you were friends?" Searra took a step back, her heart beginning to crack.

"Friend?!" Diego huffed. "I don't know this *chupasangre*.³" His dark eyes blazed with pure malice. "He attacked me and Lissette. He hunts witches Sisi! Vampires have almost wiped us all out!"

Searra took another step back, her ears were ringing. *Lissette? Diego's little sister?*

Searra felt the rising panic in her chest as it traveled to her throat and began to choke her. The idea of something happening to Lissette had her mind frozen

---

3. Bloodsucker (insult)

in panic. She was her sister in law and she loved her, even though they hadn't spoken in almost two years, ever since Diego went missing.

She was three years younger than Searra, but always acted ten years younger. She was a sweet person, an artist with winged liner and dry shampoo, but a little ditsy and naive, and a touch self-absorbed. Searra always found that charming about her.

"I don't know how he found out about you. About Jade." Diego continued, "Tell her! You fucking leech!"

Searra didn't want to hear anymore. She had trusted Juan with her daughter, with *everything*. And it was all based on a lie? Her world was tilting again, like she was in the bow of a ship in a storm.

Juan's eyes swam with guilt and his jaw flexed so hard she was afraid he would crush his teeth. "I'm not the man I was.'"

"That is such bullshit! Tell her that you didn't attack Lissette, that you didn't fucking slink out of the shadows like a monster out of hell. You tore my sister's hair out by the root as she tried to escape." His dark gaze slid to Searra who stood there, horrified.

Tore out her hair? Lissette always had a gorgeous mane of thick, black hair and it broke her heart that someone would tear it out, that Juan had done just that.

She swallowed the lump that formed in her throat, "Is she okay?"

Diego's eyes softened for a second as he said, "Yeah, only because I was her ride. I showed up in time to stop whatever fucked up, sick shit he wanted to do to her. She has fucking bald patches now!" Diego was working himself up again, huffing. "He then proceeded to beat the shit out of me, almost pulled my arm out of my socket and fucking bit me.'" He rubbed his neck as though he could still feel Juan's teeth sinking deep into his skin. "He would have killed me had Lissette not used her magic."

What? Magic? Lissette was a witch?

"Lissette is a witch?" Searra asked, her voice small, like a wisp on the air.

"Yeah, my whole family apparently. We all have *bru-ja* blood." Diego confirmed, his gaze spitting flecks of onyx at Juan as he stood there.

Blood... that's how Juan knew about her. Diego's blood memories, when he bit him. That's how he knew everything— everything about her.

Diego took a step forward, and Searra retreated further in, back to the couches. Everything Diego had said didn't change that it still hurt to be close to him. The wound in her heart had been ripped open and she was bleeding out beneath her thin skin. The farther she stayed away from him right now, the better. She was too raw.

And now Juan.

Her taste in men had plummeted as of late.

Searra dared herself to look at Juan, a stone mask had taken over his features.

"Tell her that wasn't you!" Diego demanded, his teeth sharpening for a moment in his anger.

"I do not deny it. The *brujita*[4] had stolen something from me but that is no excuse. I deserve your vitriol for what I've done, but," He took a breath, and his throat bobbed, "I'm not that man anymore." His eyes were

---

4. Little witch

brimming with emotion as he tried to meet Searra's gaze, but she wouldn't look at him.

The *brujita...* Searra remembered that Juan said she knew the witch who stole his amulet. It was Lissette. Her stomach roiled, she was going to be sick.

Could she believe anything Juan had said to her?

She wanted to leave, to take Jade and go. Anywhere. She couldn't stay any longer.

Juan's mask cracked, and he pleaded, "I—vampires, they don't have souls. What I did, it was without my soul. But then I met you," Juan gestured to Searra, all his raw pain and desperation leaked out from behind his stoic facade. "And my soul was restored."

There was a crack of warmth in her chest that cut through the ice. She wanted to believe him, but how? The trust was broken, he had destroyed it.

A loud, derisive snort sounded from Diego as he raked his hands through his dark hair, it was the longest Searra had ever seen it. She didn't think it could grow so thick, or that it had a little curl to it. And darker than she remembered, fully black, like soot. His dark brows were pinched together and his mouth pulled down into a frown. It made his face look longer.

"What the fuck does that even mean? Your soul? You're a demon, demons don't have souls. And what the fuck is going on here?!" Diego barked at Juan. He rubbed at his chin in frustration, his fingers smoothed out the hairs of his dark goatee in the process. "I can smell it on you two." His voice wavered for a moment. Before a growl began to build in his chest and his eyes flashed with heat. His hot gaze stayed trained on Searra.

Searra's cheeks flushed as she looked at Juan in her

periphery and shot back, "That is none of your fucking business!" She jumped to her feet, fingers pointing like daggers.

"You are my wife!" Diego growled. His hands fisted at his sides as they shook. His veins were bulging out of his forearms.

Searra couldn't hold back her dry laugh. "Riiii-iiight." But it still hit her like a battering ram, the sting at those words, and the shame. Shame was so much worse, it made her stomach twist up in knots. She collapsed back onto the couch and crossed her arms in front of her chest, refusing to look at Diego and stared at her Crocs.

Pushing aside her sudden nausea, Searra asked, "Where the fuck have you even been? I thought you were dead, you asshole." Searra's voice came out flat and emotionless. "You haven't been seen in almost two years, the police found your car abandoned! What else was I supposed to think?"

Searra continued to look at her shoes, refusing to see Diego's face. Her right foot twitched back and forth with nervous energy and she kept her mind trained on the movement, grateful for something else to focus on.

"I'm sorry Sisi," Diego paused, his voice faltering. "Everything is just so fucked. I hate that I fucked it all up." His words came from above as he stood over her. She was still sitting, but he had moved to stand over her, their legs almost touching. The negative space between them pulsed with unseen energy. It stung to hear how smooth her nickname rolled from his lips, how quickly he was able to slide into their old dynamic. So familiar, and yet not.

Searra dared to meet his gaze. Diego's big, dark eyes were misted with unshed grief. The pain and longing haunted him, etched into the creases of his face. He had more frown lines around his mouth now, like he never smiled anymore. The thought made Searra's heart break for him, and tears welled in her eyes.

"I never wanted to leave you and Jade. I didn't have a choice." Diego's voice was raw. "I love you, Sisi."

It was a punch in the gut, Searra fought back a sob that stole her breath and her bottom lip trembled. Searra felt the sincerity in what he said, and saw how much pain he was in. She longed to reach out, she needed to hold him, but she didn't. Her pride was wounded, no matter if he said he loved her or not. A lot had changed in two years, and she was a different person.

Would he still love this new person she was now? *Did she still love him?*

A throat cleared in the corner, and Searra looked to see Juan leaning against the wall, arms crossed over his broad chest.

"Diego." Juan's voice was cold and impassive, and rang through the room with a strange echo. "She is an *alma marcada bruja.*"[5]

All the color drained from Diego's face.

---

5. Witch with a marked soul.

Chapter 19

Marcadas (Marked)

"What does that even mean?" Searra asked, exasperation coating her tongue. She looked from Juan to Diego, but neither spoke. A massive headache was building, and she pinched her brows together, rubbing the bridge of her nose between her thumb and forefinger in an attempt to ease the blossoming pain.

"*Chupate un pedo!*"[1] He cursed under his breath. "I don't believe in your weird vampire shit." Diego spat, turning to Searra, "And anyway, that magic is long

---

1. Suck a fart.

dead. Fucking *muerte!*"[2]

"According to who?" Juan's voice reverberated, making the hairs on Searra's arms stand on end.

"What does that mean?" Searra grumbled again. She recognized the Spanish, but she didn't have the best recall or pronunciation, but she gave it a shot. "Alma Mark-mark..." She stuttered, her Spanish was more than rusty, it was non-existent.

Searra's mom hadn't taught her anything because she had her own Spanish stolen from her back in elementary school. The nuns would hit Searra's mom and her *tíos*[3] if they spoke Spanish. So, she learned not to speak it. Without speaking it, she lost her tongue and had nothing to pass on. *Pocho*[4] status for sure, but not by choice. Her culture was stolen from her.

"*Marcadas.*"[5] Juan corrected softly, his 'r's rolling off his tongue with languid ease, as he pushed off the wall and crossed the room. He sank onto the couch beside Searra, their knees brushing as he crossed an ankle over one knee. Sparks flared at the point of contact. Like fire licking across her skin, a shiver curled

---

2. dead

3. uncles

4. Slang for an Americanized Mexican, someone who has lost their Spanish tongue and is disconnected with their roots and culture / someone who mixes English and Spanish

5. Marked

up her spine. She fought to steady her breathing.

She was still mad at Juan, and didn't trust him anymore, but she couldn't help the way her body responded to him. It made her all the more furious.

A deep growl came from Diego as he stood over Searra, watching her with rapt attention.

Searra looked from Juan to Diego and sighed.

Oh lordy...

She brought her hands to her temples to smooth out an oncoming tension headache.

Juan cleared his throat, his sandy brown brows were pinched together, making his serious face all the more intense. "The *Almas Marcadas*[6] were a bloodline of *brujas*[7] ... or mystics. Their souls are bound to vampires." Juan paused and his green eyes sparkled at Searra, "They are destined for each other." And he gave her a bittersweet grin.

"Destined?" Searra shook her head, "And you think that I'm part of that?"

"*Sí,*[8] " Juan confirmed, there was no hesitation or uncertainty in his tone.

Searra let out a hiss through her teeth and stood up, almost knocking Diego over. The air was getting a little thin, and she struggled to take deep breaths. She was claustrophobic with both Juan and Diego breathing down her neck. And her skin flushed with heat despite feeling a chill move through her body and into

---

6. Marked Souls

7. witches

8. Yes

her bones. Honestly, she'd had enough of both of them for the night.

"That shit is so old, it's all rumors and legends now," Diego interjected. "No *bruja*[9] would be caught dead working with vampires." He snorted and rolled his eyes, his disgust clear.

Diego's attitude scraped against Searra's nerves, sharper than ever now that she was a vampire. Her hackles rose, fangs aching, every instinct screaming to bare her teeth and put him in his place.

"And what *the fuck* are you?" She snapped. "It wasn't too long ago that you barged in here, half monster, all claws and fur and dripping with drool. So what the fuck are you?" Searra's voice was increasing in volume the more she spoke, and she felt her wrath taking root again; her arms waved around with a fury of their own.

She wasn't sure if it was only ire for Diego, or if her feelings for Juan were bleeding into it, but she was grateful for an outlet to aim her rage.

"*Nahual*,[10]" Juan said from the couch with a casual dip of his sculpted chin.

He sat with an unconcerned air, his arms splayed across the back of the couch. His pecs twitched beneath his white t-shirt, drawing Searra's eyes. Juan noticed her staring and cleared his throat. He gave her a smug smile and a slight head

---

9. witch

10. A witch that can shift into an animal, Shapeshifter

shake in Diego's direction.

Searra's eyes flew wide as heat rushed up her neck and into her cheeks. She felt like a tea kettle about to explode. Her ears ringing in a high-pitched squeal, a ridiculous cartoon character about to blow their top.

Searra's gaze snapped back to Diego, desperate to drag her focus to whatever the fuck they'd been talking about.

"Translation?" Her dark eyebrows rose in question.

"Wolf shifter, or um... a werewolf," Diego said as he scratched his head. His curly dark hair bounced as he did.

Juan cleared his throat, "Well, a witch shifter with a wolf affinity." Correcting Diego made him sound like a professor.

Diego snorted, "Well, there's a hole in your couch."

Searra could do nothing but stare at him. She had completely forgotten about the hole Juan had made in the couch and wanted to laugh but her brain snagged on the word *werewolf.* "Whaaaaaaat?" The claws and fangs made much more sense now, but she felt like she stepped into a cheesy movie; she just needed to cover Juan in glitter.

"Is The Great Pumpkin real too? Jezuuuus...." Searra's sarcasm tasted bitter on her tongue, but she didn't care. *Of course there were werewolves, because... why not?*

"Were you always a werewolf... errr — shifter?" She directed her question to Diego, but was hoping he wouldn't answer. If he had been lying to her all this time, she might just go die in a hole.

"The night I went missing. My wolf was... awakened." Diego admonished, his mouth formed a tight line.

"How?" Searra's mouth was on the floor she was so dumbfounded.

Diego let out a long breath through his nose in a snort, he sounded like a horse. "My bloodline was touched by magic, so it activated mine." His jaw ticked and his dark eyes hardened into chips.

Searra squinted her eyes at him, trying to understand, but squinting didn't help her read him any better or comprehend the meaning between his words. "I don't understand. How would that have happened?"

The silence stretched between them while Diego bored holes into Searra, his dark eyes swirling with a storm and mouth set in a perma-frown.

"Lissette." He almost hissed the name and looked away.

"What did she do?" Searra asked, not understanding what Lissette could have done to activate their family's magic.

Diego's voice cut through Searra's thoughts, "You know, just played with shit she shouldn't have. Now we are all here... and everything is fucked." His words were clipped and cold.

"Okay. " Searra said and took a deep breath and asked the question she had been afraid to ask since he barged through Juan's front door and back into her life.

"Why didn't you come home?" Her voice came out small, a whisper. Searra wanted to be brave, to meet his gaze, but she couldn't. She stared at the floor, she didn't want him to see the hurt he caused. She wouldn't give him the satisfaction. Or she might shatter to pieces in front of him.

Diego reached for her hand, and the second their skin touched, she felt like she was falling. Her vision darkened like a fish eye lens and she felt like she was breathing through oil. Drums beat a hard rhythm in her ears, and her own heart beat was sluggish in her chest, and each thump was a painful slog.

Searra struggled to catch her breath and blink away the fog. Her vision slowly returned to her, and her breathing returned to normal, but she was somewhere else. She recognized it as Evelyn's, her mother-in-law's, house in East LA.

It was a large white Victorian-style house with black trim that she had converted into a two-unit. It had a sizable driveway between the front house and back units that she also rented out to three different families.

She stayed in the back half of the front house and her tenants were in the living room off the main door and the entire upstairs. It was a regular-sized house, so splitting it made her living space a little cramped. Which is fine for someone by themselves, but it was a bitch with family gatherings.

That was the case now. Searra was standing in the middle of her mother-in-law's living room and she was not alone.

She saw Diego's brothers, Josué and Lalo, and his other sisters, Nayeli and Lety. All of Diego's siblings were accounted for except for Rizos[11] . Searra also clocked that Lalo's girlfriend, Yaya, was sitting in the

---

11. Curly

corner on the cat chair.

Diego's mom had a penchant for fostering neighborhood cats and had a spot she dubbed the 'cat chair'. The seat was covered in cat fur and the extra fat, orange tabby, Coco, would always claim her spot.

The kitchen was open to the living room, so it was all one big, cramped space with everyone hanging out there together. Most were standing and leaning against the walls in the living room and entry hallway, since there was limited seating.

Time-wise, it didn't feel like she was in the past. This moment had not come to pass yet.

The recent future.

CHAPTER 20

BLOODLINE

The understanding that she was witnessing the future washed over her, and with that clarity, her vision solidified. Like she was looking through a fogged window pane, and in the next moment, she was in the room, standing in the crowd, though no one could see her.

The smell hit her first, like ozone mixed with the

scent of a *fuchi*[1] dog, and a hint of a bitter floral note she couldn't quite place.

That was the scent of magic she realized. Her eyes widened with comprehension, a room full of *brujas*[2] and magic hung in the air like perfume.

Searra heard Lalo speak first, he had the loudest voice out of the group. They used to joke that you could hear him laugh from halfway down the street.

"Okay, okay! Everyone CAN IT!" He shushed the room and they quieted down.

"We are just waiting for Abu, Diego, and Lissette to get here, and then we can start." Lalo nodded, his face grim. Abu was a nickname for their Mom, Evelyn. Shortened from *Abuela*[3] by the grandkids.

Lalo had deep bags under his eyes and five o'clock shadow that had passed well into midnight. He removed his *Dodgers* baseball hat to reveal his thinning mop of curly salt and pepper hair. Searra noted the impression that dug a deep groove into his forehead.

It was getting hot with all those bodies in that small space.

Josué snorted from his seat on the couch. His arms were spread along the back cushions showing off his tattoos. He had two sleeves, the delicate script looped over his forearms like smoke, spelling out the names of his kids.

He bounced one leg with nervous energy as he

---

1. stinky

2. witches

3. grandma

crossed an ankle over his knee. With that, his foot wiggled in response. There was a haunted expression in his dark eyes that Searra had never seen before.

Josué had always been the calmest and most easy-going of the siblings, but he definitely had a combative air exuding from him now.

"I don't want to hear it, Josué." Lalo waved his hand in dismissal.

"I don't blame him." Lety's smooth voice came from behind Searra. She was sitting at the kitchen table, the back of her chair against the wall. "I haven't spoken to Lissette since it happened. As it is, I'm barely on good terms with my mom. She keeps taking up for her and not seeing how she has affected all of us. So, I don't have time for that shit." Her short dark hair bounced as she spoke, getting more and more animated as she went on.

"No. I get it. It is not helping though." Lalo said, exasperation weighing his shoulders down. For a tall guy, he had a tendency to hunch, but it was exacerbated by the tension in the room.

"That's easy for you to say! *¡Dios mío!*" 4 Nayeli's voice carried from their Mom's bedroom, which was right off the living room, having clearly heard them. She walked out in a red turtle neck, black leggings, and calf-length black boots. Her chocolate brown hair was parted to the side and slicked down into a low ponytail.

"Eli..." Lalo breathed, rubbing his face in frustration. "This is not about you!"

---

4. My god!

To Searra, Nayeli looked put together, but there was a wildness in her eyes that she recognized in Diego's, and the unmistakable smell of dog. Realization dawned on Searra.

Eli was a wolf.

Searra felt bile in the back of her throat, but she pushed it down.

"You just have to deal with magic! *¡Soy un pinche perro aullándole a la luna!*" [5] Eli's anger was aimed at Lalo, who had his hands up in submission, having clearly had this argument many times before.

"You know he can't control that," Lety grumbled from her chair, not making eye contact with Eli.

"Like that is any different?" Josué snorted. And Lety cracked up.

Searra was surprised Lety had uttered anything at all, since the sisters hadn't been on speaking terms for years.

Eli crossed her arms and looked away, pretending no one had said anything.

The front door swung open and Evelyn, Lissette, and Diego walked in.

Searra was feeling claustrophobic now. There were too many bodies in the small room and the heat was rising with their body temperature.

"It's about time!" Eli growled. Her delicate nose scrunched with derision.

Lissette's peridot eyes narrowed at her older sister. Searra noticed the lavender silk wrapped around her head like a headband, and Searra shuddered guessing

---

5. I'm a fucking dog howling at the moon!

that she used it to cover up her bald patches.

Bald patches caused by Juan.

Searra might really be sick now, her stomach began to roll with acid.

"We had ingredients to gather." Lissette sniffed.

"Yeah, your 'ingredients,' fucking *bruja*[6] ." Josué sneered from the couch.

"No te hagas. [7] You are one too, *pendejo.*" [8] Lissette clicked her tongue. "Except your magic is to attract *pulgasitas.*[9] " She waved her hand, "Anyway, Diego has an interesting story to tell you all about our niece," Lissette said in a sing-song voice, her dark eyebrow arching.

An icepick of dread skirted down Searra's spine. Her own hackles rose at the mention of her daughter, and she let out an involuntary hiss so aggressive she spat.

Yet, no one heard her.

"Jade?" Lety asked from the kitchen. Worry colored her tone.

Diego's mouth pinched, and he worried at the side of his lip. The muscles in his jaw flexed with the mounting tension.

"Goddammit Lissette." Diego   looked around the room at his siblings with a pleading expression on

6. witch

7. Don't pretend.

8. Dumbass.

9. Little fleas

his face. His dark eyes were ringed in hollow circles that made them look sunken in, like a living skeleton. Searra's heart hurt to see him like that.

"Go on." Lissette urged, flicking her high pony like a horse as she said it. But Searra didn't miss the violet light that flashed in her eyes and the sweet floral scent that permeated the air around her. Lissette was using magic on Diego.

Diego's shoulders stiffened and a growl built in his throat.

"Good dog." Lissette mocked, an impish smile illuminated her face.

"Traviesa." [10] Evelyn chided with no real heat in her words. The corner of her lip rose and she tucked her dark hair behind her ear.

Lety rolled her eyes and Eli huffed from the other end of the living room.

Diego cleared his throat and swayed back and forth on his feet, his hands were behind his back like a soldier standing at attention. "Jade is from the *Almas Marcadas*[11] line."

"Fuuuuuck." Josué breathed. "*Bruja*[12] squared?" His dark brows were raised high and his eyes were wide.

Lalo shook his head, "That's an ancient bloodline... and dead."

"Wait, what about Searra then?" Yaya asked. She and Searra had gotten closer throughout the years.

---

10. Trouble maker.

11. Marked souls

12. witch

"She would be too..." Her voice trailed off.

The whole room was silent.

"There's more," Lissette said, encouraging him with heavy side eye.

Diego cleared his throat again, but the words were stuck, like he had just eaten a spoonful of peanut butter. "She's... she's a vampire."

CHAPTER 21

CHUPASANGRE (BLOODSUCKER)

*V*ampire.

The word floated in the air like a poisonous mist.

Diego almost choked on it. The corners of his mouth were downturned, and his expression haunted. He looked every bit the ghost she had thought him to be these last two years.

Searra couldn't believe what she was hearing. These people had been a huge part of her life for the last seven years. They were her family. And yet, the ease with which they were talking now made her think she didn't know them at all.

How was all this real?

Did they even care about her at all?

Lety, Eli, and Lissette were bridesmaids in her wedding! Josué and Lalo were groomsmen. Rizos would have been one too, but he was so antisocial and didn't want to be out longer than he had to. Her heart hurt thinking these people who had such a huge impact and importance in her life... didn't think the same about her.

They had cut her out so easily.

"How?" Lalo asked from his standing spot in the kitchen, he had been pacing a hole in the floor since his younger siblings arrived.

"She was turned in the last day or so." A big sigh escaped, "That same *pinche*[1] vampire that attacked us claimed she was descended from the *Almas Marcadas*.[2]" Diego said, his mouth tight.

"*Chupasangre...*[3]" Evelyn spat under her breath and performed a quick sign of the cross. Lissette shook off a cold shiver as her peridot eyes clouded over with fear.

Diego gave his mom some side eye, but said nothing.

"But, but... what about Jade? She can't be safe!" Eli growled.

"No, we can't assume shit like that." Josué protested

---

1. Fucking

2. Marked Souls.

3. Bloodsucker

from the couch. A little of his former, sage nature shining through. Searra was pelted by a wave of sadness at the changes in Diego's older brother. He was a lot more volatile now.

"Yeaaaah." Lety agreed. "We need to talk to Searra first. And gauge from there. Moms have a special bond with their babies, and we shouldn't mess with it."

"Vampires are dangerous, period. They kill our kind." Lalo rang out, his voice clear. "And that's not a place for a toddler."

"She seemed to be adjusting." Diego ran a hand through his longer hair. The curls caught the shine in the overhead light.

"We should put it to a vote," Lissette announced. "Yes, we should take matters into our own hands, or no, we should leave everything as they are. And see how it all shakes out."

The room filled with affirmative grumbles. So Lissette continued, "All for yes?" As she stuck her hand in the air.

Lalo also raised his hand while nervously biting the cuticles of his other hand. And Eli lifted hers, a scowl on her face, dark eyes like flint. "I don't like separating a mom from her child, but vampires are more dangerous than wolves. *Son demonios.*[4] I wish someone had stepped in for me." She looked to the ground, shame pinkening her cheeks. "Thank God Bani is old-

---

4. They are demons

er. I couldn't imagine if he was still a baby. *Dios mío.*[5]

No more hands raised, and Searra breathed a sigh of relief.

Lissette continued, "Okay, all for waiting it out?" Her hand went down, and as it did, the silver on her delicate wrist glinted at Searra. It was so sharp her eyes winced in pain and she swore she heard a harsh metallic whine that made her want to cover her ears and hiss.

She was struck with the sudden sense of déjà vu, swearing she had seen that bracelet before.

But, where? It made her think of rain and lightening.

Turning her attention back to the room, Lety, Josué, and Diego all raised their hands.

"Wait, where is Rizos?" Diego asked. He was always the tie breaker among the siblings. Although, he probably preferred he wasn't.

Josué clicked his tongue. "You know he's been all messed up since Friend." He raked his hand through his thickened curls. "He hasn't been the same."

"Yeah," Diego breathed. "He fucking loved his piggies."

Rizos had an obsession with guinea pigs. At one time, he had seven set up in his room. They had their own special habitat, workout space, and thick blankets to cozy up into. His room was a bed, a place for guitars, a big screen, a gaming system, and a huge pen for his guinea pigs.

"That wasn't his fault, but I get it," Lety said, staring

---

5. My god!

at her hands. "I would die if I accidentally ate Buddy or Nibbler, or one of my *preciosas*.[6]" Those were Lety's pets, two dogs and two cats.

Oh my god... Rizos ate Friend?! Searra held back a gag.

"He couldn't help it!" Eli snarled. "Y'all don't know what it's like!"

Eli's rage bubbled over, so hot, it pulsed from her like a radiator. The heat caused her bone structure to shift beneath her skin, and her nose and mouth elongated into a muzzle.

A blood-curdling scream ripped from her throat and ended in a deep, guttural snarl as black fur began to erupt from her flesh. Her eyes glowed a pale yellow as her gaze was trained on Searra, right where she stood. Eli's nostrils flared as she took a deep inhale and let out a low, menacing growl.

Could she see her? How is that possible? She isn't even here? This hasn't even happened yet!

Eli's teeth elongated to sharp points coated in a viscous drool. Muscles were shredded, and her spine arched into an unnatural angle. Her fingers cracked and snapped backward as her nails lengthened into gigantic claws. Eli grunted again and a dog-like whine escaped as she fell to the floor. Another ear-shattering crack, and it was no longer Eli standing in the room with her siblings, but a giant black wolf.

Nahual...[7] werewolf.

---

6. Precious / lovelies

7. A witch with the power to shift into an animal.

Chapter 22

Sol (Sun)

The giant black wolf lunged for Searra, its razor-sharp claws raking the air inches from her face.

Before Searra could even think, her arms shot up in defense. A searing warmth burst through her chest, down her arms, flooded her muscles and exploded from her hands. The power of it blasted Eli's wolf form across the room and into the wall with a bone-rattling thud.

The force sent powerful shockwaves through her, and the strength of her power traveled back up her arms and knocked Searra back, careening through the air. Her head cracked against the ground in one sharp burst of pain and everything went dark.

Searra opened her eyes. Diego and Juan were looking down at her.

She was sprawled on the floor, in Diego's lap. Juan was kneeling over her, jaw tight and eyes lined with worry. She wanted to wipe those lines away with her touch but... not in front of Diego.

A pang of guilt hit her low in the gut.

What was she doing thinking about Juan? Diego was alive, and her husband.

..But he left them.

The thought nagged at her, like an open sore she was picking at.

That notion left a bitter taste on her tongue as she pushed off Diego to sit up. Her head swam, a dull throb lingering in the back of her skull, though the pain was fading fast.

"What happened?" Searra asked, her words unexpectedly made of gravel that crunched between her teeth. She touched the tender area at the back of her head and felt the wetness clinging to her roots. She must have been bleeding but it was healing over thanks to her newfound vampiric abilities. Searra brought her hand back to look at her fingers; the tips were covered in congealed, clotted blood.

It didn't make her hungry though? *So that was so*

mething...

"You tell us," Juan said. His eyes narrowed with suspicion. *Did you have another vision?* Juan's voice bounded around inside her brain like a bell.

It would take a while to get used to him inside her head. It was already making her headache worse.

"I'm fine," Searra said as she stood up. She tried to recall the exact feeling when it happened, but it was the oddest sensation that started deep in her chest. A warmth spread outward until she felt tingly in her fingertips and toes. She sensed something was awakening within her, something old.

Something powerful.

And it knocked Eli on her ass. But... how did Eli see her?

Searra pinched her brows trying to reason it all out, but it just made her headache pound with increased ferocity between her temples. She tried again to massage the pain away with acupressure and grabbed the fleshy skin between her thumb and index finger and applied pressure.

Can vampires take Excedrin?

Juan took a step towards her, worry etched into his face."Searra? Are you alright?"

Before he could reach out to her, Diego sidestepped him and made it to Searra first. His hands reached out to her face and cupped her cheeks. She tried to pull away, his touch felt like it burned her skin and she flinched, it was like hot oil splashing out of a pan, but Diego wouldn't budge.

Did he not feel that pain too?

His dark eyes searched hers, lit with a frantic

desperation. "*Vida*[1] , before you hit your head, you were *glowing.* It was like you were a... a fucking sun or something." His face was so close to hers, his hot breath on her cheeks.

Searra stared into Diego's dark eyes and wanted to fall right back into them as he held her face in his hands. As if the last two years didn't happen, and nothing else mattered, it was just him and her.

Relentless, raw emotion crashed into her like a tidal wave. She thought of their wedding day — the walk down the aisle, his eyes waiting, her tears falling faster than she could catch them. Powerless to stop, joy spilled over in sobs, her makeup forgotten. She remembered how the apples of her cheeks had ached from smiling so much that day.

It all came flooding back: their lazy Sunday mornings, making oatmeal, and watching *Gargoyles* and *I Love Lucy.*

She remembered one of the many concerts they had gone to together, how they made out in the nose bleeds and wound up missing most of the actual music. They had been so shit faced that they took a limo for late night munchies to *King Taco*[2] and bought burritos as thick as a human thigh —at three in the morning.

At some point, she blacked out the rest of the night, but she would never forget that burrito.

Her thoughts turned to the day Jade was born. Diego had cut the umbilical cord. He was so nervous,

---

1. Life (Term of endearment)

2. Famous taco spot in East LA.

he held the scissors like a complete weirdo, one side in each hand like it was a pair of gardening shears.

When he held Jade, she was so small in his arms. There was the biggest smile on his face, and his eyes glowed with such pure joy.

Jade had looked just like him when she was born. The tears stung the corners of her eyes and her throat clogged up with a sob like a wad of hair stuck in the shower drain. She didn't want to cry, but she still felt the wetness spill onto her cheeks.

Then the burning became too much to bare.

The fiery pain was building on her face beneath Diego's palms. The pain intensified until it started to feel like she had laid her cheeks on a cast-iron skillet. She jerked her head back with a feral hiss that sounded more feline than human. Diego's eyes widened in confusion as his hands hovered in the air where her head had been. He let them fall, hurt fractured his features and his mouth settled into a thin line.

Should she tell him about her vision? About what everyone said?

That his touch burned her?

Her gaze flicked to Juan's in silent question, his emerald eyes softened when hers locked with his. He gave an almost imperceptible shake of his head. *No.*

She couldn't explain it, but she trusted Juan *more* than she did Diego. Something deep within her wanted to reach out and lean on Juan, let his arms wrap around her, and never let her go. Which was insane, she had known him for less than a few days, and he had already lied to her... broken her trust.

Yet, still…

Diego and she are married. They have a child together. Searra's known him for over seven years. How can she trust a virtual stranger over him? What about everything they had been through?

But Juan wasn't the one who abandoned her and their daughter. Juan's family wasn't conspiring to take her child away from her. Juan didn't show up out of nowhere after letting her grieve for him for almost two years. Diego let her think he was dead.

He may have gotten his wish.

Was he truly dead to her now?

The guilt stabbed her like an ice pick to the heart. She didn't want to hurt Diego, that was the last thing she wanted.

He was the love of her life. *Who left.*

Her husband. *Who left.*

The father of her daughter. *Who left.*

"I'm sorry Diego," Searra said with newfound steel in her spine. "My headache is getting worse. I think… I need sleep." Her eyes shifted to Juan, who played it well but she saw the smugness hiding in the corners of his upturned mouth. She looked back at Diego, who was breaking in half before her eyes.

"Sisi." His voice cracked and the lines around his eyes hardened like cement. "Please."

Her heart splintered, and the pain almost made her flinch. "You can come back tomorrow, okay?" She maneuvered the muscles on her face into a smile, but knew it didn't reach her eyes.

Juan stepped forward and clapped Diego on the shoulder. The gesture was stiff, but genuine. "Come back tomorrow, yeah? Jade will be up and you can have breakfast together."

Searra thought the idea was sweet, but didn't want to say that Jade wouldn't recognize him. That knowledge would kill Diego.

He chose to leave.

She steeled her heart and turned from the room, leaving Juan to escort Diego out. She didn't want to see him go. Yet, as she forced herself further away, something tore deep inside her soul, and fresh tears burned at the corners of her eyes.

Something inside her was splintering, crumbling apart until it was beyond repair. She felt his dark gaze burn into her back as she walked away but Searra didn't turn back, and only silence followed in her wake.

Chapter 23

Alma (Soul)

After checking to make sure Jade was still asleep, Searra waited in Juan's room while Diego headed out. She sat on the edge of his bed, adrenaline coursing through her bloodstream as butterflies gathered in the pit of her stomach.

She should be mad, furious.

Juan had lied. He viciously attacked and almost killed Diego and Lissette.

But was she?

She tried to distract herself with the bedding, tracing the black silk patterns with her fingertips. Inhaling slowly through her nose and exhaling through her mouth. Searra focused on the rhythm, anything to steady her frayed nerves.

Minutes passed before she heard Juan's footsteps return. The air no longer held Diego's scent; it had faded entirely.

He must have left the property.

In that same instant, Juan opened his bedroom door. The moment their eyes locked, her entire body relaxed.

"I'm going to need you to explain," Searra said, although she couldn't ⬚control the pleading in her voice. She couldn't control much of anything right now. Too much was happening at once to process it all. She was disconnecting hard, piece by piece. Her mind began to grow numb and quiet. "Because you aren't looking too good right now."

Juan remained standing, looking down at her where she sat on the bed. His eyes were soft, liquid pools of green that drew her in. She longed to drown in them; and she cursed herself for it.

Juan let out a deep sigh and his shoulders caved in. "I regret that I didn't tell you about Diego sooner."

"Why didn't you? You knew he was alive this entire time." Searra didn't understand why he had kept Diego a secret from her.

He raked both hands through his light brown hair. His biceps strained against the sleeves of his fitted tee, but his gaze remained fixed on the floor, refusing to meet hers.

Juan sat next to her on the bed. The weight redistributed on the mattress beneath her and her center of gravity shifted to lean toward him. Her leg pressed against his as they leaned into each other on the bed.

He put his large hand on her thigh, spreading his fingers wide to take up the entire breadth of it, and gave a reassuring squeeze. Sparks flew at his touch and gooseflesh pebbled her skin.

His light brown hair hung in his eyes, casting them in shadow. "The night I turned you." He paused, his voice gruff. "I went there to... " He trailed off.

"To what?" Searra urged.

He looked up at her, his emerald eyes shimmering with rubies, tears of blood. "I went there to kill you.'"

Searra went still. The quiet itself held it's breath.

Juan continued, "I found out about you through Diego. I had been hunting his *brujita*[1] sister because she stole a precious relic of mine, but when I drank from him, I saw you. In his memories, I could sense your magic." He sighed as if searching for the right words, "I went to eliminate you, and your bloodline. It is what I do. But, there was something else, I was drawn to you. I needed to hunt you. I had to see you, just once."

"What do you mean? Why?" Searra pushed.

Juan raked his fingers through his hair in frustration, "I was caught in your thrall, an inescapable pull I've never experienced. And when the time came, I couldn't do it! I couldn't kill you. So, I turned you instead." Juan explained, his hands moving in blurs of nervous loops. "I told myself a lie—that I would use you. Once I had my amulet, I'd deliver you and Jade to The Council and be done with it. I needed to believe that... to make what I did feel... acceptable." Juan snuck a look at Searra from beyond the shadows cast by his own sandy hair.

---

1. Little witch

Searra blanched. "And who is *The Council?*" She didn't want to believe him.

Juan let out another breath, like he was steeling himself up for a heavy weight to crash down. He had fisted his hand on her thigh and the knuckles were stretched white.

"The ruling class of vampires, think of them as an old world Elitocracy. We have been at war with the mystics, or *brujas,* for centuries. We have been on a mission to wipe out all magical bloodlines."

Searra was quiet for a long time, struggling to make sense of all the new information coming at her.

"Why?" Searra breathed. "Why are you at war?"

The worry lines in Juan's face deepened. "Magic is the only thing vampires are susceptible to."

That made the pieces start to click in her head. There was no war. Vampires were simply taking out a threat, through magical genocide. The idea sent a cold, sharp sliver of dread up her spine and bile rise in the back of her throat.

"So, what is your relationship to this zealot vampire gang?"

Juan let out a brief chuckle and the corner of his mouth lifted in a dry, sardonic smirk. "I'm one of their leaders. The oldest of us, we rule together, but. .." Juan swallowed, "I specialize in eliminating magic wielders."

Searra's eyes widened in surprise. A sudden chill enveloped her and a sharp, bitter loneliness stung her deep. She really didn't know Juan at all, and that knowlege hurt.

Specialized? ...One of their leaders? Searra had known he was old, but assumed there had to be more ancient vampires walking around. *Was he one of the oldest still living?*

"How many witches have you killed?" Her tone was hard and cold. Searra wasn't even sure she wanted the answer to that question. The idea made her stomach hurt and wished she could reel it back in and swallow it.

"I've lost count and the faces have begun to bleed together." He paused. "I don't want to lie to you." Juan's gaze returned to the floor as he let out an exasperated sigh, "I *can't* lie to you... not anymore."

Searra didn't know how to feel, if Juan was even telling her the truth... *now.*

"Where do Jade and I fit into your plans now?" Searra needed answers. It gnawed at her, not knowing if he was just going to hand her off to the other vampires when he was done with her. "Are you still going to turn us over to The Council?" A pit had formed in her stomach as the question hovered in the air between them, his answer would determine the way the pendulum swung.

Juan's expression turned to stone, almost unreadable except for the hurt that flickered across his features. "I had those intentions, yes." And he went silent.

Searra's blood ran cold through her veins and she tasted her own fear skittering through the air.

Juan scented it too and rose from the bed only to kneel at her feet. "Don't do that."

Searra retreated into herself, retreating behind her sturdy mental walls when shit got real. The sharp pain in her chest was beginning to throb and if he didn't let go of her, she was going to make him.

"I have no intention to do that anymore." Juan's desperation to get through to her was so palpable that he shook her a little. His large hands rested on her thighs as she sat. "I told you that I get flashes of memories from blood when I drink. So I went to your house, I was intending to kill everyone inside."

Searra tried to get up, to push past him.

He would have killed Jade, her mom and her sister.

Her heart wrenched at the thought and hot tears pricked her eyes, but she refused to let them fall.

"But, then I saw you," He licked his lips, "And I *knew* you. Something within me recognized something within you." His fingers tucked a dark strand of her hair behind her ear as he whispered, "Searra... the goddess with the most enticing scent I've ever encountered in my entire existence."

Searra's mouth had gone dry and her tongue had stuck to the roof of her mouth. It took her a moment to speak, to remember how.

"Earlier, you mentioned something about..." Searra paused, not quite sure how to ask. "Your soul?"

Juan grimaced. "Vampires, we—we don't have souls. Or a conscience." He looked at the floor. Shame was a weight bowing his shoulders. "I haven't felt one way or the other about things I've done for a long time. Truthfully, I haven't felt much at all. Numbed by time."

Searra began to shake her head. That was impossible. She had met a few people— even dated a couple that would have rated high on the narcissism scale, people she'd peg as soulless.

But not Juan.

"You have a soul. I can see it." Searra argued. Placing her hand on his chest above his heart. "I can feel it." She said in a quiet whisper.

Juan looked into Searra's eyes, his emerald gaze held a hypnotic sparkle that took her breath away. "I do now. Because of you."

Searra was speechless for a moment, caught in the starlight of his iridescent expression. But then she blinked and tried to shake it off with a laugh. "You're serious?" She searched his face for a hint of humor that she didn't find. "Because of me? How?" Searra didn't understand at all.

"Your *bruja*[2] line. The magic from your ancestors. It is said they used powerful magic to bind themselves to vampires for protection. It was a smart move, calculated. But a vampire without a soul has no loyalty, no trust. You can't have a true alliance. So, when one binds to a witch, they regain their soul." Juan chuckled. His smile was hesitant, but she sensed a sadness within it.

Searra's heart squeezed. It hurt to see him in pain and she wanted nothing more than to wipe that despair from his face. "I didn't think it was real, until I bit you *y sabías a cielo*[3], a heaven I don't deserve."

"Why?" Searra asked, shaking her head in disbelief. *Why her?*

She was already so broken, a ghost walking through her own life. Up until a few days ago, she was a stress-ball of grief and pain, numb to everything and everyone around her. What could she even offer anymore?

Juan's brows creased, and fire lit within his jewel

---

2. Witch

3. And you tasted like Heaven

toned eyes. *You are not a ghost to me, corazón.*[4]

The words floated to her on the wind. Juan's voice inside her mind held such raw emotion, such longing. His hand fisted in her hair at the back of her head as he pulled her in for a gentle kiss. His soft lips were an intimate caress against her own and she felt her body melt into his. She felt her heart melt into his. This kiss was so different than their previous kisses. Before, it had always been frenzied desire, urgent and wild. But this was different. Sweet. Tender... Loving.

When he pulled away, his face was glowing, "You are my mate. *Mi alma gemela.*"[5] His words felt like a claiming in themselves. The tension of the silence pressed on her, as if all of creation were listening to their conversation, holding its breath for her answer.

Searra's mouth fell open and and her breath caught in her throat.

My soul mate.

---

4. Heart

5. My soul mate.

Chapter 24

Mate

*D*id she believe in soul mates?

"My soul." Searra watched as Juan gazed down at his own chest, like he could see it through his skin and bones. "I feel like I've been asleep for centuries, only half alive walking the earth." He looked at his hands, wonder on his face, as if he saw them for the first time. "I didn't know it though." At long last, his gaze met hers. "Everything I'm feeling is so intense, it's hard to control."

Searra swallowed down the sudden lump that formed in her throat. "If vampires don't have souls, why do I still have mine?" Searra asked with genuine confusion.

Juan flinched at her question. Regret was clear on his face, and the light in his eyes dimmed. Did he want to undo what he had done to her? He had said no, but was that the truth?

Did she regret becoming a vampire? Was she fully one yet? It had only been a few days and Juan had said it took almost a week to change. Maybe she would feel different by then? She didn't feel soulless, though; if anything, she had felt more alive in the last few days than she had in a while. Was it because she was a vampire? Or because she met her soul mate?

Maybe both?

"I have a theory on that," Juan interjected, startling her from her thought spiral. "I think it's because of your ancestry. You would never have lost your soul because of your *bruja* blood." His eyes flashed with a dangerous heat. "Or, since you were mated from the moment you turned, you didn't have a chance to lose it." That heat from his possessive stare seared her, making her body shudder with pleasure.

Mated since she turned? Did a mate bond need to be sealed? Or agreed upon? Did they need a court or a judge? A signature at least? Would there be a box for 'magically mated' on her taxes?

"We sealed our bond that second night. When I showed up in your backyard." Juan answered, seeming to have read her thoughts. His expression alight with mischief.

"Can you read my mind?" Searra blurted, more than a little mortified, especially now that she thought about it... it seemed obvious.

A quiet chuckle escaped from Juan before he said, "*Más o menos.*"[1] The corners of his mouth upturned in a devilish grin that brought to mind a villain in a fairytale. A tremor of fear and anticipation snaked up her spine.

"What does that mean?" Searra edged, trying to keep the scent of her fear at bay.

"The more connected I am to someone, the easier it is to mind speak. The magic level makes a difference too." Juan smiled again and Searra's heart almost stopped with how devastating he was, even with his sharp canines winking at her in the dim light of the room. "Someone powerful would be louder." His brows raised pointedly.

"Louder?" Searra mumbled, half in her own head.

"Yeah, sometimes you're practically shouting at me." Juan's breathy chuckle came out as a low rumble that sent pleasant pulses through Searra, down to her toes. She could never get enough of that sound.

She was getting distracted and she still needed answers from him. *What were they talking about?*

"Why... why didn't you tell me about Diego?" Searra pulled the question from out of nowhere, since her head was truly turning to mush.

Juan stood, and the scent of crisp citrus and bergamot wafted from him as he sat next to her. It brought to mind images of a fresh shower and a warm, spicy drink she wanted to savor.

Juan's eyes were full of green fire as his hand came

---

1. More or less.

up to stroke her cheek.

Her breath caught in anticipation of his touch and sparks danced beneath her skin.

He pinched her chin between his thumb and forefinger and pulled her face to his. His lips brushed against hers, slow and deliberate, like a warm promise. The kiss lingered, tender and unhurried, making her head go fuzzy until she completely forgot what they'd been talking about. His tongue explored the seam of her lips. Gentle and strong. Her toes curled as liquid heat gathered in her core.

His strong hand grabbed her by the back of her neck as he deepened the kiss. The air stalled in her lungs as she forgot how to breathe.

An ache was building deep inside her and she felt herself surrender to him.

Abruptly, he pulled back, but not before brushing a final featherlight kiss that lingered, leaving her lips tingling.

Then he leaned back on the bed, elbows propping him up on either side, a smug, satisfied smile on his face. She was flushing hot. Her head swimming with incoherent, aching thoughts. She could see his pecs straining against his shirt as he lay, and she bit her sensitive lip to keep her drool in.

"I should think that was obvious." His gaze was intense and probing as he stared at her.

"Tell me," Searra said rolling her eyes, having almost forgotten she had asked about Diego. Her entire body was buzzing.

"I wanted more time with you," Juan admitted, a startling softness to him, unguarded and raw. "And I'm sorry for that." He lifted himself off the bed, his eyes were shadowed, and his face suddenly gaunt. "I'm so sorry I turned you. I *stole* your life and gave you no choice. I was overwhelmed, so full of these *emotions*," he grimaced as he spat the word. "I acted out of fear and desperation. For that, my deepest shame." Searra could see the remorse written in the lines of his face. "I don't, however, regret that you are now immortal and strong. I couldn't let my mate be at the mercy of mortality." His eyes resembled a lush green forest, wild and untamed. "I couldn't bear it if something happened to you."

Something softened in Searra's heart, and she melted at his words.

He knelt at her feet and gripped her knees in his hands. "There's more, *mi amore*,"[2] Juan whispered, his deep voice was low and full of gravel that made a sweet heat bloom in her chest. "I felt your emotions when I drank from you that night. I *knew* how much you grieved for Diego." He breathed and gave her a sad smile. "And I was... jealous. So I didn't tell you, because if I had... I knew I had no chance."

There was a brewing storm in his eyes. Passion, pain, and shame were a potent combination.

"I'm in love with you, Searra. I am *yours* and...you are *mine*." There was a finality in his tone that left no room for argument and his possessive gaze set her ablaze in the most delicious way.

Her heart began to hammer in her chest and her breathing quickened.

Love?

---

2. My love.

The word didn't scare her like she thought it would, even though they had only known each other for a few days. If anything, *she liked it.* She liked the idea of being *his.*

A thought intruded at the back of her mind, making guilt claw at her gut. *What about Diego?* She had no answers for that voice, for the part of her that felt like she was betraying her husband.

Juan's face was etched with worry, and Searra reached out to smooth away the lines that had settled in the corners of his eyes. Her thumb felt the fire along her skin where they touched. Butterflies fluttered in her stomach. She tried to give him a reassuring smile, but exhaustion was finally settling in. Searra could feel it in her bones. An aching tiredness washed over her and her vision began to blur.

Reluctantly, Searra admitted, "I'm so tired," as she fought back a yawn. "Can we finish *this,*" she waved her hands in circles, "in the morning?" Searra knew her brain was melting like a cake in the sun the longer she stayed awake. Her eyelids felt heavy, and a slow, sinking fatigue crawled up her limbs like a numbing blanket.

"Of course, *mi amore*[3] ," Juan said as his fingers played with the ends of her long dark hair. "Sunrise is coming soon and the sun brings on a weighty lethargy. You may not awaken until the afternoon at the earliest. It depends on how far along your change has progressed."

Searra's eyes grew wide with worry. "What about

---

3. My love

Jade? She is going to wake up in an hour. Is Piche—"

"I've already called ur mom and sister." Juan gave her a sly grin full of too white teeth. "They will be here by the time she wakes up. I gave Pichi the day off."

"How will—" Searra started.

"I gave them the codes to get in," Juan interjected. His smile crinkled as his eyes glowed forest green. "I know you will feel better knowing they are here watching her."

Searra felt a warmth spread throughout her chest at his thoughtfulness and felt a genuine smile bloom across her face. "Is it safe for them to come here?"

He nodded, "It should be. No one would come here without my permission first."

"At least they got an actual invite." Searra's statement dripped with sarcasm.

While she was abducted?

"Abduction is the ultimate invite," Juan said, his fangs gleaming.

Searra gave him a deadpan look. Juan hung his head, pinched the bridge of his straight nose, and let out a breathy chuckle. "Yeah... that was me acting on heightened *emotions.*"

Searra looked at him from the corner of her eye and pursed her lips as if to say *no shit.*

"I apologize for the way I went about that. But I was like... like a dragon that just found a hoard of treasure. I had to secure you away, somewhere I can keep an eye on you and Jade." His grin was sheepish, and yet his fangs glinted at her with a sinister promise that sent a tremor of anticipation over her entire body.

With a devilish gleam in his eyes and matching

smirk, Juan moved to the head of the bed, adjusted the pillows, and pulled back the covers. "Get in. You're swaying. Any longer and I might have to scoop you off the floor."

Searra looked down at her worn and dirty pajamas— the same ones she'd been wearing for days. They were definitely on the ripe side. "I need to change really quick." Her own voice reached her ears, but it sounded all wrong— Like a record on the slowest speed. It was deeper and warped, and underwater.

"I'll get them for you. Newer vampires are more susceptible to the sun." Air rushed around her in a flash of preternatural speed, flooding her senses with his cool and spicy citrus scent. She breathed in deep, the calm cascaded over her as her body sank, heavy as stones she was too weak to lift.

In an instant, Juan was kneeling in front of her, a wad of clothes clutched in his hands. He brushed her dark hair from her face and removed her tank. Her bare breasts hit the cool air, and she quivered as the crisp fabric of a new, clean tank skimmed over her flushed skin.

She was surprised she was not embarrassed as he swapped out her panties and pajama bottoms for fresh ones. His hands were gentle and quick as he worked. Soon, she was in a clean set to sleep in. She felt ten times better smelling the crisp laundry smell on her clothes. It was the intimacy of the gesture that made her heart stutter, heat rising in her chest as tears pricked the corners of her eyes.

Juan's handsome face was glowing as a genuine smile lit him from within. He removed his shirt in one swift motion, his muscles on display for Searra to peruse.

She wanted to touch each one and rake her teeth over them.

And bite them?

The thought sent a thrill of excitement through her but she shook her head to clear it from her brain. She was *waaay* too tired.

Wordlessly, he climbed into bed and wrapped his strong arms around her waist. He drew her closer, nestling her against him, and pressed a soft kiss to her shoulder.

Her entire body shivered at his lips against her sensitive skin. Searra wiggled her hips closer to him in the guise of getting comfortable. Gravity was weighing down on her but she continued to grind her ass against him with a big, silly grin on her face.

Tease. The word cascaded over her, sending delicious shivers in it's wake.

Juan chuckled into the back of her neck and she could feel his lips smile against her skin. It sent gooseflesh pebbling down her spine.

"Go to bed, *mi amore*[4]," Juan whispered into her hair as he gripped her tighter against his body and she molded into him like memory foam.

Searra yawned wide, so wide she felt like she might unhinge her jaw, "I still have a few choice words for Diego too." Searra said, her eyes shut and her voice in slow-mo.

"I bet you do." Juan said with a chuckle. *Sleep.* His

---

4. My love

smooth voice echoed through her mind as she sank into the numbing dark.

Searra slumbered as one of the immortals, silent and still —dead to the world.

CHAPTER 25

CAGED

Searra was walking down a long hallway lined with old terracotta colored tile that had chipped corners from years of use. The walls were covered with ancient shiplap that ran down the length of the passage. The sound around her was muffled, like she was listening through a thick pane of glass.

Was she underground?

The air tasted stale, carrying a damp scent she couldn't quite place— like a bathroom after a shower, but without the clean trace of soap. Her footsteps echoed as she walked, each sound lagging behind with an unsettling delay.

Grand double doors of dark heavy oak hung open, leading into a cavernous ballroom. A raised stage dominated the center, encircled by dark wood and black velvet, the room lit only by the trembling glow of torchlight.

Voices bounced off the walls, whispers she couldn't quite make out. Hooded figures stood against the railings on either side of her, like viewing boxes in a court proceeding.

Darkness swallowed the stage so completely she could only just make out the silhouette of a massive metal cage at its center. Shadows cloaked it, writhing and ebbing like it breathed in the gloom.

As if it were alive.

Searra's feet moved of their own accord. Setting a sluggish pace, like walking through wet cement. Dread bloomed in her stomach and began to gnaw at her. There was something horribly wrong and the knowledge of that, the certainty of it, grew and grew until she was standing at the base of the stage, looking eye level at a cage that was big enough for a medium to large dog.

The shadows split open without warning, a gaping hungry mouth. Through the rift came a flash of yellow. Sunflowers. Familiar sunflowers. Ones she knew.

Jade!

Sitting at the bottom of the cage, dirty and without her shoes, was her baby daughter, Jade. Searra's heart dropped to the floor. Hot, angry tears clogged her throat and burned her eyes.

"Sweetie pie?" Searra's question came out as a threadbare whisper. And she reached out with hesitant fingers. Disbelief halting her for a heartbeat.

Was this a vision, or a nightmare?

Dirt crusted her rosy cheeks, tear tracks cutting pale lines through the grime. Her puffy brown eyes locked on Searra, wide and pleading.

"Mama! Mamamamamama!" Her little voice screamed. Her pink fists gripped the thick dirt-encrusted bars and stood up. Her screams melted into desperate cries as she reached through the bars to get to her.

Searra's heart cracked. Then she was moving. No thought, only Jade. Fear surged through her veins, adrenaline sharpening every movement. In one fluid leap she was on the stage, sprinting for the cage.

Just as quickly, the shadows enveloped the cage once again. Jade's keening cry split the air, echoing in Searra's ears. Panic clawed up her throat, choking her.

But it didn't stop her from charging the cage like a fucking battering ram, hoping to bend or knock out the bars. But instead of hitting metal, the shadows formed an impenetrable wall. When she hit, Searra felt her shoulder crack against it.

And then she was falling, and she could only hear Jade's screams echoing around her.

Searra sat up in bed and bit back a sharp stab of pain. Her hand clutched her shoulder, trying to soothe the throbbing ache but only one thought cut through.

Jade.

She was up in an instant, out of bed before she even

realized she'd moved. Juan stirred beside her, muttering something, but his voice barely registered. She seized the door and wrenched it open. It ripped free of its hinges, crashing against the wall with a sharp crack.

"*¡Qué demonios—!*"[1] She heard Juan exclaim in surprise behind her but she was already at the end of the hallway.

Searra reached out with her new vampiric senses, seeking heat signatures. Through the door, she saw three bodies, two large, one small. Relief dulled the edge of her panic. She clutched the handle and yanked the door open in a blur of wood. Panting, she fought to steady her breathing.

In the cream-colored room, her mom, sister, and Jade sat together on the bed. Searra released a shaky breath. Her whole body collapsing into jelly, shoulders slumping, knees buckling.

A second later, a puff of air rushed next to her, dark hair moving around her like wisps of smoke. The crisp scent of cedarwood and spicy citrus let her know that it was Juan, waiting for word from her. She sent her thoughts out into the ether, hoping that Juan would be able to read them.

Everything is okay. But I have a really, bad feeling. I think I just had... a fucking nightmare.

Searra could still see Jade in that cage, screaming for her. Searra's stomach flipped with nausea, the acidic sting of bile climbed up her throat. Her panic was rising again as she looked to Juan to anchor her.

---

1. What the fuck? / What the hell? (Arcaic saying)

His emerald gaze was like a balm that soothed her fraying edges. He reached out holding her hand, giving it a gentle squeeze. The pad of his thumb lightly caressed her knuckles. Each stroke comforted her, like a wary street cat with raised hackles being soothed by a determined cat lady.

Jade screamed in her grandma's arms, "No booo! No booo!" And made a dramatic frownie face.

Jade had been reading with Grandma from a composition book Searra's sister had created. A makeshift alphabet book with cute drawings. Although, it started off rocky since the first few pages were filled with terrifying sketches of demented cats and dogs that Searra's mom had drawn. They were like something out of Shel Silverstein, which gave Searra the creeps.

Searra was relieved her mom and sister were there but the last thing she wanted to do was freak them out. They had enough stress as it was. So she decided not to discuss any of the vampire, *bruja*,[2] or vision shit within their earshot.

Searra noticed her mom's hair looked thinner than the last time she saw her. She could see scalp peaking out through the short pink mohawk.

Was that only a few days ago?

There was also a distinctive smell of sour rot, a scent she had never experienced before. It was coming from her mom and she bristled.

Was that the cancer?

She snuck a look at Juan and he gave her

---

2. witch

a short, curt nod of affirmation, having heard her thoughts. He squeezed her hand. Hot tears pricked the corners of her eyes, but she refused to let them fall in front of her mom.

"Ma? Your hair's falling out again?" Searra asked, concern lacing her tone. It was the first thing that popped into her head. A distraction, but a real worry all the same.

"Yeah." Her mom croaked and cleared the phlegm from her throat. "The doctor said these new pills were gonna make my hair fall out again." Her wrinkled hand patted her head. A few purple bruises splotched her yellowed skin from where the nurses had drawn blood. They always had to stick her extra because she had such tiny veins.

"But it's sore. I got a couple of sores on my scalp." She had a pinched expression, and her thin lips were pressed together so tight they almost disappeared.

"I'm sorry Ma," Searra told her.

"Yeah, she is at that stage again. Full dandelion." Syd interjected, a manic glee in her eyes. She blew into her hand for emphasis and mimicked the spreading of dandelion seeds with her fingers.

Searra snorted because she couldn't help it. Sometimes shit was just sad and stupid funny.

"Or like those baby orangutans!" Searra added, unable to stop from laughing.

Syd smiled wider and looked to their mom. "See!" Pointing to her sister with a triumphant finger.

But their mom's mouth only hung open, eyes wide like she couldn't believe the barrage of insults coming from her own daughters. It only made Searra laugh harder.

Jade began to repeat again, with more adamance and an exaggerated angry face that said she was fed up with not being listened to, "No booo! No booo! No booo!" This time Searra looked to her sister, and gave her a questioning look.

Syd pointed to her hair and the two light blue streaks framing her round face. "It's blue. I didn't want blue. The box said 'tonal silver' But it came out blue." Her eyes were wide and full of drama, as she gave Jade a face of bewilderment.

Jade repeated, "No booo! No booo!" Her little brows were set in a tight, angry line as she held her mimicked expression. She then, immediately broke out in a huge smile, showing a mouth full of teeth, with eyes like twinkling crescent moons. Mischief danced within her gaze as it landed on Searra.

"Mama! Mama! Bye-bye!" Jade shouted at Searra, then at her grandma and auntie. She wiggled off Searra's mom's lap and grabbed her blanket, blowing kisses as she got to Searra. Short, plump arms raised to be picked up. "Up! Up! Up!" Jade demanded. Each "up" progressively louder and more aggressive than the last. Her little brows knit together in a scowl, the step right before the screaming starts.

Searra reached down and plucked Jade from the floor.

Jade bounced and squealed, burying her face in the crook of Searra's neck. Searra held her close, squeezing tighter until Jade began to squirm and demand, "Down! Down! Doooown!"

Reluctantly, Searra brought her back to the ground and gave her a big kiss on her cheek while Jade tried to wriggle away. Searra watched her run, knees lifting high as she stomped away, making circles around Pee-Paw at dizzying speed.

Searra's heart stung. She'd give everything to prevent what she just saw. She would not let anything happen to Jade. Searra felt the resolve burn through her, hot in her blood. She turned to Juan, who continued to hold her hand, like he was her own personal anchor and needed the contact as much as she did. Her dark gaze met his and he gave her a slight nod, confirming he had been able to read her thoughts.

They had to protect Jade.

"Hey..." Suddenly, Syd was at Searra's ear, leaning in to whisper, "Can I talk to you outside? Like the hall or something?" Eyes flashing with determination, shifting from Searra to Juan.

Searra was taken aback, "For sure. Lets go." She gave Juan a quick, questioning look and then asked her mom "Ma? You gonna be okay with her for a few minutes?"

"Oh yeah, me and little one will be fine." But her gaze slid to Juan, her expression pinched, like she wasn't sure whether to trust him or not. Searra couldn't blame her. Her mom lost all trust in men years ago, when her parents divorced.

Plus, he basically kidnapped her daughter and granddaughter?

Searra said to Juan, "Watch out for this one," while she pointed at her mom. "She is tricksy."

Juan's eyes widened in surprise, amusement flickering in a forest of green as he looked down at the tiny, older woman.

"Whaaaaaaaa?" Her mom gasped with such indignation that Searra couldn't hold back the loud snort as she followed her sister out the door.

They walked down the hall a ways until Syd spun around and faced Searra. Her arms were crossed over her chest and she looked... non-plussed.

"What's up Squee? What's going on?" Searra asked. She had no idea what Syd wanted to tell her. Maybe it had something to do with their mom and her latest doctor's appointment?

"WHAT. THE. FUCK. SISI?!" The forcefulness of her words impacted Searra like physical blows.

"What?" Searra's mind had gone completely blank.

Syd's hazel eyes sparked with rage, the type of drag-on rage Searra hadn't seen from her for years. She had done a lot of work, a lot of therapy, to control her volcanic temper, but it appeared her grip on the leash had slackened today.

"You and the baby just up and disappeared in the middle of the night and DIDN'T SAY ANYTHING?!" Her voice got louder and louder the more she spoke. "We almost called the police! ...Sisi! The fuck?!"

Searra's mouth hung open in shock. Syd was right, she realized. She hadn't even thought to text them that she was alright. Everything had happened so fast, she was still processing it all and had no idea how to put any of that into words.

"Shit Syd..." Searra breathed. "You're right! I'm sorry. I had no intention to keep you guys in the dark."

Syd snorted at her. Her arms were still crossed, with her weight shifted onto one leg so her hip stuck out.

"I deserve that. And believe me *I get it.*" If anyone understood what it felt like for someone to leave and never come home again... it was Searra. "Trust me when I tell you that some crazy shit has been happening and I'm still making sense of it. But I will tell you everything soon." Searra took a deep breath, her voice laced with compulsion, with magic. The air around them was heavy with plumerias and sunshine, "Trust me."

Syd gave her the harsh side eye, but her stony facade was cracking. "Like what?" She said through pursed lips.

In show of good faith, Searra shared what she thought was safe. "Diego is alive."

Searra's words were like an anvil as they hit Syd square in the face. Her eyes widened in disbelief, "WHAT?!"

"Yeah... I know."

"Are you sure?" Syd's round eyes were practically popping out of her head.

"Yes... I talked to him yesterday." Searra rubbed her eyes in frustration. Saying it all outloud was getting her pissed off all over again.

Syd narrowed her eyes. "And where is he now?"

"With his family I suppose." Searra said with a forced, casual shrug.

"And where the fuck have they been?" Her sister spat, like she was ready to squish them beneath her shoes.

Searra sighed, "They've had a lot of issues come up. Shit they've had to deal with... away from us. I'll explain better when I know more details."

Syd was silent for a moment as her gaze shifted back and forth, "Soooo..." Her hazel eyes lit with mischief, "What about the beefcake in there?" Head nodding to where they had left Juan and their mom with Jade, full lips in a sly smile.

Searra laughed and felt heat in her face, "I don't know what is going on there." But she couldn't hide the wide smile that bloomed on her face. She was grinning so hard that her cheeks hurt.

Syd gave her an answering smile, "It's been a long time since I've seen you like this..." She hesitated, "Don't get mad at me... but," she took a breath and hesitated. "What about Diego?" Syd asked, her hands raised. "Don't get it twisted... I totally understand that Diego has been 'dead', I just want to know where your head space is."

Without missing a beat, Searra admitted, "I'm confused *as fuck*. One hundred percent."

CHAPTER 26

INTRUSIVE

"THE YELLOW WALLPAPER IS THE MOST BEAUTIFUL THING IN THE

ROOM, AND I AM AFRAID OF IT."
-CHARLOTTE PERKINS GILMAN
(1892)

After Searra and Juan had their liquid breakfast, they went to the backyard to talk, away from the prying eyes and ears of her mom and sister.

Chismosas.[1]

Searra's mom and sister had taken Jade to hang out in the living room. They put on a movie while Searra and Juan slipped out into the night, beneath a quiet blanket of stars.

Los Angeles was famous for how few stars could be

---

1. gossipy women / girls who gossip

seen with the naked eye due to a potent combination of lights and smog. But with her vampire eyes, she saw galaxies swirling in space like glittering marbled ice cream. She marveled at the spectacle. Entranced by something bigger than herself or her problems.

Her gaze was fixed on Juan as he stood on the back porch just outside the house. A slight breeze chilled the air and ruffled his sandy brown hair.

As he leaned forward on the porch railing, his large hands almost engulfed the thick beams. In the moonlight, he looked carved from marble— exquisite, timeless, as though the landscape itself had claimed him as its own. His hair was so shiny and thick. She wanted to run her hands through it to see if it was as luxurious as it appeared, or if it truly was made of stone.

"You had another vision," Juan said, breaking the silence. It wasn't a question.

Searra was surprised, and yet she wasn't. "How did you know?" She asked, but already knew the answer.

The corner of Juan's mouth rose. "You were shouting at me when you woke up." His emerald eyes flashed with worry.

"Ahhhhh." Searra mused and clicked her tongue. "So, how much did you glean?" She was trying to keep her tone casual, but she shifted on her feet with nervous energy. Her fingers found their way to her hair and she began twirling the long strands. A habit she'd had since she was a kid. She would twirl them so tight she cut off circulation in her fingers, and their tips had blued. Looking back, she may have been dealing with way too much anxiety as a kid.

Juan chuckled under his breath, but didn't look at

her. "I know it was about Jade. And that it frightened you out of a heavy day sleep."

Searra must have had a confused expression on her face because Juan explained, "Sunlight presses down on us during the day. Waking early would take immense strength." Juan was speaking matter-of-factly, but his eyes betrayed a haunted look. "Some don't even awaken when they are in mortal danger."

"But you woke up. I saw you. You were right behind me." Searra recalled.

Earnestness broke through his placid facade, "My mate awoke *terrified*." His deep voice cracked, "I felt it and it woke me up too. Your fear... I can still taste it on my tongue." His tone was throaty with pent-up emotion. "I cannot bear that kind of terror from you." With eyes lit like molten crystals, he confessed, "I would do *anything* to prevent that." His gaze held her captive, and she forgot how to breathe.

Juan closed the short distance between them, his long legs made quick work of it. His hand reached out to cup her face, the pad of his thumb made lazy, gentle circles on her jawline.

She shut her eyes against the onslaught of delicious fire building in her core, trying to control her emotions, her hormones, the way she reacted around him.

"No, don't do that." His voice was a whispered caress as he goaded her into opening her eyes. "Let me in." The words shimmered in the air around her.

Let me in.

She felt it then. A gentle tug she couldn't ignore. She obeyed and opened her eyes. Her dark brown gaze locked with his. Emerald eyes like a sparkling green field she could get lost in.

She was lost.

Lost in a blooming field of thick grass and golden flowers. Standing barefoot as the long blades caressed her skin, the slight mist from the morning dew cooled her toes. She reached out and the sparkling petals were so soft against the pads of her fingers, like silk.

Then she sensed it, a twitch, like probing fingers. A familiar male energy was moving around inside her mind.

Juan.

Flowing from thought to thought and memory to memory like a stream of cool water until he reached her vision from last night. When he touched it, she flinched away, making them both pull back. She was engulfed by the damp earth around her and the muffled sounds of the underground chamber.

Juan tried to push through, but Searra flinched back again. She didn't want to see Jade sitting in that cage again; it was a fresh, open wound. Still tender and raw, and his poking and prodding was like salt.

She hissed at him between clenched teeth. Panic began to set in. Her thoughts became frantic and jumbled. She wanted to stay in that field, rest her head in the pillowed grass.

There was another tug at her temple. It hurt.

An intrusive thought, not a vision, an intrusive thought— not her baby girl crying out for her.

Scared and alone.

Dirty, cold, and hungry.

Looking for Searra, her Momma, and not finding her.

Hot, stinging tears pricked the corners of her eyes.

Scared and alone.

Crying for her momma. *Just an intrusive thought.*

Jade was fine, she was with Aunty Squee and Pee Paw.

Yet, she couldn't get that image from the *nightmare* out of her mind.

The vision.

Searra's breath was coming in a shallow and rapid pace as the tears fell in wet grooves down her face.

There was another tug at the back of her mind, to get into her memory. But a familiar warmth began to spread beneath her skin. It built and built, rising with her fear, with her pain.

First warm, then hot... hotter... boiling. Her skin was slick with sweat from the heat and her shirt was sticking to her skin. She couldn't breathe. It was too hot. Sweat began to pool in the small of her back. The boiling heat in her chest felt like it was cooking her from the inside out.

Hot like the sun.

A sudden burst of energy released from her, a blazing white ball of pure fire.

She felt Juan's presence shrink back and then sharp pain blistered along her right shoulder, as if it had been burned. She cried out as she felt her flesh melt from her bones, muscle and sinew buckling beneath the torrential heat of a living sun.

But a nagging thought pulled at her. Was that her pain? Or was it an echo of something else?

Without warning, Juan's mind had her own locked down like a vise; frozen, and the heat in her chest withered like a flame under glass. Panic clawed its way up her throat as a newfound claustrophobia triggered another anxiety attack. Her heart became smothered, and she felt like she was trying to breathe underwater. Her mouth popped open and closed like a fish, thrashing in its last fateful gasps.

It's okay mi amore.[2] *Let me in.*

The words echoed in her mind and began to soothe her like a warm balm. Her aching lungs filled with sweet air and relief tingled through her body, leaving her boneless. He had pushed through the barriers in her mind and she sensed they were in the underground chamber again, where she had found Jade. She thought she would panic, but she was wrapped in a thick mental blanket and everything was muffled.

She couldn't hear Jade's cries, or smell the mold in the room anymore, but she knew the exact moment Jade began to scream because of the wetness on her cheeks from tears she could not shed. The emotions couldn't penetrate the protective barrier Juan had wrapped her in. As darkness engulfed Jade in her vision, Searra felt miles away.

Numb.

Then the ground she thought she was standing on disappeared beneath her feet. Her stomach dropped, and a scream caught in her throat as she fell.

---

2. My love

CHAPTER 27

ESTRELLAS (STARS)

"WHATEVER OUR SOULS ARE MADE OF, HIS AND MINE ARE THE SAME." -EMILY BRONTë

Searra woke and couldn't quite remember where she was. Strong arms wrapped around her and held her upright. She remembered falling and should have woken up on her back, splayed out on the floor with a potential head injury.

"Are you with me?" Juan's gruff voice vibrated in her head as she rested against his chest.

She nodded, not able to form words. "Fuuuuuuuc-cc..." She grumbled out. She was sitting in his lap and their legs were tangled together on the floor.

His grip tightened on her and she let him pull her body closer to his.

Searra's mouth was dry and she smacked her lips trying to find her words. "What?" Her voice no more than a croak, she cleared her throat, and tried again, "What was that?" She looked up at him, his chin resting on her head. Dark strands of her hair were caught in his stubble.

Juan's jaw ticked. "I used compulsion on you." His eyes looked wary, like he was dealing with a wild animal he couldn't control.

The fog in Searra's head was lifting, "And you used it so I would let you in... to see my vision." It wasn't a question, but Searra looked to him for confirmation.

Juan nodded in response. It was stiff and guarded, like he feared how she would react.

She searched her feelings and couldn't find the outrage she expected to feel. He violated her mind, without consent. He *compelled* her. And yet, there was no anger; only gratitude that he had softened the vision for her, so she wouldn't have to go through it again.

"Why didn't you just ask me?" Searra posited. Had he asked, she would have probably agreed. If it meant protecting Jade, there was nothing she wouldn't endure.

The silence stretched. Juan didn't say anything for a long time. So they just sat there, wrapped in each other under the stars.

He cleared his throat, "I *want* to tell you... that you're mental walls are so strong I needed compulsion to break them down. That you would have had trouble letting me in. I *want* to tell you that." Juan grunted with frustration, like he wasn't used to explaining himself like this. "But, I honestly didn't consider it."

Juan buried his face in her hair, as if to hide the shame within her dark tresses. "I did what I thought necessary. I got the information by any means. It didn't occur to me to ask you first." It all came out in an angry rush, not anger at her, but at himself, at his own behavior.

Frustration seemed new for him, like he wasn't accustomed to regretting his actions. He nuzzled his head further into her hair, his breath tickling the sensitive skin at her nape, which sent goosebumps down her spine. The languid pleasure at his touch almost had her purring like a cat starved for affection.

Searra looked up and blinked at him, shocked by the blatant honesty. She was already exhausted by the mental marathon they had just run and couldn't summon the energy to be angry. So she only sank deeper into his embrace and said, "Okay. Just ask me next time." She gazed into his mossy green eyes, "Deal?"

Juan kissed the top of her head which sent warmth blossoming in her chest. The tension melted from his shoulders as he said, "I promise."

"Good." A smile pulled at her lips, content to sit in that moment for eternity. But worry and anxiety for Jade bubbled to the surface and she needed to move, to do something, to plan.

When Searra tried to pull away, Juan stiffened and pulled her back in, seeming unable to go without her touch. She leaned into him, her back against his solid chest and her head lolled to rest on his shoulder.

Juan flinched. It was a small, almost imperceptible movement, but Searra noticed.

She pulled away from him with her vampire speed, dodging his arm that tried to recollect her, so she could turn around and get a good look at him.

Her mouth fell open as she took in the nasty burn taking up his entire right shoulder. His white t-shirt looked melted into his flesh and was splotched with blood and yellow plasma. The skin beneath was raised, shiny, and angry. Gnarled to the point of grotesque. It smelled like fleshy, burnt hair and she couldn't believe she didn't notice until now.

So much for heightened senses.

"Shit..." Searra whispered through her teeth. "That looks like it hurts." She wanted to reach out to soothe the rawness of his injury, but she wasn't sure what to do, and touching it was going to make it worse.

Was there a vampire ER? Could vampires use Neosporin? Why hadn't he healed already? Didn't vampires have super healing shit?

"I'm fine. It will heal again... as soon as I feed." He remained stiff while he said it, but his gaze flared, like emeralds caught in a blaze.

Searra's dark brows pinched together. "But... why didn't you feed already?"

She reached her hand out, but she hesitated mid-journey through the air, not wanting to hurt him more. Her hand hovered in the space between them and dropped like a stone. "You could have run to the fridge to get blood, faster than I even woke up. Or... you could have fed off me." The last bit tumbled from her before she even thought about what she was saying.

Did she want that? Did she mean it?

His face was grave as he said, "You were unconscious. And your mind was..." He hesitated, trying to find his words, his voice gruff with emotion. "I—I couldn't leave you. I needed to make sure you were alright first." His tone was firm and unwavering, conviction clear in every word. "And I would never feed from you when you are passed out." His brows creased and his eyes flickered with hurt before he looked away, jaw muscles flexing beneath his skin.

Searra was feeling bold; she bit her lip as she grabbed her long, dark hair and moved it all to one side, exposing her neck to him and the chill night air.

"I'm not unconscious now." She said it with much more confidence than she felt.

She had never been this forward, not even with Diego. He was always the pursuer, the initiator. Yet, here she was, waving her neck cleavage around for all to see. Although, she was never embarrassed to express herself in front of Juan, not even when they first met.

Juan's gaze flicked from her eyes to her bare neck. His sharp fangs had emerged, reflecting the moonlight. "I think you should rest." His voice had dropped an octave and his breathing had quickened.

"I want you to," Searra said. She moved then to straddle him, careful not to touch his wounded shoulder. His body was so solid and strong beneath hers, she didn't even worry about squashing him. Her body flush against his, it made flames dance along her skin. Her nipples were tight against the soft fabric of her bra. For the first time, she wished she hadn't been wearing one so she could feel herself pressed against him.

Searra angled her head in offering and Juan's breath plumed against her neck. The hairs stood up as goosebumps pebbled her flesh and shivers of pleasure traveled through her body.

"I —" Juan stuttered, but his grip on her hips tightened, and his breathing quickened. His large hands were like hot brands on her sides as they traveled down to cup her ample ass. The need for friction was pure instinct, causing a whimper to escape her throat. She tried to clear her head and suppress the ache building in her core but straddling him left her in a precarious position with her center so exposed to him.

She needed to get a grip.

Juan needed to recover.

"Feed and heal." Searra insisted, her voice was throaty with need and she fought to control her shaky intake of breath. She took in the sweet scent of him. Cedar and citrus were still lingering in the air, mixed with the spicy bergamot.

And burnt hair. She tried not to think about that part.

Juan's lips brushed against her skin and the sudden sharp sting sang through her body as his fangs pierced the delicate hollow of her neck. Searra tried to hold in her moan as Juan drank from her, her hips rocking against him as he did.

The pleasure she felt during a feeding was unlike anything she had ever experienced before. Pain and pleasure tangled into one exquisite high, dangerous and addictive. She may never get enough. She may never want to come down.

And then Juan withdrew his fangs, lapped his tongue over her bite, and she felt a tingle as the raw sting receded into nothing. When he pulled back, the cold air between them was an assault on her senses.

Complete overstimulation.

Searra did her best to focus on one thing, just Juan.

His eyes were heavy and lidded, like she had caught him freshly woken from a nap. Or like a cat that just ate a fat ass bird and was content to sleep for the rest of the day.

Before her eyes, Searra watched as the gnarled wound began to shrink and the burned edges of torn skin stitched themselves back together until the only evidence left were the stains on his shirt. As soon as the wound disappeared, the cocky smirk returned to Juan's lips as he said, "Thank you, *mi amore*.[1]" His fangs were still visible and looked extra sharp in the light of the moon but the gratitude in his gaze was genuine.

"No problem." Searra breathed and shifted her hips to unseat herself from his lap, but Juan's grip only tightened on her.

"Where do you think you're going?" Juan's voice was playful and gruff with need that mirrored her own.

Searra rolled her eyes. "I think we need to actually discuss shit right now. And from this position, I don't think either of us is thinking with our brains." And she tried again to dismount. Juan let her go this time and she stood up, dusting off her leggings of any remaining dirt. Her ass cheeks jiggled as she smacked the dust away.

Juan let out a low whistle and waggled his brows at her. "Damn, that ass is a thing of beauty. It's got a

---

1. My love

mind of its own in those pants."

Searra snorted. "Riiiiiight." She tried to act non-chalant, but the heat still rose to her cheeks. It had been so long since she flirted that she had almost forgotten how to do it.

Was she doing it right?

Searra offered her hand to Juan to help him up from the floor. He looked at it, green eyes reflecting the starlight above their heads, and he took it. Their hands clasped together like they had done it a thousand times, fitting together perfectly like puzzle pieces. Searra pulled him up easily, smiling at him when he rose to his full height without wincing.

Searra strode to the edge of the porch and leaned on the thick wooden railing. Juan followed and stood next to her, his back to the railing. Her elbows dug into the wood and she felt the bite of bark against her skin. The chill night air swirled around them, filling her lungs with crisp night and citrus.

"So, was that because of me?" Searra asked pointing at his healed shoulder with her chin. She had an idea, but wanted Juan to say it out loud.

Juan clicked his tongue before he conceded, "*Sí.*"[2]

"That's not the first time that happened right? It happened last night, in front of Diego." Searra's voice was flat and emotionless.

"*Sí.*" Juan didn't hesitate in his answer this time. "Your visions seem to trigger it. Or at least the ones that trigger intense emotions."

---

2. Yes.

"I think it has building in me, every since you bit me. It'd been getting stronger." Searra mused. "But how? What is happening to me?" There was a note of desperation in her voice.

Juan sighed, "You are one of the most powerful *brujas*[3] — turned newborn vampire, I've come across."

Searra had no words, except, *"What?"* She felt so dumb needing to ask so many questions.

"You aren't dumb. This is all new to you. It's understandable that they're are things about my world you don't know. It's that way by design. We work best in the shadows." Juan interjected, seeming to have read her thoughts.

What if he judged her by them? It sent a chill of trepidation over her entire body.

"Get out of my head!" Searra spat. She bristled thinking Juan could hear all of her insecurities, everything she tried to work through. Every intrusive thought.

The most abhorrent ones.

He had no business knowing any of that shit.

"Then stop screaming your thoughts at me." Juan kept his voice in an even tone, but his calm mask looked on the edge of cracking.

Searra immediately regretted her tone and wanted to change the subject, "How was I able to burn you like that?"

Juan's eyes lit up like green fire, something out of a dark fairytale, for a brief second before he said, "A vampire with the power of daylight."

---

3. witches

A vampire with the power of daylight?

Searra couldn't wrap her brain around it. But she was still affected by the sun? How could she wield sunlight?

"You have the power of the sun within you," Juan whispered and let out an airy chuckle. "Your *sol.*"[4] There was admiration in his gaze and a little bit of awe.

"But, why? I don't understand." Searra thought she might be getting a headache from trying to figure all this shit out. Her dark brows pinched in thought and a dull throb grew in the center of her forehead. She even contemplated taking Excedrin.

Would that even work on her now?

"When I turned you," Juan continued, his voice smooth like dark silk. "You're magic began to awaken. Your *bruja*[5] bloodline is very powerful." He paused, pinning her down with his heated, emerald gaze, "My *mate* is powerful." There was only pride and possession in his tone, written in his expression. The corner of his mouth lifted, amusement in his eyes.

That should have made Searra recoil. She was *not* someone's property. But a part of her liked being thought of as *his,* and a warmth bloomed in her chest at his words. She liked being possessed.

Possessed by *him.*

"So, I can kill vampires with this power?" Searra

---

4. Sun.

5. witch

269

hedged, fear and a little excitement coating her throat. It was nice to feel a little powerful for once, but would this make her a target? Would that even be worth it? Did she even want to kill vampires now that she was one?

"*Sí... y sí.*"[6] Juan's words emerged through gritted teeth. "I know many who would love to get their hands on you." His voice was no more than a growl as his jaw clenched and anger flashed across his handsome face.

Searra's eyes widened in surprise. "Like who? *Your* council?" She arched a dark brow. Her black gaze like ice chips from the Mariana Trench.[7]

"They do love to collect rare weapons." Giving her a possessive side glance that burned her like a brand, a branding she felt down to her toes.

Searra tore her gaze away.

"Hey," Juan demanded, his voice steady. "I would *never* let anything happen to you and Jade." A muscle on his jaw ticked and his eyes were searing. "I would burn *every single one* of them to the ground." His expression was so steely and yet soft as he looked at her. His mop of sandy hair hung in his eyes and cast shadows across his face.

Shadows that were reflected from within.

Darkness staining his soul.

He had been around a long time and had done a

---

6. Yes... And yes.

7. The Mariana Trench is the deepest part of the world's oceans, plunging nearly 36,000 feet into a dark, crushing abyss.

lot of horrible things, things she couldn't even begin to contemplate or understand. Searra didn't want to be added to his long list of atrocities he would have to atone for one day. But this man before her was not a monster, she could see the good within him, his inner light.

Something in her chest began to thaw and warmth returned to her gaze. Searra felt the sincerity in his words, and she wanted to believe him.

"If I find out you set us up," Searra laced her words with what remained of the ice in her veins. *"I'll burn you alive."* Her voice was strong and sharp. She meant it and hoped he read the intention in her thoughts.

Juan looked serious for a quick second, but the corner of his mouth lifted and relief flooded his expression. "Oh *vida*,[8] I'd expect nothing less."

---

8. Life (term of endearment)

CHAPTER 28

BREACH

"Was there anything useful at least?" Searra asked. They had moved the conversation on to dissecting her vision and what Juan had gleaned from her thoughts. "Hopefully you got *something* after poking around in my head."

Juan walked up to lean next to her on the railing. "Indeed, if memory serves, it was a council session."

Searra gave him a heated look.

Jesus.

She reminded herself to take a breath and breathe out slowly. If she lost her cool again, she couldn't think clearly enough to prevent *anything*.

"Thank you for breathing." Juan offered a sly smile

and his eyes sparkled for a moment. But the light soon went out as he continued. "But I fear I can guess why the rest of the council desires your daughter. We do not convene in such a manner for mere trivialities. Things are in motion and we need to stop it."

Searra knew it was probably her bloodline. Jade was descended from two *bruja*[1] families, one with a wolf affinity and one with light... whatever kind of light it was. She would grow up and be powerful, the idea made Searra's heart swell with pride. Any mother would want their daughter strong, but icy fingers of fear began to twist themselves through her mind. That same strength would make her a target too. Jade would know no peace... powerful beings would be coming after her. If not to use her, perhaps to destroy her.

Searra's throat clogged with worry at that thought and her mouth went dry. "Any ideas are welcome." Sarcasm dripped from her words even as her tongue got stuck to the roof of her mouth. "I'm new to this shit." She grumbled.

"I think I can rule out psychic manipulation and coercion from your vision." Juan rubbed the dark stubble on his chin. "There are a few vampires on the council known to invade dreams, manipulate a vision, or even hypnotize. But, I didn't sense any other magic apart from yours. So, we can at least rule out the vision being some sort of trap."

Fear clawed at her chest. She tried to ignore it, to push it down, but the thought had dug into her.

---

1. witch

Someone might be tampering with these visions, or creating dreams to lure her in. She could smell her own fear in the air, sharp and sweet. They had to come up with a plan to prevent it, in any case. And she needed more support, and the only plan she had... was to go straight to her in-laws.

Juan's eyes slid to hers, having obviously heard her last thought. He raised his brow in question, concern coloring his expression.

Jade's tiny voice peeled out at an ungodly register as she laughed with Aunty Squee and Pee-Paw inside the house. The sound brought a small smile to Searra's face, but it soon fell away as she realized how distant life with her family seemed from her now, almost out of reach.

She wasn't human.

This was the longest time she had been away from her daughter, *ever.*

Juan nodded his head further into the backyard so they could get more privacy, his mop of sandy hair in his eyes.

Searra made her way to the stairs on the side of the porch that led out into the expansive yard. That was when she felt Juan's hand at the small of her back, guiding her into the dark.

"There is a nice place for us to sit this way. Where we won't be overheard." He crooned, his voice like silk draping over her skin. Her body yielded to his touch like she had always known it. A rare sense of peace washed over her, like a warm blanket. She was, at last, able to breathe in deep since seeing Jade in that cage.

They soon came upon a large black pergola wrapped in gorgeous, vibrant red bougainvilleas.

The petals reminded Searra of drops of blood. In the light of the moon, the red was much deeper, richer, and the contrast of the ornate black structure was stunning and intense. Beneath the pergola sat a gigantic U-shaped white couch with a wrought iron fire pit in the center. Searra plonked down and put her feet up.

"One minute." Juan teased as he held up one finger, his face alight with mischief. Searra couldn't help the smile pulling at her lips. She liked him less serious. Then he was gone in a burst of vampire speed, and only wind and the scent of citrus and bergamot wafted around her. Her dark hair whipped around in a mini cyclone, but another strong gust of wind sent it all flying before her hair settled.

Juan had sat right beside her, his ankle resting on his knee. He had put on a deep burgundy turtleneck sweater. It brought out the green in his eyes; they were so vibrant that they glowed in the starlight. His sweater clung to him like a velvety sheen of sweat and every dip and curve of his muscled torso was on display and rippled as he moved.

Searra bit the inside of her cheek to distract herself. If she didn't rein in her thoughts, they may end up doing more than "planning" under those stars.

"You changed?" Searra's voice came out squeaky, like a teenage boy's during puberty. Her cheeks pinked as she cleared her throat, but not before she caught Juan's self-satisfied smirk.

Searra's hand collided with his hard chest as she gave him a smack. She meant it in jest, but her newfound strength ripped an "Ooof!" from him, which was covered with a cough.

"My shirt was not up to my usual standards."

A smile played at the corners of her mouth despite herself and she agreed, "Yeah, blood and burn juice isn't the best accessory."

Juan burst out in a deep, genuine laugh. The sound was so sweet that Searra's toes curled, and her grin widened. She vowed to herself then and there that it was her mission in life to make him laugh. It was decidedly the most beautiful sound she had ever heard, and she would listen to it all day if she could.

She cleared her throat, trying to stay focused, "I don't know how far into the future my vision was, but it had to be close. Jade was wearing the same outfit she is wearing now." Searra nodded with her chin in the direction of the house. Even talking about her vision gave her chills of dread that crawled up her spine and made her nauseous. The smile evaporated from her face like smoke.

Juan leaned in so their sides were touching. "Hey." His voice came soft, low. He reached up, tucking a lock of dark brown hair behind her ear. The gentle graze of his fingers lit sparks of pleasure beneath her skin.

"Maybe we should change her outfit too?" Juan suggested. He shrugged, broad shoulders rolling. But his voice had dropped an octave, rougher now, gravel threaded through every word. His eyes had darkened, lids heavy. A muscle ticked in his jaw. He looked like he was holding himself back—yet his fingers stayed tangled in her hair, unwilling to let go.

Searra chuckled, her concentration wavering, "If only it were that easy." Her gaze shot to his, an idea sparking in her chest. "Is it?!"

His dark brows raised, creasing his forehead, like time itself had carved them. "Divination is more art than science. So, there is no way to tell if a small change is enough to change the course of a vision. But, every little change we make is thought to help chart a new course." Juan offered as he scanned Searra's face, eyes searching hers as his fingers moved from her hair to trace the line of her jaw.

She swallowed, primal desire clogging her throat.

"We need backup." Searra managed to say, trying to ignore the sparks of pleasure moving from her chin, down her neck, and peaking her nipples. They rubbed against the fabric of her bra, which only made them harder.

"Who do you have in mind?" Juan asked, his brow raised and skepticism coloring his voice. His sharp teeth bit into his bottom lip as he presented her with a heart-stopping smile.

She gave him side eye. *Like he didn't already know.*

"My in-laws, but you knew that," Searra stated with a throaty huff. "I counted three witches and three wolves, just between Diego and his siblings. That *has* to be enough protection. At least for now. " She raked her hands through her thick, dark hair. Nervous energy coiled in her legs, until they began to bounce while she sat.

"But will they work with us?" Juan asked, his smile waning a bit, his fangs glinting at her in the starlight.

"I hope so," Searra said. It was a desperate plea. An ideal. She needed Diego's family to protect her daughter, just not from her.

"I think I know who I should approach first," Searra said scratching her chin. There was one member of the family who hadn't been at that meeting. Searra needed to talk to Rizos. If he vouched for her, the others would follow. Diego had to help too, but she didn't want to face him again. Not now, but she knew she had to.

All of this was his fault in the first place.

The reason she was no longer human.

Searra was a practiced avoider; she could dodge him until hell froze over.

Is that what she wanted? Searra didn't know.

The stars above their heads peeked through the thorny vines wrapping around the top of the pergola. They twinkled down at her in greeting. As if they knew she was now something eternal, too. Even though stars did eventually die. Earth was just so far away that its light still shone even after death. Were stars just another type of vampire? Only celestial?

The wind whipped her hair, carrying a chill but Searra didn't care. She'd changed earlier, ditching pajamas for bright pink leggings that hugged her big butt just right and snatched her waist and a crop top patterned with monarch butterflies. No sweater needed.

A perk of being a vampire: weather didn't matter. Not that it ever had, she was Southern Californian, born and bred.

Unless you were a weather nerd.

Diego was a weather nerd.

Her heart squeezed thinking about him. Remembering how excited he was to tell her whenever the weather was changing, when there was a heat wave or crazy winds.

Especially when there was rain.

He used to sit at the bar he built on their back porch for hours. Listening to the rain. Sipping a Modelo. A plate of salt and lime slices nearby, along with one tall shot of tequila.

He would rush her outside to hear the pitter-patter of rain as it hit the cement. Diego would come up behind her, pulling her into a tight hug and he'd breathe her in while she watched the storm. Together, they stood and inhaled the crisp, wet air, soothed by the white noise blanketing the world.

Content. They had been happy.

The familiar wet sting pricked the corners of her eyes and she blinked hard to clear them away.

Look at where they were now.

Her chest caved in with a desperate heaviness she felt in her heart.

How did they get here?

The soft pad of Juan's thumb wiped away the tears. Searra had been so lost in thought, she had forgotten where she was. Her eyes widened as she drank him in. His sandy brown hair was tousled and hung in his eyes, casting those familiar shadows. Juan's expression was unreadable, but she caught a muscle tightening in his jaw. His perfect mouth had set in a grim line as his gaze hardened into cutting gemstones.

Searra realized Juan must have gleaned her thoughts. In that moment, it felt like a violation. These were things she was still sifting through, still trying to confront. She wasn't ready to share these thoughts. Not with anyone.

"Get out of my head." Searra bit out. Her voice

sounded sharper than she intended. She wasn't even mad at Juan, not really. But, she couldn't control her mouth when she was heated. Impulsive to a fault. Even when the person she was angry with, was herself.

She didn't look at Juan. She cast her face downward, fixed on her white-and-pink sneakers. Her anger already fading.

Juan stood, taking a few steps away.

The lack of contact left Searra cold. She wanted to reach out, to reclaim the connection but her body wouldn't move. Her limbs felt like stone, weighted down by stubbornness, paralyzed by anxiety. She sank into a mental mud pit, like quicksand. A familiar, thick mire she welcomed.

Juan paced in front of her, like he was working out the words he needed to say.

She let him and said nothing.

His pacing filled the air with anxious energy. A static charge like before a lightning storm. Her nerves buzzed, jittery, as if she had drunk a whole pot of coffee. She swore sparks would start soon, the air was so charged.

Halting, Juan took a deep breath, and faced her, "Searra," her name was a tender caress on his lips, but she also sensed the rawness... the vulnerability.

Her gaze slid up to meet his. She was lost instantly. Swallowed by forest green eyes brimming with emotion so intense she forgot how to breathe. He continued, "I'm s—"

"What are you guys doing out here?" A booming, familiar voice called from the dark brush beyond the property.

Searra would recognize that voice in her sleep. She turned toward it, spotting his heat signature in the shadowed vegetation. Even his silhouette, the way it moved, was unmistakable.

Diego.

CHAPTER 29

ESPOSO (HUSBAND)

"THE WORLD SEEMS FULL OF GOOD MEN—EVEN IF THERE ARE MONSTERS IN IT." - BRAM STOKER (1897)

"Hope I'm not interrupting anything," Diego said as he joined them under the pergola. His shoulders were loose, his grin easy, if not sharp at the edges. Teeth gleamed large and bright in the darkening night, almost too perfect, like veneers. But that megawatt smile was all his own.

"What are you doing here?" The words slipped out before Searra could stop them. Harsh. Rude, maybe? But she didn't care. His presence grated on her nerves. That fact, more than anything, shocked her.

A flicker of hurt flashed across his face, only

to smother it under an even more brilliant smile. His tone was deceptively cheery, "I came to hang with Jade." All teeth and thick dark brows.

Oh shit. Searra's brows knitted together. *That's right.*

It had slipped from her memory.

Of course, he wanted to see Jade.

Her nightmare vision had scrambled her brain.

Searra rubbed the front of her head with the heel of her hand. The building pressure of a tension headache began to pulse behind her eyes. "Shit. Sorry. My mind is kinda all over the place right now." She offered Diego a small smile.

"Yeah," Diego said as he looked down at the ground and studied his Air Force Ones. Both hands were resting in the back pockets of his worn black jeans. His black V-neck shirt hugged his pecks and arms in a way she hadn't seen before. In addition to having thicker hair, he was much bigger than he had been almost two years ago. Searra was staring hard as the silence stretched.

Diego cleared his throat and it echoed in the awkward silence. Searra's startled gaze jumped to his dark brown ones and they were crinkled with amusement. He looked so much younger when he smiled, and cocky as fuck. The weight on her heart lifted a little as a giggle burst from her throat. The tension bubble between them burst and relief washed over her. A genuine smile tugged at the corners of her mouth.

"Fuck. Come on. She is inside with my mom and sister." Searra jumped up, slapping her thighs as she did, and turned towards the house. She looked back at Juan, who was following behind her. He was quiet and his face was like stone. They would need to finish their conversation later, but she wanted to reassure him that she wasn't mad anymore. She could get heated quickly and burn out just as fast.

I'm sorry too. She said in her mind, hoping he was still listening and not taking her outburst to heart.

A sudden high pitched screech came from the dark sky above them, followed by a strange hollow clacking, like banging two wooden clogs together. Searra's head whipped toward the sound. *Was that a bird?* She didn't know why, but the call made her blood run cold and the hairs on her arms stood up. Searra held her breath and listened harder, both Juan and Diego seemed to fall silent, listening too.

Then a blood-curdling scream cut through the night. It came from the house. Ice chilled in her veins as a sharp shiver of fear skittered up her spine. She recognized the voice, it was her mom. A cold stone lump dropped in her gut.

Searra ran.

Chapter 30

Hija (Daughter)

Searra cut through the air as fast as her vampiric speed allowed— feet barely touching the ground. Everything around her was a blur and in slow motion simultaneously. Her own fear coated her tongue and acid roiled in her stomach.

Not Jade. Not Jade. Not Jade.

A prayer. She never prayed, but that was what this was.

A prayer... a wish... a hope.

Juan and Diego chased close behind, moving just as fast. Only blurs of watercolors bleeding into the night.

Searra was the first one to reach the back door. Her eyes scanned the house for heat signatures. There was only one, waining on the floor in the living room.

Panic clawed up her throat and made it hard to breathe.

She wouldn't believe it.

She had to see.

Searra gripped the handle of the sliding glass door and shoved. It slammed into the frame with bone-rattling force, shattering in its casing. The bang echoed through her skull, drowning out every other sound.

She bolted through the doorway, into the kitchen and then living room. Searra froze in her tracks. Two purple Crocs jutted out from behind the couch. Winnie the Pooh Jibbitz splattered in blood.

Momma? Her ears started to ring. *This couldn't be happening.*

Searra wasn't moving, or breathing. She was paralyzed, not even present in her body. Staring at those purple Crocs, willing them to move.

And then someone was screaming.

It was Searra, she was screaming. The cries ripped from her throat like death itself had reached in and clawed it out.

Then she was moving in a possessed frenzy until she was kneeling over her mom. Her body was crumpled in a misshapen mess but she was breathing.

She was still alive.

Hope bloomed in her chest as she reached out for her.

"Ma! Ma! Can you hear me?" Searra said through shaky breaths.

Diego was on the floor in an instant next to Searra, blocking her when she reached out to grab her mom.

Searra shot daggers at him— sharp accusation in her stare.

"Look at her. There are definitely broken bones. We can't move her." Diego insisted.

Searra looked down at her mom's crumpled form. So small. *When had she become so small?* The chemo had taken weight, but Searra hadn't seen when it stole her strength, when it made her fragile. Like a broken doll.

She'd been thrown against the wall. Now she lay in a heap on the ground. A dent marred the plaster where her body struck.

Searra winced.

"There's blood." Searra's voice was only a throaty whisper. Tears clogged her airway. Diego looked at her, only sympathy in his dark eyes.

"It's not hers." Juan's deep voice came from behind them. "There is no one else in the house." Searra's brain was moving at a glacial pace.

Of course. Smart to check the house. She nodded to herself. *But that also meant... Jade and her sister...*

"The *pinche* [1] blood suckers," Diego swore under his breath. "*Chingada madre.*" [2] He was trying to move her mom as little as possible and still check her injuries. "Sisi... I don't think—" Diego started in a hushed tone but a loud cough ripped through her

---

1. fucking

2. Motherfucker.

mom's contorted body, cutting him off. Searra lurched forward to cradle her. Diego couldn't stop her this time.

"Ma! Ma! It's okay. You're gonna be okay! You hear me? Ma!" Searra's voice trembled. Her hands caressed the sparse tufts of hair on her mom's balding head. Strands came away with each stroke. Searra stared at the bleach blonde strands clinging to her palm.

Numb.

Her mom looked up at her, her dark eyes were small and clouded. "It's okay sweetie." Her voice was thin, the ghost of a whisper.

"Ma. It's gonna be okay." She wasn't sure who she was trying to convince more, herself or her mom. Like lightning, she had a sudden and desperate thought and looked to Juan.

Juan's mouth was set in a grim line. *No.* The thought echoed inside her mind with finality.

Hot tears pricked her cheeks as she said, "No! But, but... You can turn her!" Her desperation was so palpable you could taste it in the air.

"Searra..." Juan began, his voice gentle.

Searra's mom began to cough again. Blood was ringing around the inside of her mouth. "No. Sisi. No..."

"But Ma — we" Searra started, tears running down her face now.

"No. The baby—" Her breathing was labored. "They took the baby."

"I know Ma. It's okay. We are going to get her back." Searra said and tried to smile, but the muscles felt foreign, like they were made of stone. Her face was just wet and cold.

"Good. You better." She seemed so far away, her voice only a whisp of breath. "Poor... little one..."

Searra watched as her mom exhaled and her mouth hung open. A drop of bright red blood gathered at the corners and began to spider-web out into the creases around her thin lips.

She did not inhale again.

The light left her yellowed eyes and she was so still.

"Ma. Ma!" Searra screamed, her voice broke and her throat felt raw and sore. Her head was fuzzy, like thousands of flies were buzzing around in her brain.

How is this happening? This can't be happening.

Strong arms gripped her shoulders, pulling her in, and she sagged into them. She sobbed into his black T-shirt, arms searching for anything to grab, anything to keep her steady as a wail of grief raked its way through her chest, escaping as a pitiful specter of a scream.

Warm hands were in her hair, cradling her head as she buried her face in his shirt. Teak and vanilla bourbon hit her nose, along with the sharp stench of dog, but she didn't care.

His strong heartbeat, a droning rhythm she latched onto as another sob wracked her body, as an unstoppable wave of loss crashed into her again and again.

The sounds she made were broken.

Sounds she didn't recognize.

Jade and her sister were taken.

Her mother was dead.

And Searra had no idea what to do next.

CHAPTER 31

BROKEN

Searra couldn't feel anything. She just sat there, on the floor. Numb. Her mother's head cradled in her lap. The weight anchored her to the spot and she didn't dare move.

"I didn't think vampires could cry," Diego whispered under his breath in disbelief.

"It's rare," Juan confirmed, his voice reverent.

Searra wiped her face, pulling her hand away to reveal ruby red streaks of blood on her fingers.

Diego looked at Juan, and nodded to Searra, "That normal?" There was a cold bite to his voice Searra hadn't heard before.

Was his vitriol directed at her, or Juan?

Searra looked to Juan. His brows were pinched and his green eyes were clouded. "You have crossed over. You are a true vampire now." Juan looked at the ground and hung his head with what looked like shame.

She tried to absorb it, tried to take in the words. But she was already beyond normal capacity for coping and felt herself engage in autopilot. She was dissociating, and this was *really* not the time.

"Sisi. We need to move. Now." Diego's voice had a steel edge to it as he growled out, "We need to get *my daughter* back." His dark eyes glowed with menace. His veined forearms began to swell as claws elongated from his fingertips. A low growl emanated from his throat, and his bright smile erupted with rows of sharp canine teeth dripping with thick drool. The sound of his heavy breathing filled the room's silence.

The silence in her head.

In a daze, Searra looked through him, only seeing Jade in her mind's eye. Sitting on the dirty wooden floor, crying for her, all alone.

These weren't intrusive thoughts, *it was happening now.* She reminded herself.

Her baby needed her.

Adrenaline surged through her — chest heaving. She looked down. Her mother's still expression blurred as hot tears pricked her eyes and clogged her throat.

Her dark, almond-shaped eyes were semi-open, the whites having yellowed with age and the chemo treatments. Her lashes were gone, another side effect of the medication. Searra brought a shaking hand to her mother's face. With trembling fingers, she eased the naked lids closed. Her thin mouth was agape, but no air passed through to her lungs. The blood staining her lips like a macabre beauty trend.

"I'm sorry Ma," Searra whispered to her, with a kiss on her forehead, lips brushing against the low outline of peach fuzz from her widow's peak.

Baby orangutan, Searra thought and a strangled laugh escaped from her, clinging to the stupid joke, the last joke she'd made to her mom.

"I'll be back for you, okay?" Searra told her mother's body. "I'm gonna go get our baby girl back." She breathed, and her body began to shake with anger, "I'm going to kill them all." Her fangs elongated, the sharp tips poking into her full bottom lip.

A low hiss reverberated from her throat, a sound she did not recognize.

Feral.

Full of rage, full of fear. She couldn't let her mind linger on Jade, on all the possibilities of if she was even still... *She couldn't.* Wouldn't finish that thought. She had to turn off that part of her brain. Otherwise, she would be sick, she would be paralyzed in her own dread and panic. Right now she needed to act.

That was when she noticed a strange spotted feather, stained red with her mother's blood. It was so long, longer than a quill. With a shaking hand, she picked it up and twirled it between her fingers. Examining it, as though it held some mystery for her to solve, but her brain could not make sense of it.

She looked at Juan, who had gone deathly pale, eyes

wide. *"Las lechusas..."*[1] He whispered.

Diego's eyes went wide, "The fuck? Those are not real!"

Searra looked up at them, the feather smearing blood on the pads of her fingers. "THEN. WHAT. IS. THIS?" Her tone was sharp and forceful, like a blade, as she held the large feather to his face. It might have looked like a normal bird feather, if the bird were the size of a human.

Digeo stared at it, his words caught in his throat.

"They work for Ambrose, for The Council. *Brujas*[2] that sold their souls." Juan's voice was calm but she felt the tension coming off of him in waves. "They are referred to as "The Birds.""

A spark of memory at that name flooded Searra's mind. She had heard Liv say that very thing to Juan. Anger clouded her vision, and that familiar warmth rose in her chest, spreading through her veins with her rising anger and she pulled at it, stoked the flames... let them grow. Searra was starting to find this new power... comforting.

Searra was on her feet in an instant. She whipped her head to Juan as her hair began to float around her, power exuding from her very pores, "Where are they taking her? Best guess for that chamber." She ran her tongue along her teeth, feeling out her fangs with it.

---

1. a witch who can transform into a large owl (often a barn owl) to stalk and terrorize people at night.

2. witches

Talking was going to be an adjustment.

Juan nodded, his green eyes flashed with awe, his gaze dropping to her mouth and quickly back up to her eyes, "If memory serves, it's in Artesia. A decrepit Portuguese hall— that stage, I've seen it before."

"What? Why?" Diego fired off the questions in quick succession, disgust and disbelief lacing every word. If Searra hadn't been so pissed, she might've laughed— hearing that outrage spill from his half-wolf form, mouth full of teeth.

They were all monsters now.

"Not a lot of foot traffic to draw attention. But the Portuguese roots in Artesia run deep, as deep as the vampire connection." Juan explained in an even tone.

"They made a deal with the *blood suckers?*" The shock in Diego's tone was evident but because he was half in his wolf form, most of his words came out as sinister growls through his sharp teeth.

"It's mutually beneficial." Juan gave him a sharp smile and took a deep breath, and exhaled through his flared nostrils, annoyed with Diego's questions. "The council bought swathes of land outright almost one hundred years ago, including the land on which the club was built. So ... choice was an illusion." He paused, a humorless smile pasted on his face. "If they wanted to keep their club space." Juan shrugged his massive shoulders. "Real Estate in California is brutal." He cut a sharp grin at Diego. 'Plus, dissenters were always dealt with."

"And the vampires don't eat— " Searra started to ask, but Juan seemed to already know where she was going and answered.

"No. The club rents out for parties and weddings. Any drunken guests that happen to stumble off into the dark..." His smile was ruthless as his fangs glinted at her, silence swallowing the rest of his words.

Searra's blanched.

"But no one touches the club members," Juan assured. "It's part of the deal, an unspoken arrangement."

Searra tried to shake off her disgust and looked to Diego. "Can you send the address to your siblings? Tell them to meet us there."

Diego looked ready to protest, but Searra raised a hand to silence him. Heat flared in her dark brown eyes, like swirling infernos on the surface of the sun. "They're her family. We need all the strength we can get. They can put aside how they feel about me for one night to come through for her." Searra held Diego's gaze, watching the gears turn behind his dark eyes.

At last, he gave her a solemn nod and pulled out his phone.

Diego strode out of the room, phone up to his ear... his claw awkwardly wrapped around it. Hopefully, he didn't crush it trying to hang up or rip through the touch screen.

Searra looked again at Juan, "They have my sister too."

Juan was silent, waiting for her to finish her thought.

"Why do they want her?" Searra continued, eyes flashing like a reflective surface under direct sunlight. When her gaze landed on Juan, he flinched away.

"Sorry," Juan looked sheepish. "I can feel your power burning me, even now."

His green eyes flicked to hers again. "I'm starting to like it." He gave a mischievous side smile, one that lit his whole face and made her heart squeeze.

The heat left her in the same instant, and her chocolate brown eyes blinked at him.

Juan reached out to cup her face and pull her closer. "Even with the burning light of a thousand suns, I cannot resist falling into your deep brown gaze." He leaned his head down to hers and gave her a chaste kiss. His lips lingered on hers for a moment before he pulled back to look into her eyes. Even though it was quick, she felt it deep.

Juan brought his lips to her ear and whispered, "Consider me in awe, *vida*.[3] You are stunning. A warrior goddess made flesh." Juan was looking at her with such reverence, that her cheeks flushed. She didn't even think vampires could still blush, but here she was, turning into a strawberry.

Diego coughed, making Searra jump. A lump stuck in her throat. One look at him, and a crushing guilt crashed over her, and her gaze fell to the ground. Diego was looking more human than wolf now, so his siblings must have succeeded in calming him down. It was a good sign.

Diego put his phone in the back pocket of his black jeans. His mouth was a tight line and his jaw flexed hard enough to break teeth.

"Diego —" Searra started. She reached out to touch

---

3. Life (term of endearment)

his shoulder but he pulled away, his face unreadable. His dark eyes looked past her, to Juan, venom in his gaze.

Searra tried again, her heart in a vise. "Diego, it's not what it —"

"Let's just focus on Jade." His voice cut her as he stared daggers at Juan.

Juan stepped forward, his face an unreadable mask, "We need to put this all aside until Jade is safe."

With that, Diego's cold look of indignation went from chipped ice to molten lava. Fire burned in his gaze. "The fuck?!" Only pure fury in his tone. "Who are *you* to be saying anything right now? Jade is *my* daughter." His eyes flamed a wolfish yellow and his teeth elongated into rows of razor-sharp fangs. "You don't think I would do anything to protect her? To save her from *pinches malditos*[4] like you?!"

Diego had stepped forward, invading Juan's personal space. "How do we even know we can trust you?" Diego shot a glance at Searra before landing his scorching gaze back on Juan. "I mean how the fuck did this council know where to find them?" His dark brows were raised and had grown bushier the longer he spoke. "Who else knew they were here? Just us, and *you!*" Diego's voice reverberated in the air, his gruff half-wolf voice like a bass she felt in her chest.

Juan stepped forward, a storm in his lethal gaze. "I would not betray Searra or Jade." His fangs erupted

---

4. Fucking bastards

like a snake fit to strike. "I would *die* first." Juan hissed at him through his teeth.

"The fuck you would! Your kind don't give a shit about anyone but yourselves!" Diego spat.

Without warning, he swung at Juan, the blow landing squarely on Juan's jaw. The impact sent Juan tumbling back a few steps. His arms flailed for balance, but Diego didn't give him the chance. He lunged, hands morphing into claws sharp enough to slice through flesh.

They crashed to the floor together. Juan's back smacked the wood floors with a sharp, sickening crack. The air punched out of his chest in a ragged gasp.

Diego's claws sank into Juan's shoulders, *like fucking meat hooks*. They dug around his collarbone, blood soaking Juan's burgundy turtleneck a wet shade of red.

Searra moved on instinct. She lunged, arms clamping around Diego's thickening neck. His body already warping, mid-shift — fur sprouting, bones cracking. Any second now, they would have a full-blown, horse-sized wolf to contend with.

She locked her arm around his throat, forearm, and bicep, squeezing tight. Diego began to thrash, his claws tearing free of Juan as he swung toward her, desperate to dislodge her.

"Stop Diego!" Her voice boomed.

His long, blackened claws swiped at her in slow motion. Searra braced for impact, for the pain. Her muscles locked, pressure unrelenting on his windpipe. She clung to him like a rider on a bucking bull in some rundown dive bar.

It was only a matter of time. Either Diego gave in... or passed out.

How long would it take to cut off a werewolf's air supply? That was probably something she should have thought about sooner, but *oh well.*

Searra squeezed her eyes shut, bracing for the pain as those vicious claws plunged toward her flesh. But the impact never came.

The scent hit first — cedar, citrus, and the sharp sweetness of hot blood.

She opened her eyes as Juan stood over them, Diego's claws gripped tight in his hands, held inches from her face. Relief flooded her chest in a dizzying rush, and she let out a ragged, trembling breath as she took him in.

Juan's burgundy sweater was glistening in the light, like the surface of a pond. He was sparkling. A majestic warrior straight out of a dark, twisted fairytale. But that was his own blood he was bathed in. The fabric was soaked in it.

Diego was grunting like a pissed off boar, and Searra's muscles were straining to keep the tension required for the chokehold, and she began to shake with the effort.

Diego's face contorted, bones cracking as his snout elongated into the skull-crushing muzzle of the *nahuaƂ* wolf. Hot, fetid breath washed over her, thick and sour, as he wheezed for air beneath the relentless press of her elbow.

Warm drool dripped from his gaping maw onto her

---

5. Witch shifter

arm. Searra paled. Acid in her throat as she gagged, barely choking it down before she almost vomited all over him. Her heightened senses made it worse, every stench magnified, every drop burning into memory.

Juan grunted as Diego shoved against his grip, raw strength straining between them. Searra held on, refusing to loosen her hold. She prayed Juan wouldn't either.

Diego couldn't keep this up forever. He'd eventually tire. Or black out.

Diego gave another strong buck, trying to throw her off. To tighten her hold, she wrapped her leg around him, trapping one foot, and began to squeeze him with her powerful thighs. Between the two of them, Diego's breathing became more labored and his thrashing weakened.

Searra whispered in his ear, "I don't want to hurt you, but you need to calm down! Stop moving and I'll let go." Her voice was stern, but the wolf stiffened beneath her and relaxed almost imperceptibly. Searra took that cue and released his throat, scooting back in the process in case he decided to swipe at her at the last second.

Juan had let Diego's arms go as well and stepped away to stand by her side. The coppery citrus came off of him in waves, filling her nose. A pang of hunger hit her stomach. She felt emptier than the plot of a porno movie. Searra pushed the feeling down, needing to focus on getting Diego in line. But she couldn't help when her gaze slid to Juan's. He was looking at her, his green eyes heated. Adrenaline spiked in her system as she looked back at Diego, her cheeks pink.

He was on the floor, hacking up a lung.

Searra flinched at every subsequent cough.

No longer in his wolf form. His black jeans and tee were in tatters from transforming while still clothed. Tanned muscle roped around his arms and thighs. She noticed his chest seemed wider than she'd remembered ...and much hairier.

Wolf genes...

"The fuck, Sisi..." Diego rasped between coughs, his hand massaging his throat. A red ring bloomed in the expanse of his neck, darkening the longer she stared. A Searra-shaped bruise. Diego's Adam's apple bobbed. Her gaze snapped to his. Confusion flickered there. Pain. But most of all... betrayal.

The knife she seemed to have plunged into her own heart twisted in her chest. The sting welled in her eyes.

"I'm sorry, but we don't have time for this. I trust Juan, and he could have killed you just now." Searra's frustration was threatening to manifest in hot red tears, but she managed to rein them in. "We have to go NOW." Searra insisted, moving toward the front door. She couldn't think of anything else. Her baby girl needed her and that anxiety was threatening to overwhelm her. Searra had to keep moving. "Are you cool enough to ride with us?" Searra glanced over her shoulder, back to Diego.

He was already on his feet, moving toward her with an expression carved from the stone these past two years had hardened in him.

Diego didn't stop. His shoulder slammed into hers as he passed, knocking her back a step. He stormed out the front door without a word or even glancing back.

"I'll find my own way there," Diego growled to the cool night air; his own voice adding to the chill.

Searra let out a shaky breath. She hated how much Diego was hurting... but so was she.

If she lost Jade too...

She shook her head, trying to dispel those thoughts from her head. She wouldn't spiral now. Jade needed her.

Searra tried to calm herself down, to ground herself in the physical world. She felt her feet in her sneakers and wiggled her toes, a soreness that was beginning to throb in her elbow. She might have twisted something or have a nasty bruise later.

Did vampires even get bruises?

She was starting to feel grounded again — back in her body, back in the moment.

Inside the house, Juan emerged from the hallway leading to his bedroom, tugging a black tee over freshly mended skin.

"Are you okay?" Searra asked, warmth coloring her voice.

"Yeah." Juan gave a sardonic chuckle, fangs glinting with his dry smile. "Good as new."

"I'm sorry about Diego," Searra said, her gaze drifting from Juan to the bloodstains behind him on the hardwood floors.

That would stain if they didn't clean it soon.

Something caught her eye in the blood, something gold.

Crossing the room in long strides, Searra looked down and saw it was a golden ring. Goosebumps pebbled her flesh as recognition flashed through her. She bent down to pick it up.

Diego's wedding ring.

Chapter
32

Fortune

Her husband's wedding band, covered in the blood of her mate.

The moment the cool metal touched her skin, she felt as though she were falling... falling through that pitch-black void she was becoming all too familiar with.

The room with Juan faded around her into darkness. A dim light led her down a familiar tunnel, and the familiar stench of moldy stone wafted to her nose. Sound was muffled as her pink running shoes waded in an inch of cloudy gray water.

She was underground again, walking through

the tunnel leading to The Council's chambers.

There was a sudden bang, like a bomb had gone off on the other side of the stone walls. Searra burst into a run, scaling the tunnel with her vampire speed, only a blur to anyone watching her.

She reached the end of the stone hallway and stared at that familiar wooden door that haunted the inner recesses of her thoughts. Her hand hovered over the eroded steel knocker. She gripped the cold metal as it leeched into her flesh, and pulled the door open. Even with her vampire strength, it was an effort to get the door to move.

Inside the chamber, chaos reigned.

Searra saw herself, Juan, and Diego — backs pressed together in the center of the wooden ballroom. Figures in dark, billowing cloaks swarmed them from every side.

Members of the Vampire Council.

It had to be.

In the center of the chamber, Searra glowed like a holy beacon, her dark hair floating around her as though she were swimming underwater. It was unbelievable and hard to look away.

She dragged her eyes from the scene and found Juan. Breathtaking in his own right.

In his hands, his long sword gleamed, daylight playing off the emerald stone embedded in the pommel. Flaming light shimmered along its two-sided blade. It was the same ethereal glow that burned deep inside Searra.

Was she able to transfer her power to weapons?

This was one way to find out.

Searra looked back at herself, meeting her own eyes.

The recognition she saw unnerved her.

Could she see herself? Was she actually here? Was this not a vision?

Future Searra nodded imperceptibly, as if in answer to her internal question, and flicked her eyes to the stage, as though urging her to look that way.

Tearing her gaze away, Future Searra spun back into the fight.

A hulking vampire lunged onto Diego's back and Future Searra seized the beast by the leg, yanking it off in one swift motion. Her hand blazed with white, daylight power.

The vampire let out an ear-piercing shriek of pain. It was otherworldly, like nothing Searra had ever heard before. A high-pitched screech, part creature and part demon. Goosebumps rippled over Searra's skin, the sound leaving her a little dizzy.

Searra scanned the stage and spotted her sister in the corner, with thick chains on her wrists attached to the wall. She was covered in bite marks. From what she could see, the two deepest ones were on her inner thighs and neck. Syd was awake, but her eyes were glassy. Blood was dripping from the chains on her wrists.

Next to her was Jade... trapped in the steel cage. Adrenaline spiked in Searra's veins. Her body screamed to sprint, to tear that door open, but she froze. Sneakers squeaked against the wooden floor as hesitation rooted her in place.

Searra noticed no one was guarding them. If her future self could see her, there was a good chance others could too. Crouching down, she crept quietly from the door into the stands.

She took the steps two at a time, her pink sneakers squelched with every step since they were still soaked with dirty tunnel water. She kept herself low once she got to the landing.

A low, reverberating growl echoed from the tunnel as more creatures jumped into battle. She looked through the benches and caught sight of Nayeli and Josué barging in. Both were half-transformed.

Josué let out a huge roar. Bones popped. Crunched. The sickening sound echoed through the wood–clad chamber.

His black tee was shredded. Gray sweatpants split apart, falling to the floor in useless tatters. Thick ebony fur erupted across his skin, swallowing him entirely.

Then the wolf rose.

Darker than shadow. Larger than Diego's. A creature born for war.

The stench of dog burned Searra's nose as Nayeli joined Josué.

Her mouth elongated first — teeth sprouting in jagged rows, bone–crushing and unending.

Dark eyes ignited with animal fury.

Searra watched as Nayeli surrendered to the change. Anger bled into something wilder.

A beast no one could control.

She lunged at the vampires, feral and unstoppable. Her jaws clamped around a massive one, lifting him like a ragged dog toy. Eli shook the vampire with savage violence. The motion was relentless — side to side, like a predator breaking the neck of its prey.

Centrifugal pressure ripped through flesh and bone. The sound split the air. Wet. Fibrous. Obscene.

Her jaws clamped tighter, bone splintering between her teeth like toothpicks. A sharp crack echoed, followed by another.

The vampire's torso twisted unnaturally, pulling apart at the seams. Limbs dangled uselessly before tearing free altogether, blood arcing through the air in wide, crimson fans.

When Eli finally stopped shaking, nothing whole remained in her jaws.

Searra was nearly at the stage now. The last row of elevated seating loomed behind her. Metal benches that reminded her of the school bleachers she used to dread during pep rallies.

She crept down the narrow stairs at the back, each step groaning under her weight. The staircase hugged the side of the bleachers, leading straight toward the edge of the stage.

Searra ducked behind the deep red curtains bunched up in the corner, slowly making her way up the short set of steps that led to the stage.

A loud bang shook the ground beneath her and she heard Jade scream in fright.

Searra turned to see Josué's gigantic black wolf had been thrown clear across the room, through the side wall of wood and stone. A sharp whine rang out as he tried to stand, but failed.

He couldn't.

There were three horrific creatures, vampires, closing in on him as he attempted to rise. Their true faces were showing: bumpy, demonic ridges across their brows and glowing yellow eyes. Their fangs were dripping with anticipatory saliva as they closed the distance between them and Josué's broken form.

Searra looked around for anyone to help.

Eli was trying to shake off two vampires that were hanging onto her by fistfuls of her dark fur.

Searra saw herself a few paces away.

One vampire had her by the hair, yanking her head back with vicious force. Another lunged low, clawed hands snatching for her feet.

Juan was pinned against the wall by an especially menacing-looking vampire, his glowing sword pressed to his own neck as they struggled for dominance. Sweat gleamed on Juan's forehead, tiny rubies sparkling in the light of the blade.

Diego was still in human form, sprawled on the ground. His forearms lifted to shield his face as a red-haired vampire stood over him, raining blow after blow.

Searra knew that face.

Recognized it.

Liv.

The redhead's face contorted into something monstrous. No trace of the delicate beauty Searra once saw. The demon beneath her skin was bare now, grinning as she drove her fists down in a relentless storm. Each blow cracked through the air, sharp and wet, the sound of flesh meeting flesh. Diego's body jolted under every strike.

No one would be able to help Josué.

Searra looked back, Jade was only a few feet away. If she could just grab her and get her somewhere safe, she would come back for Josué. By then, it might be too late.

Searra took a deep breath.

She would kill them all.

Searra twisted on her heel and broke into a sprint across the room toward Josué and the vampires surrounding him. Warmth bloomed in her chest as she ran, and she focused on it, urging it to grow. Her sneakers squealed against the hardwood floor as she gained speed. She willed the heat into her hands and stopped just behind the group of vampires.

A guttural rage-filled scream ripped from her and echoed throughout the chamber. Light shot from her hands, bathing the three vampires in all her anger, frustration, and sadness.

The vampires shrieked as Searra's light seared their flesh.

High pitched. Half creature, half demon. The sound carved straight through her bones. They writhed, thrashing against the invisible fire consuming them from the inside out. The stench hit next—burning flesh, acrid and thick in the air.

Searra swallowed, fighting back the urge to gag.

Their charred husks collapsed to the floor with a dull thud. Smoke curled from blackened limbs. Searra lifted her gaze — straight into the burning eyes of Josué's massive wolf. Confusion and gratitude in their dark depths.

Time began to press down on her. She didn't have much more of it. If this was anything like her other visions, she could be pulled away at any moment.

She spun on her heel and bolted for the stage, vampiric speed turning her into a blur.

In one bound, she cleared the lip of the platform and landed hard, knees bending to absorb the impact.

Please, let them stay distracted. Let no one follow.

Both Syd and Jade were still behind the curtains

on stage. Her sister was staring at her, eyes no longer clouded, still chained against the wall. Syd's gaze was penetrating. Cutting. The scent of fear permeating the air around her was palpable, and a little intoxicating, like sweet candy.

"Momma! Momma! Momma!" Jade's scream echoed through the chamber and Searra winced, hoping that no one was paying attention.

"*Sí,*[1] Sweetie pie. Momma is here." The blood-red tears threatened the corners of her vision, but she held back the flood with only bald-faced will and adrenaline. "I'm getting you out of here *mi vida.*[2] You're safe, okay?" Searra soothed, her voice quivering.

Jade's tiny hands poked through the bars of the rusted metal cage, reaching for Searra. Her little pink face was dirty and her diaper was bulging. Searra's heart sank seeing Jade's delicate skin touch the filthy wooden floor of the stage. Her eyes pricked again with wet heat, willing herself not to cry. The last thing she wanted to do was scare Jade with her bloody tears.

"It's okay sweetie. Mommy is here. Mommy is here." Searra soothed, chanted like a prayer. Trying to calm Jade down long enough to free her sister. Searra moved her legs close to the cage and let Jade grip her leg through the bars. The contact quieted Jade, and Searra felt immediate relief, feeling her daughter's touch.

Searra bent down to pull at Syd's chains to see if she

---

1. yes

2. My life

could dislodge them with her newfound strength. She grabbed the thick chain, her sister's gaze following her every move in silence. There was steel in her eyes, as thick as the chain in Searra's hands.

"I'm so sorry Syd." Searra swallowed. "I never meant to get you involved." She knew her sister's temperament, and this was bad. Syd had never missed the opportunity to chew Searra out. She seethed like a volcano about to erupt. Vitriol boiled inside her, fury coiling tighter with every breath. When it burst, it would rain down and decimate everyone around her.

It would be deserved.

Searra focused on the heavy chains anchoring Syd to the wall. She didn't dare meet her sister's icy stare — colder than the metal in her palms.

Searra pulled.

The metal screeching, a metallic whine that made her ears ring.

She felt the chains give. With a final grunt, the links snapped apart, clanking to the floor at their feet. The shackles still clung to Syd's wrists, but that could wait. At least now, she could move.

Searra turned to Jade's cage and gripped the bars with both hands.

"Okay Sweetie, you need to let go of Mommy now and step back. I don't want this to hurt you." Searra instructed Jade, knowing that she would not understand, or listen. Jade looked at Searra with her big brown eyes and impossibly long dark lashes, and screamed, "No, no, no!"

Searra started waving her hands, "Back, back, back." And by some miracle, Jade began to inch backwards in the small space. Searra breathed in deep through her nose, and out through her mouth, steadying herself.

Her grip tightened around the cold metallic bars and she began to pull. She chose the ones on hinges, hoping to exploit a potential weak spot. This metal was different than her sister's chains. These bars were a lot stronger, and the surface of the metal was covered in a rust that made it sharp against her palms, and a little itchy. Searra pulled even harder, muscles bulging, gritting her teeth as the corrosion bit into the skin of her palms with each tug on the door. Her muscles strained as she used all of her power. Her hands began to burn, but with a satisfying crack, the door to the cage broke free, and fell to the floor with a loud, echoing thud.

Searra opened her arms and Jade sprinted toward her. She caught her mid-stride, scooping her up, crushing her to her chest. Relief washed over her in a crushing wave and she tried to control her shaking breaths.

Searra buried her face in her daughter's tangled hair and breathed her in. "I love you so much, Sweetie! I'm so sorry!" She stole a big, fat kiss on Jade's dirty pink cheek, which Jade protested.

Burning tears gathered at the edges of her vision and Searra tried to wipe them off in Jade's hair.

Hopefully, she didn't just wipe red streaks all over her own face.

Jade had gotten an "owie" before, falling on the cement in their backyard, so she knew what blood was. There was a whole two months straight where Jade would point to her already healed scab on her knee and ask "Owie?" She would then give it a kiss and say, "Better?"

Searra looked to her sister, who had gotten to her feet. Her bite wounds began to leak steady streams of blood as she moved and Searra couldn't help but wince. "Let's go."

Syd said nothing, only nodded once. The bite wound on her neck stretched with the movement, making it look gnarled, like the vampires used her as a chew toy. The wound glistened, like crystals. Her pulse was a deep, steady rhythm that sang to Searra. She tore her gaze away, refusing to be swayed by the hypnotic beat. Searra hoped the rest of the vampires in the chamber were too distracted to notice. Because if *she* found her sister's blood enticing, they sure as hell did too. "Follow me."

Searra retraced her path, her sister close behind, staying low as she ducked beneath the raised bench seats. Jade clutched her collar, quiet for once, as she was balanced on her momma's hip. Searra sent up a silent prayer of thanks to the universe for keeping her that way.

The battle raged around them. The last set of bleachers rocked beneath their feet, swaying so violently that Searra feared they'd be thrown off.

Searra saw that Juan had thrown Liv into the side of the platform. A loud hiss escaped her fanged maw as she got up from the debris that littered the floor around her. Liv shook the dust from her wild red hair, a gray cloud pluming around her like steam, and sped towards Juan in a blur.

Searra kept herself moving, her sister following on her heels.

They were soon at the entrance. Searra pulled the heavy door open but it bumped against a body on the floor, a fleshy door stop. Searra spared a glance. It was Pichi.

Juan's familiar, and his last living relative. His pink hair was stained by the deep red leaking from his temple. More blood had clotted around his nose and dribbled down his chin, like he had gotten hit square in the face with an iron skillet.

He was alive. Barely. A faint heartbeat thudded under her palm. Searra grabbed his limp arm, dragging him through the door into the wet tunnel. Her vampire strength made it easy to pull him along and carry Jade.

Her sneakers splashed in the familiar gray water and a chill snaked up her spine. She almost cried out in shock. A moan came from below, and she realized the freezing temperature was waking Pichi up, now that he was being dragged through the murky water, half-submerged.

Jade was still quiet as she clutched Searra, head resting on her shoulder. Searra turned to Syd. "I need you to take her and get somewhere safe." Searra's voice was strong and clear, surprising herself.

Syd looked at her in confusion as her brow knitted together. "What do you mean? We have to go now." Her voice came out thick, anger barely restrained. Searra didn't blame her for it.

"Syd..." Searra started.

"And what about him?" she asked, nodding toward Pichi, who was now choking on the dirty water.

Searra shook her head. "I don't know how much time I have. I'm in a vision." Searra paused, her nose scrunching as she thought, "Or am I projecting here from earlier tonight?" The possibility was over-whelming, that she might be time-traveling? Everyone could see her, and she was affecting things, not just seeing them. It was a crazy idea. She barely liked being in one timeline.

She continued, "Any minute now, I may disappear on you, and you'll need to get Jade somewhere safe. Far from here." Searra's earnestness must have convinced her, since Syd just looked at her thoughtfully. Her eerie calm was a little unsettling.

Searra looked down at Pichi, the blood wisping around him in the murky water like smoke. "Priori-tize Jade. If he wakes, try to get him out. But if not, at least he is over here and not back there." Searra said, thumb pointing back to the chamber door.

"Okay. Where do we go?" That was all she said, no questioning any of the other batshit things that just happened, or this random dude Searra was dragging behind her.

Syd could be going into shock though?

Searra couldn't rule that out.

Another deafening bang from the chamber rattled the tunnel. Water surged around their ankles, slosh-ing like ocean waves breaking against their legs. Sear-ra double checked to make sure Pichi's nose and mouth were still above the water line.

"Go to my in-laws," Searra said turning back to her sister after the ground ceased its shaking. She tried passing Jade into Syd's awaiting arms. "They can protect you," Searra explained when Syd's reti-cence showed on her face. Syd hadn't gotten along with Diego, or his family in the past, but they had no choice right now.

Jade had latched onto Searra like an aggressive tree frog, pulling at Searra's shirt and crying, "No! No! No!" Her little face scrunched up in anger and her lips pouted. It broke Searra's heart to hand her over, but she couldn't risk having her and then disappearing back to her own time.

What would happen to her then?

Searra detached Jade and gave her over to her sister as she continued to scream. Searra's anxiety prickled, glancing around to make sure no one heard.

Just at that moment, she heard herself scream from beyond the threshold. Her hackles rose as she whirled toward the open door. She turned to look at her sister one last time, "Run Syd!"

Then Searra ran, speeding so fast she was through the tunnel and halfway in the chamber before her brain registered what she was seeing.

Liv was standing, Juan's glowing daylight sword in her hand. Buried to the hilt, deep in Diego's chest.

CHAPTER 33

TERCA
(STUBBORN)

"LEARN FROM ME, IF NOT BY MY PRECEPTS, AT LEAST BY MY EXAMPLE, HOW DANGEROUS IS THE ACQUIREMENT OF KNOWLEDGE..." - MARY SHELLEY (1818)

Diego was kneeling, mouth opening and closing, gasping for air. Liv pulled the sword out with a callous yank that emitted a loud, wet, sucking sound and Diego fell to the floor in a heap.

Something savage reared its head within Searra. There was only a roaring in her ears. All she saw was Diego's limp body on the ground. She was going to rip Liv's fucking head off.

She couldn't lose him again.

Not again.

She *wouldn't* lose him again.

Searra ran at Liv, not caring if everyone saw her. The thundering in her head manifested from out of her own throat like a savage beast. Before she took even a few steps, she was overcome by that familiar falling sensation.

Her breathing hitched, she was dizzy, her vision spotted.

Disoriented, she staggered to a stop.

The world around her faded and she was swept away by a numbing darkness.

Searra awoke on her back, her body sore, as if she had just run a marathon. She blinked as gorgeous emerald eyes gazed down at her. His hand stroked her hair, sending tingling sensations through her body that traveled down to her toes.

In an instant, it all came flooding back. The chamber, saving Jade and her sister, the battle, and... Diego.

Diego.

"Where's Diego?" Searra asked, sitting up in one quick motion, with utter surprise on Juan's face.

His perfect mouth was set in a grim line. "He left remember? He said he would meet us there with his family." His tone was guarded and his eyes scrutinized her, a flicker of hurt within them.

"*Sí*,[1] Eli and Josué both show up," Searra said absentmindedly, her brain still working through everything she had just seen.

"You want to tell me what you saw?" Juan asked, concern lacing his question.

Searra's brows shot up and her eyes widened as she thought about Diego. "I need to warn him." She fished her phone from her pocket and went to call him, realizing she no longer had his current number. Of course, he changed it. Otherwise, when he went missing, the police could have tracked him if he had used it. Which would have messed up his whole "faking his own death" plan.

"I don't think I'm having visions," Searra admitted. "I think I'm astral projecting... but through time."

Juan's eyes widened in shock. "I've never heard of someone being able to do that." His brows pinched, anger suddenly clouding his green eyes, "You could have been killed."

She huffed out a frustrated sigh, ignoring Juan as she stared at Diego's contact entry in her phone, her face heating with a helpless anger as she stared at his picture, a still from their wedding photos. His hair was shorter, like how she was more accustomed to seeing him, and his tie was crooked.

Diego always complained that no one told him his tie was off-center and mentioned it every time they looked at their wedding photos. Searra never cared about his tie, only that he looked happy. That he *was* happy.

---

1. Yes

She closed her palms to scratch at the inside of her hands. Her palms were so itchy. She brought them up to her face and inspected them. They were red and raised in a thick line traveling straight across both hands. Filled with tiny cuts that hadn't closed yet. That made her pause, fear and confusion skittering up her spine.

She wasn't healing.

Searra looked up at Juan, "Do you have his number?" Her voice sounded so small to her own ears, she could taste her own fear in the air.

Juan shook his head, "No." His gaze was heated as he stared down at her, searching, trying to read her mind. Probably to find the source of the fear he could scent on her.

In a blur, his hands gripped her wrists and tugged them into the lamplight for inspection. "You aren't healing." Alarm in his voice. Juan brought her hands to his nose as he gave them a quick, cautious sniff, his brow wrinkling with concentration.

"*Ruda y ajo.*"[2] Juan spat. His gaze flicked to hers, and they glowed like twin flames in the lamplight. "It got into your bloodstream, it will dampen your powers for a bit until it's out of your system. *Lávate las manos.*[3] Immediately. Use alcohol to disinfect."

"I pulled that door off its hinges, to save Jade from that fucking cage," Searra explained under her

---

2. rue and garlic (strong herbs used for protect, cleansing and repelling evil spirits)

3. wash your hands

breath.

"The Council coated the bars in an herbal power dampener, to prevent escape." His brow arched at her. His gaze was still searching, looking for the rest of the information in her head.

Searra flinched, no. She didn't want him to see. He couldn't see what she planned to do about it.

Searra snatched her hands back and turned on her heel, heading to Juan's room. "Where do you keep your *lucky* sword?" She called from over her shoulder.

The leather squeaked as she shifted in the passenger seat. Searra had been holding the steel sword in her lap, trying to channel her daylight. It was much heavier than she anticipated. From films and television, you would think a sword was easy to brandish, but it was not. It weighed almost four pounds and was not something you could just wave around, especially one-handed.

Juan was concentrating on the road. Driving like a blue shell was hot on his tail in a round of Mario Kart.

They had chosen to take the least inconspicuous of Juan's cars: an older, black Mustang. That was what she thought anyway, but as soon as he turned it on, she knew she had made a terrible mistake. It was the loudest car she had ever heard in her life. The muffler made a low, threatening growl, like a goddamn tin dinosaur every time Juan pressed on the gas.

Inconspicuous indeed.

Searra gripped the sword between her hands, her palms on the flat side of the blade. Her grip wasn't tight enough to cut, but if anyone yanked the hilt, she was sure to get sliced.

Searra didn't know how to infuse the sword with her power. In truth, she was having trouble summoning her daylight at all, which was most likely due to the rash plaguing her hands and blocking her power.

"What are you trying to do?" Juan asked as he sped through traffic, his eyes glued to the road.

"I told you." Searra sighed in frustration. "I'm trying to infuse the sword with light."

"Because you saw me using it in your vision earlier." Juan reasoned, his voice even.

"I was actually there earlier, I know I can do it because I already did." Searra's head was starting to hurt from trying to make sense of the last few hours; the last few days of her life.

Life had changed exponentially in the last few days. She was a single mom battling depression and intense grief, trying to make it through the day. And now? She was still a single mom, and chances were, she still needed to deal with her depression and grief, but she was immortal now. Plus, a Vampire Council had killed her mother and abducted her sister and daughter.

Her heart felt like it was carved from stone when she thought about her mom. The image of how still she had been at the end clung to her thoughts. Frozen and unyielding. An image forever burned into her.

Searra could still hear it. Her mom's last breath,

jagged and incomplete, as if another one should've followed. She couldn't bear the thought that she'd never speak to her mother again.

Her face burned as the blood-red tears threatened to sear the corners of her eyes. She tried to shake it off, to slough off all the oppressive grief she had been living with for the last two years.

Juan's voice cut through her thoughts, "My condolences... about your mom." He slid a glance her way, his eyes flashing like a cat in the oncoming headlights. It was unnerving to see how inhuman he was... how inhuman she'd become.

And yet, Searra could also feel a new warmth blooming within her chest when he set his bejeweled gaze upon her. One that still felt achingly human.

"Thanks. I know I'm not processing it right now... and don't want to think about it. Or talk about it."

Juan nodded and looked back at the road, "We are almost there."

Searra took a deep breath, reaching for her daylight again. This time, she felt the warmth pool in her chest. She pulled at it, willing the power into her hands.

It sputtered out.

Searra let out a frustrated hiss through her teeth.

Juan made a sudden turn down the neighborhood streets from the main road. Searra stared outside her window, trying not to cry with frustration. He zigzagged through the neighborhood and slowed to a stop in front of a random peach house with a dark gray roof. The king palms on the curb outside swayed in the night breeze.

Juan cut the engine. The silence was deafening. Only then, did Searra realize how much she'd grown used to the beastly rumble of the muffler.

"We are two blocks away, we can speed there easily, but they won't see us coming," Juan said as he looked her up and down.

"You need to feed," Juan said, deep lines creasing his brow. "My blood may move the magical dampener through your system faster." A spark flickered across his face, but she couldn't read the emotions.

Searra couldn't help it, her fangs sprang from her gums, the pressure and pain of it spurring her hunger on. She hadn't felt hungry initially, but now she was starting to feel like a yawning pit, aching to be filled.

Her gaze slid to his thick neck, tracking the blood pulsing through his veins with the same rapt focus she saved for a Food Network bake-off... or one of those reality shows where housewives flip tables at each other.

Searra wanted to straddle him right there. Her hips grinding against his as she pressed her aching body to his hard, muscled frame. When the friction became unbearable, she'd sink her teeth into his waiting neck. Her thighs would clench around him as she drank her fill of his sweet, honeyed blood. Her tongue would lap at his wound in a slow and aching motion, with all her longing and desire. So he would know just how much she wanted him. How much she needed him.

Juan chuckled low to himself, a smug smile on his face. His eyes danced with mischief, lit from within. Amusement brought out the most beautiful shade of emerald in his eyes and Searra couldn't get enough. A warmth spread in her chest like the first relaxing sips of wine, she was drunk on it, on him. But she didn't want to examine what that truly meant for her, for them.

"You need to stop looking at me like that," Juan said, his tone playful, but she did catch the edge in his voice that betrayed the desire smoldering just beneath, his self-control on the brink of snapping.

Cars drove by, and the reflection of their headlights refracted within his green eyes. A true predator sat beside her and she watched as he dragged his wrist across the blade.

He let out a breathy chuckle. Fangs gleamed through his dry smile, catching the light and pulling her gaze to his full lips. She licked her own. Without fail — his eyes followed, locking on the wet curve of her mouth.

He cleared his throat, "I think this way will be less distracting." His voice was huskier than it had been only a moment ago. "The mate bond can be intense." His sandy eyebrows rose.

Fuck yeah, it can. Searra only nodded in response, her entire being trained on the blood flowing from his offered wrist.

She seized his arm, sparks leaping from her fingertips at the contact. Her tongue lapped at the wound. Sweet, hot blood sang across her taste buds and slid down her throat like molten honey. She drank deep, like someone dying of thirst finally finding water, a groan tearing free as ecstasy flooded her senses. Another pull, and her eyes squeezed shut, sparks bursting behind her lids like fireworks. She bit back another moan, heady from the magic and the taste of him.

It washed over her at last, the rising warmth in her

chest as her power grew. She opened her eyes and saw that Juan had his head against the headrest, eyes shut, his long sandy brown lashes like fans along his cut cheekbones. A growl reverberated from his throat but escaped his lips as a deep moan.

Watching him unravel from nothing but her lips made heat curl low in her belly. It left her aching to see what else her mouth could do — what sounds she could drag from him if she touched him...*elsewhere.* Her eyes flicked to the hard bulge straining against his jeans, proof of just how much he wanted her. The sight made her lips curl against his wrist, a quiet promise she'd cash in on later... once the chaos was over.

Searra pulled away, but not before lapping along the wound to close it. Tasting honey and salt from the sweat on his skin.

She felt him shiver and he opened his eyes.

That heated look told her all she needed: he would take her right here, right now—inside the car, on top of the car, against the palm tree—and make her scream his name into the balmy California night.

Then his head swiveled to look outside, his entire posture stiffening, a hardened mask took hold of his features and he looked every bit the demon lurking beneath his usual handsome facade.

She caught the scent a moment later, the sharpened aroma of dog, with hints of soft blueberry, rich vanilla, and teak.

Diego was here.

CHAPTER 34

IMBUEMENT

Searra and Juan sped from the car, taking only the sword.

Diego and his sisters, Lety and Lissette, had parked only a block over, a little closer to the building than Juan and Searra had.

Searra called out, "I'm glad you could make it."

Diego looked up, fury flashing in his expression. "We had supplies to pick up. You want protection, don't you?" And nodded his head over to where Lissette and Lety were setting up. They had come in Lety's black Prius. It was old, a little beat up, but reliable. Searra smiled at her peeling "I Rescue D ogs... Unless It Is A Full Moon" bumper sticker.

The irony.

Her trunk was a makeshift altar. Herbs, bowls, candles, crystals, and corked bottles of clear liquid were scattered across the space, along with what Searra guessed was rock salt.

Perfect for the bruja[1] on the go.

"Hey Searra!" Lety's kind face lit up in a genuine smile. She was always so welcoming and open with Searra. She had missed her.

"Hey Lety," Searra said, with a small wave, and nodded to Juan. "This is Juan. He is on our side. So, don't try to curse him or anything."

Lety laughed, almond eyes crinkling into small slits. "Oh yeah, I got you." She hefted a *molcajete[2]* already packed with herbs and began grinding with the *tejolote*,[3] wincing at the effort. "I swear, I need to start working out if I'm gonna keep doing *bruja* stuff. My arms are always sore now." Her own breathy chuckle made Searra smile as she watched Lety pulverize the herbs into dust.

"What are you guys cooking?" Searra asked, looking from Lety to Lissette, who was pulling more candles from a canvas tote bag that said *"Botanica Reina"*[4] in elegant black script across it.

---

1. witch

2. stone bowl made of volcanic rock, used to mix

3. the stone grinder or pester used to crush various herbs, used with the molcajete

4. Spiritual Shop that sells a variety of herbs, candles and spiritual tools, + queen

Lissette's cautious peridot gaze lifted to meet Searra's. Her dark hair was pulled into an intricate braid that trailed down to the small of her back. A constellation of freckles dusted the bridge of her nose in the soft lamplight.

Searra had known Lissette since she had been a young teen and still viewed her as a kid sister. It was a shock to see her all grown up. With the braid, Searra could barely tell that she had patches of hair missing, but her black mane was definitely not as thick as it once was.

Searra noticed that Lissette's wary gaze avoided Juan's direction, seeming to look around him as if he wasn't there, making sure to keep a healthy distance between them. Searra's heart twisted at the fear and mistrust, but she knew it was earned. It was up to Juan to prove himself, to change Lissette's mind.

Lissette turned back to the candles she had meticulously placed and gave a casual shrug. "You heard Diego... protection." She struck a long match against the worn edge of an old-school matchbox and stared into the flame. It flickered in the night breeze, then steadied — growing under Lissette's powerful gaze. The scent of gardenias curled through the air as her magic wrapped around them. She lit each candle in turn, moving counterclockwise in a slow circle.

Lissette extended her long, slender arms toward Lety, wordlessly taking the bowl. In silence Lety grabbed the vial of salt, drawing a circle around the car and where they were standing.

"Salt is purifying. Powerful protection." She glanced down, checking that the salt lines were solid and unbroken. "Plus... delicious." A snicker slipped out before she schooled her face back to serious and kept working. Shaking the salt out with rhythmic movements, like a dance.

Lissette had finished with her concoction, a muddy substance that looked similar to wet ash filled the *molcajete.*[5] She dipped a finger in, "D?" she called, and Diego sauntered over from his leaning spot by the hood of the car, where he had been staring Juan down since they first arrived.

"You're first," Lissette announced with a small smile.

"Alright, Lis. What do you need me to do?" Diego asked, towering over his little sister, his dark gaze locked on her. He had been careful not to make eye contact with Searra. It hurt, and she wasn't sure if she preferred it that way or not.

"Just close your eyes and don't move," Lissette instructed, her words were playful, but Searra caught the hesitance in them, like this was the first protection spell she had done.

"How often have you done this?" The question spilled from Searra the moment the thought passed through her brain.

Lissette gave her a thin smile, "I've read enough about it." Her light green eyes gleamed like gemstones in the dark, "We haven't needed protection until now." Searra didn't miss the accusation in her tone and it cut her like a blade.

Searra ducked her head to hide her expression and held her tongue. The last thing she needed was to get

---

5. stone bowl made of volcanic rock, used to mix

into a fight with her in-laws. Especially when they were the only ones who could help rescue her daughter. No matter what, she would always be tied to them through Jade, and she needed them.

Lissette looked back at Diego, while he continued to act like Searra hadn't even spoken — then she dipped her fingers into the mixture and marked a cross on his forehead.

She began to whisper, "*Por la cruz y por la sangre.*"[6] The scent of gardenias thickened in the air. "*Que no mal te alcance.*"[7] Lissette's voice grew in strength as Lety joined in. The scent of sage and eucalyptus mingled with gardenias as magic hummed against their skin. "*Sal en mi boca, ruda en mi mano...*"[8] their voices swelled, "*Ni sombra, ni muerte, ni engaño.*"[9]

The air was charged with the energy of their magic. Searra could have sworn her hair was standing on end with all the static building around them. The muddy cross on Diego's head glowed green, like sunlight peaking through thin, veiny leaves, then it vanished. He looked no different, but Searra imagined a force field between him and any impending harm.

Searra wanted to warn him about the battle... about Liv, but she hesitated, thinking that telling him right

---

6. For the cross and for the blood,

7. Let no harm come near you,

8. Salt in my mouth, and rue in my hand,

9. No shadow, no death no deceit.

before they went in would only screw with his head and get him killed faster.

Lissette looked to Searra and Juan and hesitated, "I'm not sure if we can perform this protection on you both." Her grinding on the word 'both.' *Ruda*[10] and garlic are dangerous to vampires. It might make you safe, but it also might slow you down or inhibit your own abilities." She shrugged her shoulders with a feigned casual grace, "It's up to you."

Searra looked to Juan. She wouldn't mind protection, but she was already struggling with her daylight abilities, and didn't need them dampened any more than they already were.

Juan's emerald gaze locked on hers and she heard his voice rasp in her head. *Unfortunately, we cannot risk it. We need to be at full strength to stand a chance at getting Jade out unscathed.*

Searra nodded, "I think we will pass. Appreciate the offer though."

Lissette nodded and turned to Lety. In perfect unison, they chanted to each other, smearing small crosses onto their own foreheads. Again, the air thickened with the mingled scents of gardenia, sage, and eucalyptus as their magic swelled. The crosses flared bright, then faded. Both sisters were now draped in heavy wards of protection.

"Ready?" Diego asked, deigning to address Searra directly.

"Almost," Searra said, she held her hand out to

---

10. Rue –Known as the "Herb of Grace" — often used to sprinkle holy water in Catholic rituals.

Juan.

Without hesitation, he flipped the sword, catching it by the blade, and handed it to her, hilt first.

Searra took it and walked around to the front of Lety's Prius. She put the sword down on the hood and took a deep shaky breath. She was tempted to crack her knuckles, but what good would that do? Closing her eyes and looking inward, she placed both hands on the blade of the ancient sword.

She almost didn't want to bring the sword, since it was the weapon of choice that Liv used on Diego, but, it was Juan's lucky sword. She didn't want to jinx coming out of this fight alive. A six-hundred-year streak seemed like pretty good odds. Searra didn't want to risk changing too much; otherwise, something might affect Syd and Jade's rescue.

Searra concentrated, trying to find that familiar heat, that fiery thread she could pull on to summon her magic. Nothing happened. Air whistled through her teeth as she breathed, frustration peaking. She shook out her hands and rolled her shoulders, trying to ease the tension from her muscles. Breathing, she placed her palms again on the surface of the blade. The metal bit into her skin. She inhaled again, reaching within. Then, Searra felt the familiar warmth simmering in her chest, right above her heart. She smiled to herself, "There you are."

Juan's blood had worked to push the magical dampener from her system.

Keeping her eyes shut, she willed the heat to travel down to her outstretched hands. The heat obeyed and though her eyes were closed, she could still see the light as it traveled down her arms and into her fingertips.

Suddenly, the cold steel of the blade leeched into her skin, sending a shiver down her spine.

She heard Juan in the background, "Maybe you should stop, *Vida?*"[11]

There was a guttural growl, followed by a bone-chilling snarl, the kind of sound you only hear in documentaries of large jungle cats or grizzlies. "You don't tell her what to do." It sounded like Diego, and Searra wanted to roll her eyes, but she was afraid to lose concentration.

She blocked out everything except for her and the blade beneath her fingertips. The chill of the steel began to travel until she could no longer feel her fingers all the way up to her knuckles. Instinct told her to push back, to use the warmth of her daylight against the cold metal.

Searra took a calming breath, breathed in through her nose and out through her mouth, and willed her daylight to fight back, to give warmth to her fingers, to push past the icy steel, to force fire into the blade.

Not since its creation had it known heat, and now it will know heat again. Like being reborn.

She felt it... the light surged from her hands and flooded the sword. Heat roared through the steel, building until it felt like it would brand her fingerprints away. It burned like gripping a cast iron pan pulled straight from the stove— unbearable, but she held on through pure stubborn will.

She only needed a little more, just a little more.

---

11. Life (term of endearment)

The pain intensified. Searra gritted her teeth against it. Heat from the daylight prickled her face, like the start of a bad sunburn. Her stomach lurched in protest. The oppressive warmth was incredible, but the pain was pure agony, drowning out every other thought until she wanted— needed— to let go.

She was desperate to let go.

Let go! A strong, deep voice laced with panic echoed inside her head. Searra's eyes snapped open as her fingers unlatched from the now-burning steel. Her eyes stung with the brilliance of the living flame cascading like a torch all along the blade sitting on the hood of Lety's car.

There goes the paint. Searra grimaced at the thought, needing to apologize for the sword-shaped burn on the hood of her car.

Strong hands seized her shoulders, spinning her hard enough to steal her breath. Juan's face filled her vision. Worry warring with horror in his eyes as they locked on hers. "*¡Por todos los infiernos, ¿qué fue eso?*"[12] He demanded, his voice cracking with emotion.

His Spanish was too quick for Searra to catch, but she was pretty sure he was cursing at her.

In an instant, Diego was in his face, "She doesn't have to answer to you, bloodsucker. She is doing what she fucking needs to."

"I made you a weapon." Searra couldn't help the smugness that seeped into her words as she smiled at Juan, ignoring his distress. She winced as her

---

12. By all the hells, what was that?! (archaic saying)

cheeks stung with the movement and she tore her dark gaze away from Juan's emerald one. They were streaked with gold veins, like furious lightning had cracked through them.

Searra saw her reflection in the darkened car window. Her skin had puckered like crumpled foil, little welts and angry, fat blisters swelled along her jawline, the part of her face that had gotten the most exposure from the daylight sword. She brought up her hand to probe the sensitive skin and felt the inflamed, peeling wound there. When she pulled away, her breath hitched, her fingertips had been burned away and scorched bone was poking out beneath her cooked flesh. Bile climbed up her throat, but she swallowed it down.

Why didn't it hurt? Had she gone into shock?

Was she numb — was that a vampire thing now?

Searra looked to Juan, but his expression stayed stony, fixed on Diego. Diego had already turned his back on Juan and was heading toward his sisters by the trunk.

Juan turned back to Searra, heated gems met melted chocolate as he explained "You will heal. Daylight wounds are slow to mend for vampires, but you just fed, so you should be good as new in a few moments." *I couldn't stand you in pain, so I took it on myself.*

The words wove through her mind like a gentle caress. A shiver of pleasure ran through her and her heart softened.

It was then she noticed the stiffness in his posture, the way his jaw muscles flexed as he clenched and unclenched against the agony he was taking on... for her.

Her eyes pricked with hot tears as she blinked them back, determined not to cry in front of everyone.

Thank you. She whispered to him on the air, hoping the words floated over to him with everything she was feeling, everything she was carrying inside her heart.

Juan gave a slight nod, his expression burning with heat, desire, and desperate longing. It was something like love, but fiercer, deeper than anything she'd ever known. Searra was lost in it. She was falling, hard, terrified of the moment she'd hit the ground.

Diego cleared his throat with all the finesse of a bull, "Jesus Christ. Can we hurry it up here?"

Searra glanced his way, an apology on her tongue. Her reflection in the car window stopped her cold. The welts and blisters were gone. Only faint pink patches remained where they'd been the worst. She was already healed.

Searra smiled up at Diego, her fangs erupting from her gums, "Let's go get our daughter."

It was then, that a strange, ominous echo danced toward them on the night air... a strange beat, making Searra's head turn toward the sound.

It was like clacking.

The clacking of beaks.

CHAPTER 35

LECHUSAS (OWL)

"The fuck?" Diego was looking up into the darkness of a nearby tree, eyes wide and nose wrinkled in disgust.

Searra followed his gaze, only for her eyes to snag on two large glowing eyes staring down at them. Fear choked her, making it hard to breathe and yet, she couldn't look away. The aroma of dry grass, rich earth and dusty wood with an underlying sourness cloyed at her nose. It reminded Searra of a barn and her hackles rose.

"Lechusas... "[1] Lety hissed under her breath.

In the shadows of the camphor tree, Searra could make out the feathered body of what looked like an owl, but larger, much larger. In place of talons, what gripped the branches of the tree were gnarled hands, human hands. It was so unsettling that Searra wanted to look away and her stomach turned. It's knuckles were white with the tight grip it kept, bark biting into the skin of it's palms. It's glowing gaze instantly snapped to hers, two bright, yellow pits that stared deep into her soul.

Without warning, it tore through the hushed silence as it began to clack it's beak together and let out a high pitched screech. It was warning The Council, and now they knew they were here.

"We gotta go!" Searra screamed, trying to cover her ears fromt he piercing assault on her eardrums.

Lissette reached into the trunk of Lety's car and grabbed something and pulled it up to the dim light of the street lamps. It was a feather.

Lissette began to chant, holding up the feather and making the sign of the cross on the air, *"En el nombre de Dios, no entras aquí. Vuela lejos, bruja. El diablo llama el nombre.* "[2]

The enormous owl spread it's massive wings and puffed out it's chest. The two glowing orbs continued

---

1. a witch who can transform into a large owl (often a barn owl) to stalk and terrorize people at night.

2. In God's name, you will not enter here. Fly far, witch, the devil is calling your name.

to stare unlinking as it's neck began to roll. It's own hackles rising.

Lety joined Lissette in her chanting and the scent of their combined magic filled the air, overpowering the smell of rotting barn. The creatures wings began to flap as it retreated from the tree and back into the darkness of the surrounding night.

Lety and Lissette waved Searra away, not dropping their gazes or letting up their chants. It kept the wards in place and strengthened their spell.

Diego grabbed Searra's arm, "We got to go, now. There is no way they didn't hear the warning."

With one last look, Diego, Searra, and Juan took off for the building's side entrance.

"Eli and Josué are on their way. He just texted me. 'ETA 5 mins.'" Diego's voice was rough, barely audible while he was half shifted in his wolf form. It was hard for him to enunciate with rows of sharpened fangs and to text with his fingers now ending in long bone carving claws.

Searra nodded, knowing Eli and Josué were almost there meant she had seen the majority of the battle. Which meant the Council was waiting for them, no chance for the element of surprise.

As they made their way across the little courtyard, past an old white wooden pergola with a small bench, and to the steps leading to the side entrance, Searra said, "We won't get the drop on them. They must have heard that warning." Her tongue stuck to the roof of her mouth, fear making it's way through her veins like ice water. "I've seen this fight already, and they surround us. But... Jade makes it out."

Her dark gaze crashed into Diego's, "Watch out

for that sword, yeah?" Scarra nodded to the day-light sword glowing in Juan's grip.

Diego's eyes went wide with shock, and a flicker of fear, before it vanished beneath the smile she loved. The same thousand-kilowatt grin that had pulled her in the first time they met.

"Just don't bury it in my back, *Pepita*."[3] He purred at her, using her pet name purposely. His voice was silk— soft and tantalizing— as though they were alone and Juan wasn't standing three feet away.

A small scream bled through the walls, chilling Scarra to the bone. Diego growled low in his chest, the sound reverberating into the night like the engine of Juan's Mustang.

Jade.

---

3. pumpkin seed (term of endearment)

CHAPTER 36

CHUPACABRA (MEXICAN GOAT-SUCKER)

"THE MOST MERCIFUL THING IN THE WORLD, I THINK, IS THE INABILITY OF THE HUMAN MIND TO CORRELATE ALL ITS CONTENTS." - H.P. LOVECRAFT (1926)

That was Jade's cry.

Diego ran ahead, barreling through the thick, ancient wooden door. Sharpened stakes flung from all sides as it disintegrated into nothing but splinters, dust, and metal hinges.

Searra tried to keep sight of him, but Diego was lost

to the dark abyss he left in the wall.

Another scream peeled through the air and Searra's hackles stood on end.

Then she was moving— fast.

Searra didn't need to glance at Juan to know he was at her side.

She used her vampire speed to cross the threshold. There was an immediate drop as the steep, crumbling steps led them underground to the chamber.

She remembered traveling down a dark, wet tunnel like this before — but this one was different. No nasty, gray water. Only stone, dirt... and rats. Her vampiric senses were so sharp she could practically taste their mangy fur. Gooseflesh prickled her skin as her stomach churned. She tried breathing through her mouth, and prayed for blissful ignorance of the rats scurrying through the shadowed corners, chewing and biting and shitting everywhere. It didn't work.

There was no light to guide her, but she didn't need it. Her eyes had gone nocturnal. They drank in the darkness around them, following whispers of breath and heat. Yet still, no sign of Diego.

Anxiety sharpened in her blood and she picked up speed, only the sound of her and Juan's quick steps carried through the passage.

The tunnel widened into a corridor that opened onto the stage's far side — where Jade and her sister were. Searra caught their scents in the moldy wooden air, and her shoulders eased a fraction. She didn't dare look their way. Couldn't risk anyone realizing she knew exactly where her daughter was.

The chamber was filled with dozens of billowing cloaks that seemed to float in the air like blackened smoke. The sharp sound of heavy metallic chains rattling had her gritting her teeth. Attached to those chains, were three of the most horrid creatures she had ever laid eyes on.

They resembled grotesquely large, hairless coyotes — warped by what nightmares are made of. Spiked spines erupted along their backs like jagged fin bones. Rib cages jutted at unnatural angles, each bone pressing against the mottled gray flesh of its chest.

Its breath rasped out in a low croak, like water gurgling through a broken drainpipe. The noise crawled up Searra's spine, lifting every hair on her neck in cold warning.

Worst of all...they had no eyes. Just black pits burning with unholy red light. Their maws gaped with rows of needle⬚like teeth, yellow drool dripping as they panted at their master's feet.

What the fuck are those things?

The pungent smell of sulfur permeated the air around them, as if these creatures had clawed their way out of Hell — brimstone still clinging to their talons.

Chupacabras.[1] Juan whispered into her mind, fear palpable in his words. Searra's eyes went wide and her jaw almost hit the floor. She had heard stories when she was little, but never in her life, thought they were real.

Don't let them bite you. Chupacabra venom is deadly to vampires. Juan's warning skittered through

---

1. Mexican Goat Sucker (legends say they attack cattle at night)

her mind, spiking her adrenaline as her stomach dropped to the floor at the prospect of being bitten by something with that many teeth.

They were circling around the chamber like demonic hyenas and her breath caught in her throat as they surrounded a figure in the center of it. Their croaking growls echoed so loudly her head was beginning to vibrate, as their long, barbed tongues probed their captive.

Diego... They must have grabbed him as soon as he entered the tunnel.

He was on his knees, and a silver collar had been fastened to his neck. Both hands clutching it, trying to wrench it off, inhuman snarls ripping from his throat. Searra could taste his blood in the air. The collar was weeping blood, and more dripped down his chest, soaking his black shirt the more he struggled.

Brilliant, truly. Juan's sarcasm snaked through her head like a gossiping Greek chorus. She wanted to roll her eyes and give a real-life face palm because the last thing they needed was Diego adding himself to the hostage list. She gritted her teeth so hard her jaw began to ache, her frustration growing.

The collar, they are spiked on the inside. Silver keeps wolves from shifting. Juan's voice had gone as sharp as the blade in his hand, edged with anxiety.

Then one of the shadows spoke, its billowing black facade solidifying into an older man's handsome face. Gray streaking his temples and a southern drawl. "Juan, you are late." The words were drawn out, pulled like taffy, sweetened to the ears.

The gentleman's dark eyes glowed gold as he stared

at them, a smile widening his rugged face.

His golden gaze was fixed on Juan as he chuckled to himself. "Oh no, hoss. You set the table, poured the wine, and brought the guest of honor. Ain't no leavin' now." He pinned Searra in place with his icy stare, as his arms gestured to her, thick, dark brows raised in a confirmation and in question.

There was a pause, and he tilted his head, eyes flashing. It was like he was listening to the air, or to someone who wasn't there.

"You always had a stubborn streak, brother. Still do, seems." The vampire answered, amusement in his tone, his voice was raspy velvet.

It dawned on Searra that Juan was speaking to the gentleman in his head and she shot him a glare. "What is he talking about? What are you telling him?"

Juan's jaw ticked, the lines of his face deepened as he said, "It was my charge to bring you here." His tone was as hard as steel, but she could see the remorse on his face.

"I was just telling Ambrose that he needs to let Diego, Jade, and your sister go. Or he is going to have me to contend with." Juan continued, his stare never wavered from the disarming older gentleman.

A deep groove began to form between Ambrose's salt and pepper brows, displeasure clear on his face. "You brought the daylight bearer to our door. Your duty's through, friend." His velvet twang had gone from sweet tea to a cold gin and tonic, all trace of civility gone.

Searra's gaze flicked back to Diego. His wolf strained beneath his skin, swelling and clawing to break free...but the collar held it down. A frustrated whine tore from his throat, cracking her heart wide open.

The sharp warmth rose in Searra's chest, feeding on her anger.

"Ah, ah ah..." Ambrose chided. "We won't have none of that darlin'." He shook his head like he was chastising a toddler. "You light up any brighter, and my babies will be having wolf for supper." Eyes that were black as pitch grew golden again and his fangs gleamed in an impossibly charming smile. "I mean, they do prefer goat, but wolf would do just fine."

Ambrose pulled on their chains, the metal scraping against the wooden floor, and they all pulled back, their barbed teeth dripping with venomous drool. The beasts whined as they tried to inch their way back, closer to Diego, their black pits glowing with hunger.

"Wait, wait!" A panicked voice called from the stage. It was Juan's *primo*[2] Pichi. His short pink hair was disheveled, and his dark eyes full of confusion.

"Juan. What are you doing? You know they just want the *bruja*[3] and her daughter." His dark eyes searched Juan's, an emploring expression on his face. He was moving with nervous energy as he played with the straps that dangled low from his backpack.

Juan's jaw locked so hard she thought he might crack his teeth. "You dare to act in my name, without my command." He hissed at Pichi, eyes full of bitter rage.

"What command?" Pichi began to wave his arms

---

2. cousin (can also be used for close friend)

3. witch

around, panic taking hold. "It's not like this is the first time. This is the shit you love to do." Exasperation raising his voice and his thick dark brows until they were practically in his cotton candy hair.

What? Searra almost spat at him. She had liked Pichi, now she was pretty sure he was the reason they were all standing there.

The reason her mom was dead.

He told The Council where to find them.

He was the reason why Jade was in a fucking cage right now, and her sister was bitten to shit and chained to a fucking wall.

Without stopping to think, Searra ran at Pichi, and her elbow connecting with his square jaw. He might've been taller than her, but he was mortal. She was not.

She wasn't afraid of him. She wasn't afraid of any of them.

Not anymore.

Pichi doubled over, grunting in pain, her blow landed hard.

The scent of warm blood welling in his mouth wafted to her, making her fangs erupt. Saliva pooled in her mouth and she licked her lips in anticipation. Her hands shot out, clutching his short, pink hair. She yanked him down as she drove her knee up to connect with his face. A satisfying crack echoed out as his nose broke, blood leaking from his nostrils like an open faucet.

It made her think of her mom.

Dead.

Lying in a pool of her own blood.

Her daughter in a cage, crying for her.

Her sister covered in gag-inducing bites, used like a

chew toy.

Heat swelled in her chest. A bonfire gone wild, starving for fuel. It roared through her veins, ravenous, unstoppable. The wood and stone beneath her threatened to liquefy under the blaze.

She didn't stop.

She couldn't.

The fury swallowed her whole, a red haze flooding her vision until there was nothing left to want but fire. Nothing left to do... but *burn it all down.*

Searra, stop!

Juan's command bounced around inside her head, but she ignored it. She felt the invisible chains of his compulsion and shrugged them off like silk. The heat in her chest had traveled to her entire body, unadulterated power surged through her veins like hellfire.

Heat burned through her hands, her eyes. The surge of her power lifted her hair, like a mermaid underwater, but suspended in pure daylight.

Her burning gaze slid past Pichi — crumpled on his knees, clutching his face — and locked on the smirking figure behind him: Ambrose. His polished obsidian eyes flinched from her light. Then his lips pursed, and a high-pitched whistle cut the air. The signal for his *chupacabras.*[4]

The three beasts snarled and lurched for Diego, their fangs poised to rip flesh.

Searra screamed, throwing her hands wide to stop

---

4. Mexican Goat Sucker (legends say they attack cattle at night)

them.

A white-hot beam of daylight erupted from her chest. One massive, explosive burst that punched straight through one of the *chupacabras.*

There was a keening whine, the smell of burning, rotted flesh and then there was nothing. Her daylight had disintegrated the abomination mid-lunge in a mini-explosion and the ground beneath them rolled.

Searra looked around for the other two, whipping her head back and forth trying to spot them.

One was on the floor, having been kicked in the face by Diego. Who was now on his back, scrambling backward to put distance between himself and the rabid hell beast, his sneakers squeaking on the hardwood with his efforts. The heavy silver collar weighed him down, like he was moving through sludge.

The other was circling Juan, his daylight sword poised defensively.

Searra locked eyes on Ambrose, a snarl ripping from her throat, and she charged.

Amusement flickered in his dark golden gaze and his fangs glinted at her in the dark of the chamber.

Before she could get to him, several of the billowing cloaks standing behind Ambrose began to materialize. Surrounding them like a pack of hyenas. Her eyes narrowed on the wild red hair and pitless gold eyes.

Liv.

Searra snarled at her, remembering that she was the one who would plunge Juan's daylight sword into Diego mere minutes from now, but not if she could help it.

A wet yip sounded behind her. She spun, catching

Juan as he drove his daylight sword through the *chu-pacabra's*[5] chest. The beast had lunged atop him, fangs inches from his throat, before the blade impaled it and its weight slumped lifelessly against him.

Juan grunted, heaving the hulking weight aside. In a blur of preternatural speed, he shot to his feet, daylight sword slicing the air with acrobatic ease. his skill with the blade on full display as it arced around him in a smear of light and heat. He looked like a long lost knight, a king returned to exact vengeance. Green eyes blazed gold as he snarled, a deep roar tore from his chest, and he charged at Ambrose.

One second Ambrose was there, the next he was behind Juan, black smoke floating around him like tentacles, his fangs flashing in the light.

"Behind you!" Searra screamed out. Juan's sword sliced through the air, a ray of light in shadow as he pivoted, his movements almost too fast for Searra to see.

Ambrose ducked, but not fast enough. His guttural scream tore through the chamber as he clutched his face, staggering back. When his hands fell away, Searra saw there was a raw, burning gash slashed from his hairline to his neck. It was deep and jagged through his right eyebrow. She winced at the sight. His right eye had been cooked by the daylight's heat... soft and ruined, like a boiled egg.

Ambrose's one good eye was filled with pure, black hatred as he spat, "All this fuss... for *that?!*" He jabbed

---

5. Mexican Goat Sucker (legends say they attack cattle at night)

a finger at Searra, then touched his marred flesh with a humourless chuckle. His gaze slid to Liv, standing poised to strike.

"Kill them all."

With a violent rush of black smoke, Ambrose and his last *chupacabra*[6] were gone — ripped from the chamber in a swirl of shadow and ash.

---

6. Mexican Goat Sucker (legends say they attack cattle at night)

CHAPTER 37

OBLIVION

As soon as Ambrose vanished, the vampires descended. A feral horde closing in, circling them like jackals around a fresh kill. Plagued by a gnawing hunger for the last few eternities, give or take a century.

Anticipation and the promise of blood was thick in the air.

Searra felt the stare of familiar eyes and she looked up. Near the main entrance, her own dark brown eyes stared back at her.

Searra gave a slight nod, letting herself know every-one could see her, she was really here, and they needed her.

Her gaze snapped to the stage. *Jade and Syd. On the stage! Over there!* She shoved the thought out like a scream, praying her past self would hear it.

Searra returned her attention back to the battle. She felt Juan step next to her. His fingers brushed against the shell of her ear, gently tucking the strands behind it.

"Be careful, I'm still glowing." She quipped.

Juan's gaze seemed to devour her face, burning every detail into memory. His hand locked onto the back of her neck, pulling her close. Emerald eyes blazed, un-flinching, with awe and truth. His voice — low and steady despite the chaos around them — cut through the noise.

"You shine with the fury of the sun itself... incredi-ble...and impossible to ignore. Even if I turned to ash in your light, I'd count it as a blessing."

Searra's adrenaline spiked and heat flooded her face, ragged breaths shaking her. She clung to his gaze like it was the last tether keeping her in this world.

And in a blur of red, Liv lunged at them— fingers hooked like claws, slashing low for Searra's belly. The strike meant to spill her open... meant to kill.

Searra dodged back, vampire reflexes kicking in. She dove, rolled hard, and came up in a crouch several feet away. Sneakers screeching against the wooden floor.

She turned to find Liv, who was now circling Juan as he stood between Searra and Liv.

"*Pinche pendeja.*"[1] Searra hissed under her breath.

A guttural roar sounded in front of her as Diego grappled with a tall, gangly vampire whose spider-like limbs clung to his back, dragging him to the floor.

Searra lunged, her speed a blur of color and sound. Heat gathered in her palms, glowing white hot as she closed the distance between herself and Digeo. She clamped onto the vampire's long leg; sizzling flesh hissed under her grip. Power roared beneath her skin and exploded through her palms in a rush of burning light.

A blood curdling shriek tore from the gangly vampire's throat as he crashed to the ground. His leg shriveled from the knee down, flesh desiccating until nothing was left except gray dust. His scream knifed through the chamber, his mouth a wide "O" —red tongue waggling like a worm. The echo continued to crawl along the walls long after he'd fallen silent.

She remembered when she had first heard that sound. It was the most ungodly thing she had ever had the displeasure of hearing. It was like nothing from this world, a creature born straight out of hell itself. But after the *chupacabras*,[2] this paled in comparison.

Searra spun toward Diego and froze, spotting her past self as she climbed into the stands, sneakers squeaking on the boards. The sound cut through the chaos, impossibly loud in her ears. She winced, pray-

---

1. fucking bitch

2. Mexican Goat Sucker (legends say they attack cattle at night)

ing no one else heard it.

One had. It's head snapped toward the sound.

It was a much larger vampire with arms thick as steel cables, that took notice. Discarding the cloak, his massive frame was fully revealed. A frame built like a truck — for brute force and bloodshed. His thick, curly hair — black and wild, like Diego's — framed a face fixed on her past self. A ravenous, manic grin split his features as his dark eyes flared to an unearthly gold. Grotesque ridges rippled across his brow, demonic and sharp. His wet, pink tongue flicked out, moistening his fangs in anticipation.

Searra cringed, bitter disgust flooding her tongue. Heat flared low in her gut, sharp and angry.

The massive vampire lunged for Past Searra, oblivious to the danger. He was a hulking blur that tore across the room. A menacing howl sounded near the entrance, cutting him off, freezing him mid-stride.

Josué and Eli burst into the room, half transformed and snarling. Josué tore his his shirt off, unleashing a deep, low growl that rattled the ground beneath Searra's feet. The sharp stench of dog filled the air as Josué's bones crunched, the popping sound ricocheting off the walls, off the floor, like cooking demented popcorn.

Eli joined him. Her jaw cracked, bones grinding as it surged forward. Flesh stretched and split into a muzzle, canine and snarling... but the rest of her head remained horrifyingly human.

It was so unsettling, Searra knew she would have nightmares about it.

More bones crunched, Eli's cries twisting into something feral. At last, two massive wolves stood before her.

Josué's wolf was a walking shadow, pitch–black and fathomless. Beside him, Nayeli's was deep chocolate, rich and earthen, like warm soil after rain.

Nayeli wasted no time. She charged the vampire barreling toward Past Searra, jaws splitting wide. She scooped him up like a dog with a rubber chicken, whipping him back and forth in a violent blur.

The vampire's screech tore through the chamber—piercing, jagged, like porcelain grinding on porcelain. The sound vibrated through her skull, setting her teeth on edge until her jaw ached.

Dark blood poured from Eli's clenched jaws as she bit down. Bones crunching, sinew snapping. The giant vampire shoved at her muzzle, ropey muscles bulging, face purpling with effort, but her grip didn't falter.

Then came the pop.

A fountain of blood erupted, drenching the wooden floor as his body tore in half. Two slick halves hit the boards with a meaty slap, blood pooling fast and wide beneath them.

Searra saw her past self reach the stage, relief flooding her body and she slumped like a tired jellyfish.

The ground jerked beneath her. The entire chamber rocked with the force of an earthquake.

Josué, still in wolf form, slammed into the far wall with a sickening crack. The beams above groaned, then gave way. Stone and wooden splinters cascading down in a choking cloud of dust, covering him.

A high-pitched keening ripped from the rubble, sharp and wolfish, slicing through the chaos. Searra's gut clenched tight. He was badly injured.

Jade's scream split the chaos. Searra whipped her

head toward the stage, primal instinct roaring to life. It didn't matter if her past self had her already; her anxiety was peaking. She needed to hold her baby girl. She needed her safe. Far, far away from here.

A sudden blinding pain ripped through her scalp as a vampire yanked a fist full of her hair, dragging her backwards. Searra cried out, spinning on her heel.

He was *fucking strong.*

She was shocked she still had hair with how hard he wrenched her head back.

Searra began to panic as she was dragged backwards. Her arms flailing for balance as he hauled her across the floor by her hair.

Searra dragged in a deep breath, panic coursing through her veins. She willed her mind and her muscles to remember all the times she had fought off someone in this very situation during her classes.

Women teaching women to survive. To fight back when it counts.

Hair pulling? As classic as it gets.

Searra reached up to grab the hand in her hair. It was cold and bony compared to the women she practiced with, and it sent a icy shiver of fear up her spine.

Letting her body guide her, she spun on the ball of her foot, now facing her attacker. She couldn't meet his eyes — not with his fist yanking her hair —but she could see his shoes. Shiny, patent leather oxfords. She wanted to stomp the fucking shine right off of them.

Using her weight, Searra swung backward while keeping a grip on his hand, pulling his hand into her hair so he had no leverage.

She hit the ground hard, right on her ass and rolled onto her back. With his hand pinned in her hair, she dragged him down with her.

The vampire bucked, wavy blond hair whipping with the effort. But she'd already locked her thighs around him, forming a tight defense triangle. His arm and head were trapped, exposed and begging for a swift, strong strike.

Searra drove her elbow down again and again, every strike packed with daylight and raw force. Heat flared against her skin, blunt bone and burning sun... a tempest given flesh.

The impacts rattled through to her bones. If she weren't a vampire, she'd be bruised for weeks. Hell, maybe even now.

The grip on her head suddenly loosened. Searra seized the moment and wrenched his wrist away from her scalp.

The blonde vampire scrambled, trying to escape, blood dripping from a gash in his head. It was a deep one, judging by how fast it stained his golden waves. He transformed from towhead to ginger before her eyes. Even with vampire healing, the wound kept gushing. She must have hit something vital.

A high-pitched whine split the air, followed by snarling.

Searra eyes darted around the room. Two vampires clung to Nayeli's back, clawing at her fur, trying to drag her down.

Eli snapped at them like a rabid beast, foam gathering at her bloodied jaws. Her coat glistened with dark red blood.

The scent hit Searra's nose like a punch and saliva gathered in her mouth.

Without warning, a dark haired vampire with

corpse-white skin, snatched Searra by her ankles. His claws sank into her flesh like fish hooks as he yanked— hard. She was sure he would rip her legs from their sockets.

Searra reached for her power, for her daylight, and felt the warmth quickly build in her chest and travel throughout her body.

The vampire yanking her feet let go the instant her daylight licked at his skin. He hissed, spittle flying from his mouth in a wide, furious arc.

As her daylight spread, the blonde vampire screamed, his mouth stretched so far his jaw was in danger of unhinging, fangs bared like a snake's.

He thrashed in her grip, bucking like a frantic goat as his skin began to shrivel beneath her fiery touch.

Searra willed her daylight hotter and hotter and hotter, until her own skin dripped with sweat.

Ruby beads rolled down her brow and upper lip as she cranked up the heat like she was baking a loaf of sourdough straight from Hell.

The blonde vampire went still, turning to dust between her thighs. His ashes floated in the air around her. She tried not to breathe in and choke on his death.

Searra scrambled to her feet and saw her past self ablaze on the other side of the room, burning even hotter somehow. She saved Josué and turned three more vampires to nothing but dust and air.

It was so disturbing to watch herself do things she remembered having just done, like she was on a reality show with a quick turn around time.

A few feet away, Diego was on his back, being straddled by the wild redhead, Liv. Her golden glare collided with Searra's. Pure hatred radiated from her in waves. In a sudden blink, Liv was a blur as she barreled down towards Searra.

Searra summoned her daylight again, wanting to take this bitch out once and for all.

Another streak of color caught the corner of her eye, and a strong, familiar arm intercepted Liv— tossing her like a sack of flour clear across the room and through the top level of the wooden bleachers.

She crashed into it with a raucous bang. The entire chamber shook with the impact as bits of wood, stone, and plaster rained down on them, coating the room in a sandy, white haze.

Juan gave Searra a quick wink and a small smile. With vampiric speed, he intercepted Liv just as she stood, shaking the dust and debris from her mop of copper hair. Then they were a blur of blows, crashing into the walls, the ceiling, and floor. The damage was piling up around them, like demolition day on a home design show.

Before Searra could react, the meaty vampire, the one she swore she had already dusted, ran at her, murder in his demonic gaze.

Did he have a twin?!

He must have, because this one had his cloak on still and she distinctly remembered seeing the other one's gigantic arm muscles.

Before he got close enough to touch her, Diego came in from the side with a swift tackle, his face and arms covered in blood, both landing in a heap on the floor. The air must have been knocked from Diego's lungs with the impact, because he began coughing so hard she thought he might tear something.

Another sudden and loud crash shook the building.

Plaster, stone, and wood rained down on them from the ceiling, making it hard to see. Searra knew they didn't have much time if the ceiling was beginning to collapse. It was only a matter of when, not if, it would all come crashing down.

Jade's high-pitched scream echoed down from the tunnel outside the entrance. Searra's hackles rose on instinct, hearing her daughter's fear. But she remembered that meant Jade and Syd were out and just needed to get through the tunnel. That knowledge was enough to calm her already frayed nerves.

Plus, now she knew that Lety and Lissette were both outside the building maintaining protection spells and could get her daughter and sister to safety. That was all that mattered to her.

There was grunting as Searra saw Juan and the thick vampire go at it, wrestling to grab the daylight sword that had clattered to the ground a few feet away.

What happened next, was all in a blur.

Liv sped over and swiped the daylight sword, the metal whining against the floor as she dragged it up to examine it, her face lit with gleeful malice.

Juan and the beefy twin were distracted and fighting each other for a sword no longer in play.

Liv's expression was cold as she made eye contact with Searra, an evil smile stretching her thin pink lips. Golden eyes blazing, red hair wild, and her demonic ridges even more prominent on her brow. Her fangs glinted with deadly promise and she broke out in a sprint, making a beeline straight for Diego.

The daylight sword cast nightmarish shadows around her as her arms cut through the air, gain-ing momentum. Liv was a blur of motion, but Scarra tracked her with her vampire eyes, and she was moving *fast,* too fast.

Scarra was not going to let her do this!

She was not going to lose him again!

Not again.

Scarra pumped her legs, hard, trying to intercept Liv before she was able to reach Diego. He was still on the floor, struggling with that damn collar they had put on him that prevented shifting.

She wouldn't let it happen, no matter what.

To Scarra, everything was moving in slow motion, like running in a dream. Her thighs burned with the effort. Adrenaline coursed through her veins, giving her more speed than she thought possible. She just kept thinking, *faster.*

Faster.

Faster!

Scarra reached Diego first, pushing him aside, spinning on her heel to face Liv. Arms crossed to protect herself, gauntlets of blazing daylight.

Liv was already bringing the sword down to strike and Scarra closed her eyes. Thinking about Jade and her beautiful, toothy smile, how she laughed in a high-pitched squeal, her scrunchy face and pouty lips she made when she wasn't getting her way, and the fact that Scarra was going to miss her growing up.

She would miss it all.

Jade would grow up without her mom.

Jade was so young, she wouldn't remember Scarra, and know how much she loved her.

Hot, blood tears stung the corners of her eyes, but she stood her ground. Jade would NOT lose her father again, not like this. She would protect her family with everything she had, even if she didn't survive.

A beat passed, two. But the blow did not come. Only a low grunt and a wet sound like metal sliding into flesh. She felt nothing, no pain. And she knew, with a sinking pit in her gut, something had gone horribly wrong.

Searra's eyes snapped open, only to see a large, dark figure right in front of her, standing between her and Liv and the daylight sword.

Juan.

Chapter 38

Volver (Come Back)

His tall and imposing figure crumpled to the ground without warning, like a sun setting on the horizon or a dying star collapsing into itself, both final and infinite at the same time.

Searra's breath stuttered. She felt something deep within her, a corded string tying her to Juan, pull taut. A sharp pain began to radiate from her chest, making it hard to breathe.

"JUAN!" His name tore from her throat, the naked desperation palpable.

Something broke within her. She was both raw and numb, a live nerve, and in so much pain she couldn't quantify it. Searra crashed to her knees with the weight of it. Clutching Juan, believing that if her hold was tight enough, she could keep him there.

The daylight sword was buried deep in his chest, the light dimmed to a flicker. The hard lines in his face deepened as he looked up at her, the light in his emerald eyes was fading. His fangs had retracted as he fought to stay conscious a little longer.

Searra was gripping him so hard, leaving half-moon marks in his ever-growing ashen skin. Her face was warm and streaked with dirt and blood red tears that tracked down her face.

"Why?!" The question was an attack, an accusation. Full of confusion, along with maddening, brain-scrambling, unreasonable rage, and utter sadness. Her heart was broken, impaled by the daylight sword she created. "Why did you do that, Juan?!" She choked out. "I was handling it." Her brows knit together, and she added in a threadbare whisper, "I just found you."

His gaze never left hers, "I couldn't let you do it." Juan's hands rose to tuck a strand of wild brown hair behind her ear; his fingers lingered to graze her dirt-stained cheekbones, sending light flutters over her skin.

She laughed through her tears, "Fucking mind reader."

His fingers pinched her chin as he smiled at her, a breathy chuckle escaping his paling lips, his eyes lighting up for one last moment.

Searra looked down at his wound. He was starting to desiccate like the other vampires had from the power of her daylight. The mottled gray discoloration traveled from his chest outward, crawling up his neck and down his arms.

"*Ni la eternidad habría sido suficiente.*"[1] Juan whispered.

Not even eternity would have been enough. The words floated to her on a phantom breeze.

"No!" Searra choked out. "You can't leave!"

An eerie breath escaped him, and everything went as still as death. Time stopped, and Searra was afraid to breathe.

Juan was in her arms one moment, and in the next, his body combusted into dust on the wind.

Gray ash settled in her hair, stuck like glue to the tears streaking her face and eyelashes so she could hardly see.

A tall figure loomed behind her as she slumped deeper on the floor.

"I'm sorry, Sisi." Diego's voice was soft and sweet. Genuine.

Searra looked around and noticed they were the only ones left in the chamber. It was so quiet she could hear their own breath echo against the wooden planks and stone. Everything seemed so much smaller than it had only moments ago. The room even

---

1. Not even eternity would have been enough.

looked smaller. An epic battle had just taken place here, but that now seemed impossible.

"What happened to the other vamps?" Searra asked, even though she didn't care. Whatever the answer, they were gone for now.

She was still looking down at her hands, covered in blood and ash. A sudden wave of nausea hit her like a truck and yet she felt so empty at the same time. She didn't know whether to heave her guts out or curl up and die on the floor.

"They took off," Diego said. "The *zorra pelirroja*[2] took off as soon as Juan went down. She looked fucking spooked." He whistled as his arm gestured to the door. "That meathead went with her."

"What about Josué and Nayeli?" Searra asked, a numbness creeping over her, fogging her vision like dirty glass and hearing like there was cotton in her ears.

"They just left chasing after the vamps. But I don't think they will catch them though." Diego explained. "I wanted them to make sure they didn't follow Lety and Lissette, especially since Jade and your sister were with them."

Searra felt a sharp pang at the mention of Jade's name and a little color returned to the world around her.

Diego put down his hand to her, covered in dirt and dust and blood. "Need help?"

Searra finally looked up at him, her hand taking his to stand. His hand was so warm it was like touching

---

2. redheaded bitch / slut

an open flame compared to her own room temperature skin. She almost flinched at the contact, but his touch didn't burn like it had before.

Maybe she was just that numb?

Or because her mate was gone...

As she stood, her entire body ached; she was also starving and wanted to sleep for the rest of her life.

Which would now be forever... The weight of that pressed on her. It was unbearable.

"Can you give me a ride?" Diego asked, a sheepish expression on his face.

Searra looked up at him, ash flaking away from her dark hair to float to the ground at their feet.

"What? A ride? Where?" She was definitely out of it. She couldn't understand a word he said, nothing could compute in her brain.

"Lety was my ride." He scratched the back of his neck and gave her a nervous chuckle. Like he wasn't quite sure how to talk to her anymore. They used to be best friends less than two years ago, more comfortable with each other than anyone else. It's funny how fast things can change.

"Sure, sure. Where are we going?" Searra asked, not quite paying attention for the answer.

"Abu's. You need to come too. Your place is not safe and Juan's isn't anymore... if it ever was." There was an edge to his voice Searra chose to ignore. She didn't have the strength or the energy to fight him right now.

"Is that where your sisters are taking Jade?"

"Yeah. We figure, we are safer together, in a pack. They can pick us off if we are separated from each other, but all our power in one place? Makes us pretty tough to fuck with." Diego's dark eyes deepened with deadly intent and his jaw ticked, drawing her attention to the collar still around his neck.

"Hopefully we can figure out a way to take that shit off," Searra said, nodding to the collar.

"Fuck, we better! It fucking itches." Diego complained, scratching at the raw metal edge and giving her a weak smile.

Searra tried to smile back, but the movement felt so foreign to her. Half of her was gone, ripped away, the half that gave a shit. Juan's soul had been tied to hers and when he floated away on the wind, she floated away with him.

As they walked to the car, Searra's stomach rumbled. She was so hungry her stomach was about to turn in on itself. It must have been how much magic she had used. She was depleted, but she didn't feel like eating.

"I don't suppose you have a blood supply stocked in your fridge?" Searra asked weakly.

Diego blanched, his thick eyebrows raising up to his hairline. His throat bobbing as he fought back a gag.

A dry laugh burbled up Searra's throat, "Any volunteers?"

Searra was half kidding, but she needed to eat soon to keep up her strength. Who knew when the next attack would be? And she had to be ready. She doubted The Council would give up now, especially since they had been able to escape and take out a good chunk of their numbers.

Bet they weren't counting on that.

Diego's face had scrunched into an expression of disgust and Searra made a mental note: *Wolfie snacks were off the menu.*

"Hey, it's just blood. Everyone has it, and I happen to drink it. But at least I don't smell like wet dog, that is another level of weird." Searra teased, but it came out deadpan.

"At least I don't smell dead." Diego countered, hands sheepishly raking through his shaggy jet-black hair, debris falling to the ground that had just shaken out.

Dead.

Was she dead?

If the gapping, pitiless, and endless black hole in her chest was any indication...

But, she *did not* smell!

"I do not!" Her voice full of righteous indignation. "I *just* showered!" Completely ignoring all the blood, ash, and dirt coating her from head to toe. Her shoes were even making a squishing sound as they walked down the block to Juan's Mustang.

"Dead," Diego confirmed with a solemn nod, pity in his eyes.

And maybe she was.

Epilogue

I MIGHT IN PROCESS OF TIME...
RENEW LIFE WHERE DEATH
HAD APPARENTLY DEVOTED THE
BODY TO CORRUPTION." MARY
SHELLEY (1818)

Three weeks later.

Searra had been there every day. Despite the dust and debris, the building hadn't collapsed like she expected. It stood—barely—on the verge of ruin, abandoned and forgotten.

She sat in the dark room, in the middle of the floor, trying to connect to something. Feeling for the cords that tied them together, a fragment of *him* that might trigger a vision or astral projection or *fucking anything.*

Something that would take her to him.

But... nothing.

That gaping maw of a hole in her chest was yawning ever deeper, ever more bitter. Opening wider and wider like a giant beast until it consumed her and there would be nothing left.

Since that night, Jade and Searra had been staying with Diego at Abu's house. Lety lived in the back house— a one-bedroom, one-bath tucked behind the main property. She welcomed them like the past two years had never happened. It was a bit cramped with all of Lety's animals and now a toddler in the mix, but the distractions were welcome. They kept Searra moving.

Her own sister however... was not speaking to her. She couldn't really blame Syd. It was Searra's fault that their mom was dead, that Syd was now traumatized by vampires. It made sense that she needed space.

But, with her new vampire schedule, she needed family around to watch Jade while she slept. She had attempted to stay awake during the day, but it was physically impossible for her.

As her limbs became leadened, she would drop where she stood if she hadn't found somewhere comfortable to rest. A couple times, she awoke as the sun was setting to find herself scrunched on the bed after Lety tried to carry her and struggled.

But this... this was the place where Searra would come to think.

To think about him.

Juan.

Her mate.

Dead.

She sat cross-legged, her fingers tracing lines in the dirt and ash, and she let her mind reach out.

It wasn't long before she felt a presence approach.

The hairs on the back of her neck stood up and she fought a hiss as her fangs erupted from her gums. This was not the visit she had been hoping for.

In a blur, she rose and spun on her heel to face the entrance to the tunnel. The thick door had cracked down the center, and hung precariously off its hinges. Yet, from where she stood, she could still see into the dark depths of the entrance tunnel.

Slow, deliberate footsteps echoed around her, and a sense of impending doom clouded her thoughts. She was sure she should run, but she couldn't tell her legs to move.

Wings flapped above her head, accompanied by a single hollow clack. Seats looked up, but could see nothing amongst the wooden beams.

Only darkness.

But she knew with a certainty that the *lechusa*[1] was up there, stalking her.

Searra turned her attention back to the door, ignoring the witch above her head.

As the footsteps were getting closer, she could make out another sound—a strange croaking, like a dying frog, echoed from the din. A sound that sent shivers of ice-cold fear up her spine and set her teeth on edge.

Oh yes, she should start running.

Two red pits illuminated within the depths of the blackness. Searra's hackles rose and her adrenaline spiked. She knew exactly what awaited her in the gloom of the chamber's tunnel. Her breathing hitched

---

1. a witch who can transform into a large owl (often a barn owl) to stalk and terrorize people at night.

as she tried to remain calm, but she felt like she couldn't suck enough air down.

As if from out of the depths of hell, Ambrose emerged with his *chupacabra*[2] hell hound. Shadows dripping from them like wet paint. The jaws of his *chupacabra* were lathered with a musty yellow drool, perfect for killing any stupid vampire it happened to come across... someone like her.

A long, angry, pink scar traveled down his face, cutting through his right eyebrow and down to his right eye, which was a cloudy white. It seemed he hadn't completely healed from that slice Juan gave him with the daylight sword. That knowledge gave Searra a smug sense of satisfaction, and she didn't even try to hide it in her expression.

Her eyes slid from his unsettling, cloudy stare to the other exit on the opposite side of the room. Searra would have to cross their path from where she stood. She might make it, but they were just as fast as her, and the *chupacabra* might be faster.

She may need to chance it. Her hands balled into fits, as she readied herself to sprint.

A tisking sound came from Ambrose. "Oh, darlin'. I didn't come here to fight." His deep voice was raspy and sweet, like a shot of warm whiskey. And his one good eye sparkled like polished obsidian.

"Abercrombie, right?" Searra quipped. "You could have fooled me. Brought all your cronies." Her chin tilted up toward where the giant owl was probably

---

2. Mexican Goat Sucker (legends say they attack cattle at night)

perched. "Truth be told, I really don't care why you are here." She said while crossing her arms against her chest, trying to act as nonchalant as possible.

He chuckled, low and menacing, the kind of laugh where someone knew something you didn't. It sent shivers of fear up her spine, something she hadn't felt since Juan.

"When I tell you what I'm offering, you best believe you are going to remember my name." His voice slipped over her like spiked honey and his fangs glinted in the poor light of the chamber.

The beast at his side ripped a few sinister croaks from its throat and laid down on the floor, its imposing talons folded under its muzzle to rest its large head.

Goosebumps pebbled her skin and she ground her teeth against the sound, trying her best not to look at the damn thing.

In any case, Searra was sure whatever he had to say, she wasn't interested.

"Look, Albatross." Searra barbed, looking at her nails. "I'm not interested in anything you have to say. So, there is really no need to further *this*." As she gestured to the two of them with her fingers.

"What if I told you, you can bring him back?" Ambrose asked, his tone smug, a wide, closed lip smile stretching his face. He knew he had her by the throat.

The empty pit where her heart used to be shuddered for a quick moment, breathing in a heartbeat of color and emotion. The intensity was almost too much to bear... until it went still again, and all the rich hues faded with it.

Searra couldn't help herself, "How?"

ANGELOUS

THE SECOND INSTALLMENT OF
THE DEVOURANCE SERIES

Coming out Fall 2026.

Want a signed paperback and some fun little goodies
from me? Of course you do.

Grab one straight from me and you'll not only get cool
stuff, but you'll also be supporting your favorite author.
www.jacquelynmarquezbooks.com

Or be my book bestie! Check out my Tiktok and Insta
@jacquelynmarquezbooks

GLOSSARY

Almas Marcadas – marked souls

Botanica Reina – Spiritual Shop that sells a variety of herbs, candles and spiritual tools, + queen

Bruja – witch

Chingada madre – motherfucker

Chismosas – gossipy women / girls who gossip

Chupacabra – Mexican Goat Sucker (legends say they attack cattle at night)

Chupasangre – bloodsucker

Chúpate un pedo – suck a fart

Condenado – condemned / cursed

Corazón – Heart

Dios mío – my God

¡Escúchame, por favor! – Listen to me, please!

Espanto – horror, supernatural fright/ghost

Esposo – spouses

Hija – Daughter

Las Lechusas – The word literally means "owl," but in legend, it usually refers to a witch who can transform into a large owl (often a barn owl) to stalk and terrorize people at night. Said to have sold their souls to gain shape shifting powers. They lure people out of their homes and steal children. Considered to be a bad omen, or a sign of danger.

Lávate las manos – wash your hands

Lujuria – lust

Mariposas – butterflies

Más o menos – more or less

Mi alma gemela – my soul mate

Mi amore – my love

Molcajete – stone bowl made of volcanic rock, used to mix

Muerte – dead

Muñeca – doll

Nahual – a witch that can transform into an animal

Ni la eternidad habría sido suficiente. – Not even eternity would have been enough.

No te hagas – Don't pretend.

Oh pues. – Oh, fine then.

Pansa – belly

Papelita – little paper (term of endearment)

Pendejo – dumbass

Pepita – pumpkin seed (term of endearment)

Pequeña – little one

Pinches malditos – fucking bastards

Pinche pendeja – fucking bitch

Pinche pendejo – fucking idiota

Pocho – Slang for an Americanized Mexican, someone who has lost their Spanish tongue and is disconnected with their roots culture, someone who mixes

English and Spanish

Ponderoso – strength

Polgasitas – little fleas (affectionate)

¡Por todos los infiernos, ¿Qué fue eso?! – By all the hells, what was that?! (archaic saying)

Primo – cousin (can also be used for close friend)

Que demonios – What the fuck? / What the hell?

Qué diosa – What a goddess.

Rizos – curls/curly hair (nickname)

Ruda y ajo – rue and garlic (strong herbs used for protect, cleansing and repelling evil spirits)

Sinvergüenza – shameless

Sol – sun

Sombra – shadow

Son demonios – they are demons

¡Soy un pinche perro aullándo le a la luna! – I'm a fucking dog howling at the moon!

Tio – uncle

Trejolote – the stone grinder or pester used to crush various herbs, used with the molcajete

Terca – stubborn

Traviesa – trouble maker

Vida – Life (term of endearment)

Volver – to come back

Y sabias a cielo – and you tasted like heaven

Zorra pelirroja – redheaded bitch / slut

Glossary (Spells)

Translation (In Order Of Appearance)

Awakening Spell

Sangre mia
Que duerme, que despierte
(English Translation)
My blood
What's sleeping, now awaken

Scrying Spell

Luna arriba, mar abajo,
Muéstrame por donde va su paso.
Jaspe de tierra, mar de poder;
Guíame ahora al anochecer.
(English Translation)
Moon above, sea below,

Show me where their footsteps go.
Jasper of earth, ocean of power,
Guide me now in this moonlit hour

Protection Spell
Por la cruz y por la sangre,
Que no mal te alcance.
Sal en mi boca, ruda en mi mano,
Ni sombra, ni muerte, ni engaño.
(English Translation)
For the cross and for the blood,
Let no harm come near you,
Salt in my mouth, and rue in my hand,
No shadow, no death no deceit.

Ward Away Lechusas
En el nombre de Dios,
no entras aquí.
Vuela lejos, bruja.
El diablo llama el nombre.
(English Translation)
In God's name,
you will not enter here.
Fly far, witch,
The devil is calling your name.

ACKNOWLEDGEMENTS

To my BookTok besties—

Thank you for being the spark that lit this fire. Your endless encouragement, creativity, chaos, and unfiltered passion for books inspired me more than you'll ever know. Watching you scream about your favorite characters, stay up way too late reading, and fiercely support indie authors gave me the courage to believe I could do this too.

I wouldn't have finished this book without your love and hype. You made this dream feel possible. I also wanted to specifically thank my Beta readers: Alexis, Leslie, Allison, Kendall, James, Syd and Lety. You are all troopers and I appreciate all your help, guidance and feedback.

This one's for the beautifully unhinged energy of BookTok that made me brave enough to tell my story.

With all my love and gratitude,
Jackie Marquez
@jacquelynmarquezbooks

About the Author

Jacquelyn Marquez, Jackie to her friends and family, is a Southern California native, a loving wife and proud mom, and a passionate vegan baker with her own Micro-Bakery, Chaqueta Cakes LLC.

From an early age, she was captivated by the world of the supernatural—vampires, werewolves, and witches, which sparked her imagination, fueled by iconic influences like Charmed, Buffy the Vampire Slayer, Supernatural, The Vampire Diaries and Twilight. But it was Dean Koontz's *Mr. Murder* and Christine Feehan's *Dark Prince* that truly ignited her love for storytelling and spice, marking the beginning of a lifelong obsession with dark, thrilling, romantic tales.

She earned her bachelor's degree in creative writing from California State University, Long Beach, where she honed her craft and deepened her love for romantic and monstrous worlds. Blending fantasy, suspense, and the supernatural into stories that linger long after the last page.

When she's not writing, Jackie can be found experimenting in the kitchen with plant-based treats, spending time with her family, supporting other indie authors or watching trash reality TV. If she's not baking or writing, she's likely lost in another spice-filled Romantacy novel.